Inheritance

of secrets

Colin Ferguson

First edition May 2014

The author – Colin Ferguson

Colin Ferguson was born in Perth, Scotland in 1937 and when his family became homeless they moved between Scotland and Richmond in Surrey, staying there finally in 1948. He attended Tiffins in Kingston and left there on National Service in 1956. He flew with the Royal Air Force for two years and then joined the staff at the Bank of England. Married in 1960 he and Janet have been together ever since.

He left the Bank in 1967 to train as a Probation Officer in London. His work took him to Brixton, Holloway Prison and Battersea before he was promoted to a senior management post in Reading. He took a Master's degree at Reading in Criminal Justice. Later he specialised in family law and on taking an early retirement in1994 he worked as a Family Mediator until 2007 when he began to write this novel, bringing to life some of his previous experience of the secrets with which so many people live.

South London

November 2008

4

Chapter one

Too late

It was time for a tea break at the pickled onion factory where Rosie Burns had worked since leaving school. She felt very tired today so she was glad of the chance to slip out to the courtyard where the girls went for fag breaks. The smoke did disguise some of the vinegar smell though after nearly forty years she hardly noticed. It did take a lot of washing and cheap perfume to stop others commenting on the aroma she inevitably carried with her. Still, they had been good to her and the other women were good fun, especially on Friday nights at the Bingo and in the pub afterwards.

As the cigarette fell out of her hand and the ground rose to hit her, she had little time to think. She heard other people running towards her and felt them turning her over and calling for an ambulance. Then there was a searing pain across her chest and she knew that she was dying. She couldn't speak, but in her mind she had so much to say, so many secrets to be discovered.

The ambulance came quickly but not soon enough. Rosie was dead. They lifted her on to a stretcher and took her to the hospital where the duty doctor pronounced her dead on arrival.

*****

Ellie Burns was checking her till when Jill came to tell her that there was a phone call for her from the factory. She wasn't worried by this as her mum used to call from there when she was going out.

"Hello!"

"Is that you Ellie? It's Patsy, your mum's friend."

"Oh! Hello Patsy. What's up?

"It's your mum love. She's gone to the hospital. She had a fall and they took her off to St. James'. I think that's where it went."

"Why? What happened? Is she all right? Did you see her?"

"No love, by the time I knew what had happened she was gone, but Mavis saw what happened. Said she fell and knocked herself out or something."

"St James' you said? I'd better get there as soon as I can."

"All right love. Let us know how she is. Winnie says to give her our love and we'll be along to see her as soon as we can."

"Thank you Patsy. Thank you for letting me know. I'll get back to you as soon as I can." She put the phone down and found Jill.

"Jill, it's my mum. She's in hospital but I don't know why. Can you cash up for me please so I can get over there."

"Of course I can. You'd better go now."

It didn't take Ellie long to get to the hospital. She was young and fit and used to walking so she could save for her wedding. She shuddered as she walked into the large Victorian building. The smell of hospitals always made her feel squeamish.

Casualty was quite easy to find but she couldn't see her mother anywhere. She went to reception but the woman there was on the phone. Another young nurse appeared carrying a large pile of files.

"Can I help you?" She smiled as she put the files down on top of another pile.

"I hope so. My mother was brought here from work about forty minutes ago after having a fall. I can't see her here."

"What's her name?"

"Oh! Sorry! It's Rosie Burns."

"Not a problem. Hospital can be very distracting." She smiled again. "Do you know when she came in?"

"It was less than an hour ago."

"Here we are! Mrs Rosemary Burns. She's gone straight through for treatment. I'll just check. Bella!"

"A young nurse was passing. "Can you take this call, please!"

Ellie had hardly noticed that the phone was ringing and that the other receptionist had gone.

The nurse leaned over the counter and picked the phone up. "Hello. This is A and E; no Suki isn't in today! No I can't take personal messages. No I can't tell you her home number either: same to you!"

She put the phone down and spoke to the other nurse. "Sooner that girl sorts out her love life the better." The receptionist returned.

"The doctor will be coming out to speak to you soon Miss Burns. Meanwhile can you please give me some details like your address and your mother's date of birth?"

Ellie began to get worried. "Surely my mum gave you all her details when she came in!"

"It seems she was unconscious when she arrived. It will help if you can give us the details."

"It's 15 Hurley Street, Balham and her birthday is the 3rd of September 1955. She is only just fifty three!"

"Thank you. Bella! Can you take Miss Burns to the doctor's waiting area please?"

"Sure thing: it's just down this corridor. I'll let Doctor Sandhu know you are here."

"Can you tell me what is happening? Is my mum all right?"

"Sorry dear! I've been running all over the place today but it must be serious for them to bring you in here, but I guess you know that already."

"Yes; I just thought she would be getting bandaged or something."

The door opened and the doctor came in. He saw Bella and held his hand out to stop her from leaving. "Ah, nurse! Can you hang on please?"

He turned to Ellie. "Miss Burns, I am glad you are here. Do you know what has happened?"

"I know that my mum had an accident at work and was brought in here but that's all."

"It was I'm afraid a bit more serious than that. Please will you sit down."

Ellie's mind began to work overtime and she automatically sat as told.

"I'm afraid it is not good news. As you know your mother had a fall at work but it was not an accident. It was caused by a heart attack, and it was a very serious attack. I'm afraid she was dead before she even got to hospital. There was nothing that anyone could do."

Bella stepped closer to Ellie and put her hands on her shoulder.

Ellie's mind could hardly hear the words. "Are you saying that my mum is dead? She can't be dead. She's only fifty three. She's never been sick, except for her cough and that was just the cigarettes. No! She can't be dead! You must have the wrong person. It can't be my mum!"

"I am sorry, but there is no doubt at all. It must have been very swift and she would not have suffered."

The tears welled up and burst through her eyes with a scream of disbelief. Bella had tissues ready and they waited for Ellie to compose herself.

Bella asked "Is there anyone we can call for you?"

Ellie shook her head. "No, it was just me and mum. Always has been."

She paused while she wiped the tears away and took a deep breath. "Can I see her?"

Doctor Sandhu nodded. "Yes of course you can. The nurse will arrange for you to go through in a moment or two." At this Bella slipped quietly out of the room.

He continued quietly. "It is not unusual for such things to happen, especially if someone has been a heavy smoker. People tend to think it is only their lungs that will be affected but their heart is weakening day by day as well and even if they seem to be fit and well, if it is already weak then it can fail at any time. I doubt if your mother knew anything about it. We have rung your doctor for her medical records as we will have to do a post mortem. Please don't be worried about that, it is only because she died unexpectedly. I am pretty sure it was her heart."

He could see the tears beginning to fill Ellie's eyes again. "I am sorry because it must have come as a terrible shock to you. Have you got any friends who can stay with you for a while?"

Ellie sniffed and shook her head. "I can't think of anyone at the moment. Maybe Andy will help. He's my fiancé. My friend at work has five children so she can't do much."

Bella returned. "It's O.K. for you to come and see your mother now."

The body was still on a trolley, covered in a white sheet. Ellie looked at her mum's face. It seemed different but it was her.

The eyes were closed and someone had combed her hair back in a way mum would not have done. The colour had drained from her cheeks. Ellie thought it must have been the shock that made her so pale but it was still her mum and the faint odour of pickled onion dashed any lingering hope.

They were very kind to her and brought her a cup of tea while she sat in a waiting area to see the hospital social worker. There was a leaflet for almost everything and a list of local Funeral Directors that she was advised to choose from so that they could take over the arrangements on her advice. Her head was still spinning when she walked through the door of her empty home.

As she walked into the house the telephone was ringing. She answered it automatically. "Hello!"

"Hello Ellie. It's Doctor Masters here. I thought I should call to let you know that the hospital have been in touch with me about Rosie. Are you all right? It must have been such a shock for you as it was for me. Is there anything that I can do?"

"Thank you! It is a shock and I don't think I really believe it yet. Did you have any idea she was so ill?"

"Not really! I saw her a month ago when she complained about getting breathless and I checked her out then, but apart from her smoking there was no indication that she was in any danger."

"I have to see a Funeral Director to make arrangements and they are doing a post mortem before signing the certificate I need."

"Don't worry about that Ellie. I have to go to the hospital tomorrow afternoon so I will collect that for you. I think your mum had a policy with the Co-op so you should check that out with them at their office in the High Street."

"Right; I see their name is on my list. Thank you for doing that at the hospital. I don't think I want to see that place again. I can't believe she won't walk through the door again just like always."

"Have you got anyone who can come to stay with you for a while? Have you been in touch with Brian Evans yet? He might be able to help."

Brian was the Minister at the local Methodist Church which Ellie and her mum attended. "No, I have only just got in. I will ring him tomorrow when I know more. I will have to check with him about the funeral."

The thought of what she was saying suddenly overwhelmed her and she sat down and began to sob, forgetting that the doctor was still on the line. She put the receiver back and went upstairs to her bed where she threw herself down and hugged her pillow trying to hide from the horrible truth. She ignored the ringing of the phone until she had sobbed herself out and soaked her pillow.

The phone was ringing again so steeling herself she went back downstairs. She sighed deeply and answered the call. "Hello!"

Sorry Ellie, it's Doctor Masters again. I just wanted to be sure that you were O.K."

Sorry , I think that was me. Can I come to see you tomorrow please?"

"Just what I was going to suggest but you had better come at the end of surgery, say about midday. I am sure you will be able to take time off in the circumstances. - Hello Ellie! Did you hear what I said?"

"Oh sorry; Yes! I did hear. I suddenly thought about all the phone calls I will have to make."

"I am sure there will be many. If I might make a suggestion, take time to write down all the people who need to know and then tick them off when you have made the call."

"Yes, that's a good idea. Thank you doctor! I can do that now. I think I have cried enough for the time being but it will be useful to have something to do. I'll see you tomorrow."

"Right you are then. One o'clock at the surgery. I think you will have to let your mother know as well. She will have to know, whether she turns up or not. I'll see you tomorrow."

The phone went dead and Ellie put it down. She made herself a cup of tea and sat down to write the list.

Chapter two

The bureau

Ellie's mobile began to ring in her handbag upstairs where she had dropped it by the bed. By the time she got there it had stopped. She checked the number and saw that it was Andy. She looked at the phone before ringing back, remembering how mum had been so pleased when they got engaged.

She could almost hear her mum's voice. "He's a nice young man dear. Looks a bit like a young Robert Redford and he has a good job in the bank."

She wiped her eyes as the tears began to fill them again before punching in the last number.

"Hi! Andy! You rang."

"Hi! I was just ringing to see if you want to go down to the pub tonight with some of the gang."

"Andy! Oh Andy! Something terrible has happened. My mum is dead. She collapsed at work this afternoon and she's dead. I don't know what to do. Can't you come over here and just stay with me for a while?"

"Sorry Ellie but did you say that your mum has died?"

"Yes! It seems she had just popped out for a break and she dropped dead. Please Andy, just come over. I need you with me."

"I'm on my way." Before Ellie could say anything else she was talking to herself.

While she was waiting for him she began to write her list. After a while she realised that if she rang Patsy the news would be round the factory very quickly and Brian Evans would soon inform the people at church. She rang Patsy but there was no reply.

Suddenly she remembered what the doctor had said about letting her mother know. It didn't make sense because mum was dead so she knew already.

Her confusion was postponed as Andy arrived. They held each other close without speaking for a minute.

"What's happened Ellie? Are you O.K.? What are you going to do?"

"Stop it Andy! I can't cope with all these questions and I don't know any of the answers yet. All I know is that mum had a heart attack at work and died. I can't really believe it and when I do I start crying again and I just have no idea what I'm going to do."

She began to cry into his shoulder. He held her close. "I'm sorry love, but I'm rather shocked as well. Let's go into the kitchen and I'll make us a cup of tea."

"I still have one by the telephone." They walked through the living room picking her cup up on the way.

This one is cold Ellie. I'll make a fresh pot."

Ellie sat by the kitchen table. "The doctor said something funny when I spoke to him."

"What was that? I missed it when the kettle was boiling."

The doctor said I should let my mother know."

"Your mother? What on earth did he mean by that?"

"I don't know. Oh Andy, what am I going to do? I've just thought that the council might not let me stay now that mum is dead."

"Don't worry about that Ellie. I'll be able to get a bank loan next year and in the meantime I'm sure that Mary would help. After all she has a two bedroomed flat and only herself there. You two have always got on well."

"Do you really think she would help if it was needed? That would be so good. I'm not sure if I want to stay here on my own anyway. It will always be full of memories and Mary did say I should think about getting away from home."

"We can try. After all sisters must have some use."

"Don't say things like that, especially about Mary. Where would you have been if she hadn't given up going to university to look after you when your mum died? Your dad couldn't have managed on his own."

"Help; I give up. A chap has no chance when the girls gang up."

"I don't know how you can joke at a time like this. You just don't know when to stop sometimes."

"Sorry love! I do know how much I owe Mary, but she has done all right since then, especially at work. She was talking about doing her sergeant's exams soon. Anyway! What about your doctor's comment?"

"I don't know. He made it sound as if I had another mother."

"We can soon find out. Where is your birth certificate? You will need to find all that stuff to sort out the funeral and all the legal bits."

"Do you know I have never seen my birth certificate. I haven't been abroad so I haven't even got a passport, but mum always kept all her papers in the bureau so I guess it must be in there."

Andy walked over to the bureau. It was locked.

"Do you know where the key is Ellie?"

"I think it must be in her handbag."

"Is that still at the hospital?"

"No she never took it to work. It's by her chair."

Ellie crossed the room to where mum's black leather bag was tucked down by the side of her favourite armchair where every night she had religiously watched Eastenders, except on Friday. Then she had recorded it for that was bingo night.

Every Friday she went out with her friends from the factory to the Bingo and then to the local pub. Mum had always told her it was only a ginger ale but Ellie never really believed her. Perhaps the evening she had fallen over the doorstep had made Ellie dubious.

"I'm all right dear." She had slurred. "I'm really quite all right."

Ellie stopped by the chair very aware that it was only just last night that her mum was sat there as usual. She reached slowly for the bag almost feeling guilty about even touching it. As she did so her sleeve caught the edge of mum's ashtray and nearly knocked it on to the floor. The stub of what could have been mum's last cigarette was still there. She gave a gasp and then collapsed into the chair and began to cry.

Andy tried to comfort her but for some time she was beyond any comfort. She snapped at hi. "Just shut up Andy, you don't know how I feel. She gave everything to me and now some stupid doctor gives me the idea that she might not be my mum. Well she was, see, she was the only mum I ever had and if you want to look at the certificates then you just go ahead and look."

She wiped her eyes with the back of her hand and then opened the bag. The musk smell of her mum's scent hit her unexpectedly and she stopped as if she had been caught trying to pinch money from the purse.

Andy saw how she had frozen. "Here, let me look."

"Don't you dare!" she screamed at him. "It's my mum's bag."

She could see the keys so she grabbed them and threw them at Andy.

"Go on then."

Andy kept quiet, realising that nothing he could say would make matters better, so he picked the keys up and went to the bureau.

Quietly he said. "You do need the papers, whatever they say." He checked the bunch of keys until he found one that fitted.

Ellie found a tissue and gave her nose a loud blow, then dabbed her eyes with the dry end. "I know, I'm sorry I shouted at you. I know you are trying to help and I don't know what I would do, if you weren't here, but I just can't stop thinking about her. It's as if she was still here watching us. Look! There's her fag end, her teacup is on the draining board and when I opened her bag I could smell her."

Andy went over to her and they held each other in silence.

Suddenly Ellie detached herself. "Let's look together." She composed herself and almost marched over to the bureau. She had never been allowed to go into the bureau before and her grief was tempered by curiosity.

She opened one of the drawers and found it full of old photographs. Ellie could recognise mum as a child and then as a young woman in many of them. Then there were some wedding photos and pictures of a man that Ellie assumed might have been her father. Then she had her first shock. Mum was standing there with a baby in her arms but it was hardly the fashion of the eighties and mum was still very young.

"Andy, look at this picture. Do you think that mum had another baby before me? She looks really young here."

"Surely you would know if you had a brother or a sister."

"I don't really know. Mum never liked to talk about her family, just said that was all in the past. She was very secretive now I think about it, not that I'm saying anything was wrong, but I have never seen these pictures before. Come to think of it I've never seen a picture of my dad before. He looks all right, doesn't he?"

"Yes he looks quite dashing really. Perhaps that is why she never mentioned him much. Maybe he ran off with someone else."

 "Stop it Andy. This is serious."

The next picture was of a little girl with blonde curly hair. She was smiling at the camera and holding her arms out. Andy held it up to the light. "Certainly looks a bit like you."

Then the pictures showed a variety of school photos and holiday snaps which Ellie thought were at Ramsgate which is where she used to go to stay with her Aunty Flo.

"It is certainly not me. I would have remembered those pictures. What do you think has happened Andy? It's as if she has disappeared. Do you think that she died and mum couldn't bear to remember her?"

 "I haven't the faintest idea love but why don't you ring Ramsgate and ask your Aunty Flo? She needs to know about mum anyway."

"Oh no! I haven't put her on my list. She would certainly know all about it."

Andy began to look at some of the documents in the top of the bureau. "Here they are. There is a collection of certificates. Here is you mum's birth certificate for September '55. Here is her wedding certificate – Rosemary Beatrice Newton and Reginald Terence Burns. She kept quiet about being a Beatrice; Married in February 1972. Goodness she was only sixteen when she married. "

He paused. "Here's the baby. Look, Jennifer Louise born June 4th 1972. OOPS! There goes another of your mum's secrets."

"Let me see. No wonder she was so quiet about the past. I would never have guessed. But what has happened to Jennifer?"

Andy continued to rummage through the papers. Here you are, Eleanor Jane, April 1st 1988. I didn't know you were an Eleanor."

"I was named after my mum's gran, only she was called Nellie. Before you say anything, don't even think of going there!"

Andy made no reply. He held her birth certificate out to her. "You had better sit down before you read this."

Ellie knew by the look on his face that something was not right. She took the paper from him and read the secret her mum had tried to keep from her all these years. It read 'Eleanor Jane Burns, born April 1st 1988, mother Jennifer Louise Burns, father unknown. She read it again and again with the reality refusing to sink in.

Andy sat next to her and put his arm round her shoulder.

"How could she do that to me? How, for all these years, how could she never let me know?" She buried her head in Andy's shoulder and began to weep.

He looked at the certificate again. "She was only fifteen when you were born."

Ellie raised her head. "Only fifteen! But she was only a child herself. What has happened to her? Where can she be?"

When she had recovered her composure they replaced the papers in the bureau and closed its secrets inside. Andy made the long promised cup of tea and a sandwich for them both. Only then were they reminded that it was the fifth of November as a rocket defied the rain and lit the sky with a spray of red stars. They watched the television for a while as Ellie nibbled on her sandwich.

She rang Patsy again and this time was able to tell her the awful news. Then she plucked up her courage and rang Aunty Flo. To her relief it was their answer phone. Andy was still watching the news but when that finished Ellie decided to go to bed. She was totally exhausted by the day but even in the overwhelming tiredness her mind was buzzing. Andy made up a bed on the settee in the front room so that she would know she was not on her own.

Chapter three

The second layer

Ellie's alarm woke her at the normal time and she realised that she had not rung Jill to say what had happened and to arrange to have time off work. She strolled downstairs and was surprised to see the kettle on and to smell toast.

For a moment she thought it had all been a bad dream then she remembered that Andy had stayed overnight. She walked into the front room and saw a blanket crumpled up on the floor. She smiled. "Dear, thoughtful Andy, what would I do without you" she said to herself, as she twisted the simple diamond ring around her finger.

There was a flushing noise from upstairs and Andy appeared looking rather dishevelled.

"Morning Ellie; sorry if I woke you but I have to get home to make myself look beautiful for the bank. I thought you might want to lie in after all the excitement of yesterday."

She wondered how he could be so hearty after yesterday and in the morning. Breakfast with mum had always been a quiet affair.

"Good morning Andy. Did you manage to get some sleep?"

"Well enough I think; but what about you? Were you able to sleep at all with everything that happened?"

"I think so, but I do still feel tired. Thank you for the tea and toast."

"Right, you tuck in while I put some on for myself."

Ellie realised just how hungry she was having only had a half nibbled sandwich and a cup of tea since lunch yesterday. Then she thought, 'I bet he made this for himself'.

He sat down at the table with her. The stubble on his chin and tousled hair made her think how much she loved him. He had not thought twice about coming to her when she needed him. Thank God she had him. She was not on her own, but life was never going to be the same again.

"Sorry I am rushing love but I have to go home to shave and to put my suit on. This one is a bit crumpled for the Bank. I would like to stay but we are always extra busy on Thursdays. I'll come back this evening and we can go out for a meal. Then you can tell me how you got on today and let me know if there is anything I can do to help."

"You could ring Aunty Flo. I tried last night but it was just an answerphone."

Andy nearly choked on his toast. "Come on," he exclaimed, "you know what she thinks of men!"

"Just testing to see how far you would go. No I shall have to ring her. I started to write a list of people to contact but didn't get very far last night. I must let Jill know what has happened

25

and to book some time off. Then mum's work, even though I did speak to Patsy, which is the best way of everyone finding out, but their office needs to know officially. Then I must make an appointment with our minister. After that I will try and let Aunty Flo know.

She mentally pictured her aunt. She was so different from mum even though they were sisters. Mum had always been slightly built whereas Flo was a large effusive woman who ran an art shop in Broadstairs with her friend Muriel. Both of them were well known local artists. She thought of the many holidays she had been sent on to Ramsgate where they lived. She was fond of Muriel who was a smaller but quieter version of Flo. Mum and Flo were always arguing. Flo was the older sister and felt that gave her the right to try and run mum's life for her. Ellie shuddered slightly at the thought of Aunty Flo coming.

By now Andy was ready to go. "See you later Ellie. I'm sorry I can't stay but just take things easy and only do what you can cope with. I'll be back as soon as I can but Thursday tends to be a later finish. I'll see if I can take some time off."

He blew her a kiss. She watched him running down the road and blew one back to him as he disappeared round the corner. Then she picked her house phone up and rang Jill at work. As she expected Jill was a s helpful as possible and told her to take tomorrow off as well and then to come in on Saturday morning to let her know what else needed to be done. She rang mum's work and as she expected they did already know but did also offer to help her in any way she needed. Then she rang the Co-op Funeral Parlour and made an appointment to see them later in the morning.

She looked at her list of names. Most of them now were from mum's Christmas card list and she thought they could wait until she knew when the funeral would be. She was surprised at how calm she felt. It was useful to have something to do. She tidied up the tabled and washed the cups and plates as she had so many times before, then she returned to the front room and gazed at the bureau.

"How many more secrets have you got?" She said out loud. She began to poke among the papers. Most of them were bills which had been paid. Mum was always very meticulous about paying bills on time as she had a dread of going into debt. Then a blue piece of paper caught her eye and she pulled it out and read it. It was a letter headed H.M.P.Wandsworth.

'Dear Mrs Burns, I am sorry to inform you that your ex-husband, Reginald Terence Burns died in the prison last week. We have been trying to contact his daughter Jennifer as we understand that she is his next of kin. We have been unable to contact her at the given address and we wondered if you might be able to furnish us with her present address.

I am sorry to put you to this trouble, but would be grateful for any help you can give. Yours Faithfully; Gerald Bull, Deputy Governor.'

It was dated five years ago. Ellie looked at it for a long time. What else? She thought. What else is waiting to be turned up? She put it back where she had found it and went back to her phone calls.

*

Ellie was in the front room surrounded by different piles of paper when Andy returned.

"What on earth are you doing?" he asked.

27

"I've gone through the whole of the bureau trying to find an address for Jenny or anything that might tell me where she is. I suddenly remembered that we always got a Christmas card from Jennie but mum never did tell me who she was. Now I know who she is and I'm sure we must have an address somewhere. I went to the Co-op this morning and they have made a provisional date for the funeral next Thursday at the crematorium. Then I went to see Doctor Masters. He had just been in touch with the hospital and confirmed that she died from a massive heart attack. He said they will have the death certificate ready for tomorrow and I will have to go to pick it up then. He said I should make several copies for places like the Council and the bank as well as the Co-op."

"What about the church? Won't they want a service or something?"

"Brian Evans is away today but I left a message with his wife and she said to ring him tomorrow morning and he will make time to have a chat with me."

"What about your Aunty Flo/"

"I left a message for her but I will have to ring again shortly. Jill has told me to take as much time as I need. I can have three compassionate days before I need to touch my holiday. The Co-op told me not to worry about the cost of the funeral because mum had a policy with them to cover everything. Just like mum to think of everything.. I 'll go and ring Aunty Flo again now.

As she was ringing Andy scanned the contents of the bureau and he too spotted the blue prison paper. "Oh no!" He pushed the letter back when she put the phone down.

"Ellie turned to him. "Did you say something? "Then without waiting for him to reply she continued. "That's funny! Muriel was just going to ring me to say that Aunty Flo is on her way to help me with the funeral. That's just what I was afraid of. She was always trying to organise us."

Visions of holidays on the beach at Ramsgate came back to Ellie. "Fish paste sandwiches every day for lunch. Every single day we had fish paste sandwiches to take down to the beach. I think that's why I can't stand fish."

Andy smiled. He had heard about the infamous fish paste sandwiches before.

"You carry on there and I'll make us a cup of tea, then we can go out for a meal after six thirty. I have the car tonight so we can go wherever you want."

"Didn't you hear Andy? I just said that Aunty Flo is on her way. She could be here at any time."

"That's all the more reason for us to try and slip out. There is a meeting at the church tonight remember so we do have a good excuse."

"I don't know if I feel like facing anyone yet Andy."

"You will once Flo gets here."

"You know, my mum had more secrets than just Jennifer. I began to wonder who my dad is?"

"The way things are going you may not want to find that one out!"

"Thanks a bunch Andy. You do know that I still want to scream, so just take care."

By the time Aunty Flo had arrived they had finished sorting out the bureau but there was still no further mention of Jennifer apart from a few old photographs and a school report in which the teacher commented on Jennifer's disruptive behaviour. She was only eight at the time.

Chapter four

Aunty Flo

The door- bell rang and there was a loud knock. They looked at each other. Ellie smiled. "Get ready Andy, Aunty Flo has arrived."

As she opened the door she was almost smothered by and enthusiastic hug.

"Eleanor, my dear, dear child; what a terrible, terrible thing to happen; I always told her that all that smoking would kill her, but she wouldn't listen would she? And she had such a hard, hard life, but I know she was so proud of you. How long is it since I saw you? My you have changed. You look quite the young woman now. Is the kettle on? I'm dying for a cup of tea; you don't dare drink on the trains now you know, not since they got privatised. You just don't know how often they use the tea bags. It's all profit. No concern for the passenger."

Ellie stepped back coughing from the sudden exposure to her aunt's perfume and moth balls.

"You poor child; you must take something for that cough. Now I must just pop upstairs to the toilet. You daren't use them on the train you know."

"Hello Aunty" Ellie spluttered, "thank you for coming to help."

"No trouble, no trouble at all. I just couldn't stay at home knowing how much needs to be done and dear Muriel insisted that I should come and help you at once. She would have come as well but our babies need someone to look after them." She finished her sentence half-way up the stairs.

Ellie wished Muriel had come as she had a way of calming Flo down. They had been companions for over thirty years. She had always seemed like a shadow behind Flo when they had visited Ramsgate. Mum had hated Muriel and called her 'that woman', never even giving her a name. Ellie knew that nearly all the photos she had seen of Flo showed her arm in arm with Muriel. She also remembered the many times Flo had declared how all men were useless and she could do without them in her life.

Andy called from the kitchen. "Is it three cups of tea?"

"Yes! But please Andy, Aunty Flo likes her tea very weak. Just pour out the boiling water and dip the tea bag in it, count to three and take it out. That's what she taught me."

"One cup of flavoured water coming up; one- two- three: Shit! I dropped it but I got it out again quickly. I don't think she will notice."

"I wouldn't bet on it." As she spoke there was a flushing sound upstairs and Flo emerged shaking her hands. "My favourite towel isn't here, can you find it for me please. It's the one with little poppies on it."

"Sorry, Aunty Flo, I forgot with everything else going on. There is a paper towel in the kitchen and Andy has made us a cup of tea. I told him how to do it the way you like."

"Paper towels! Really Ellie, they have those on the train!"

Andy appeared at the door with a paper towel in his hand for her. "Hi, I'm Andy, Ellie's fiancé. Here's a towel for you to dry your hands."

Flo stepped back but did take the towel from him. "Fiance! But aren't you still at school Ellie? Did you mother know about this?"

"Of course she does, I mean did?" The need to change her word caught her unawares and the tears were quick to follow. "Andy, take her coat please!" and with a loud sniff she ran into the kitchen.

Andy smiled at Flo. "Let me take your coat and hang it up, then I'll take your bag upstairs. I think Ellie said you always like the small back room?"

"That's perfectly all right young man. I can manage by myself."

She grabbed her bags and clumped up the stairs.

Andy went in to the kitchen where Ellie was drying her eyes. "Are you all right love?" He put his arm round her.

"Not now Andy! Not while Aunty Flo is here."

"Don't be silly. You are a woman now, not a scared little girl. It's just that she needs some time to realise what has changed."

"I think I will always be a little girl to Aunty Flo."

They could hear her coming down again. Ellie called out. "We're in the kitchen with a cup of tea."

Flo walked in. "About time too. I'm completely parched, completely! Two sugars and cream if you have it otherwise I can have the top off the milk."

She looked at Andy and then at Ellie. "So you are engaged are you? After all we told you as well. Your mother already had enough to worry about."

"Please, Aunty Flo! It's not Andy's fault that Mum had a bad time. She got on really well with him, didn't she love?"

Andy spluttered. "Yes, oh yes she did! Even said I looked like Robert Redford."

"She would. She always had fancy ideas, even as a child she spent most of her time pretending and then she was always watching old films on the television. When she could she would go out to the cinema. That's how she met Reg. He reminded her of Cary Grant and look at the mess he made of her life."

"That's what I want to know about Aunty. I want to know about mum and especially about Jennifer."

"Who told you about Jennie?" Flo's voice got quite sharp.

"I had to find all the birth certificates and stuff for the hospital so we looked through the bureau and found them. It was a horrible shock for me to find out that she wasn't my mother at all. But I know now that Jennifer was my mother but I don't know anything else apart from her being disruptive at school when she was only eight."

"I told Rosie a long time ago that she should let you know but she was so ashamed of Jennie and of that evil husband. They said she was disruptive did they. Disaster is more like the word, and I blame her father for most of that. He spoiled her completely and she never showed any respect for Rosie. I'm sorry Ellie but Jennie was no good and it is really sad that after all the years of treating you with all the love and care she had, as if you were her actual child that you should discover it when Rosie isn't here to tell you herself."

"But why did mum never tell me. It's terrible to find out this way. I should have known even if she was no good, and what happened to her, where is she? After all she should know about mum. I know she is still around because she always sends a Christmas card."

I really don't know. Rosie never wanted to speak of it after she left home. Left home and you just a baby, that's what she did you know. Rosie brought you up on her own as her own baby. She gave you everything and that no good mother of yours never did a thing except to bring suffering like her father."

"What was wrong with him and what happened to him?"

Andy spoke without thought. "He's dead as well."

"How do you know?" asked Flo.

"It was in the bureau, a letter telling her that he had died. I didn't want you to be upset anymore because the letter was from prison. He died in prison."

Ellie put her hand out "I am sorry Andy. I found that letter this morning but with everything else I forgot. It was just another of these awful secrets mum had kept from me."

Flo needed no invitation to launch into her own view. "He was always in some sort of trouble was Reg. Even the army kicked him out after only six months. Rosie never did tell me why. I don't want to speak ill of the dead but that man had some very nasty ways about him and it was the best thing that happened to Rosie when he left her. That was just before Jennie left home as well and then it was just her and you. It was like she had been given a second chance at life because it had been a miserable existence before then."

"Why on earth did she marry him?"

"He took advantage of her innocence. Rosie didn't know anything about men except from the pictures and he got her pregnant with Jennie. He tried to pretend it wasn't him but our Dad wasn't going to let him get away with that. Not even Reg could ignore our Dad."

Ellie looked down at the floor. "Poor mum. First of all she has to marry a man she ended up hating and then the baby she had ran away leaving me with her."

Flo snorted. "Now you have some idea why I don't trust men. They only want one thing and it's not responsibility."

Andy felt it necessary to defend himself. "We're not all like that. I would never treat Ellie in that way. We want to get married not be forced into it."

Flo snorted again. "I didn't know he ended up in prison but I'm not surprised."

Ellie took hold of the letter and read it again. "It says here they want to know where Jennie is. Oh Andy, what shall we do? I have nobody except you and this stranger who is my mother. I don't know if I want to know her after all I've heard but I have such a strong feeling that I must find her. Even if it is just to tell her that her mother is dead."

Flo sighed. "You know that you were everything to Rosie. You gave her a reason to live. I don't know where Jennie is but I believe she is still in this area, probably in some doss house as they call them these days."

Andy looked up. "That's where Mary works. If anyone can find her she can. I'll give her a ring and see if we can go over to her place for a chat."

As he left the room to use his mobile Flo asked, "What on earth does he mean? How can his sister help?"

"Mary's a policewoman and she probably knows all the local villains."

"Oh dear! I don't know if you would call Jennie a villain, her problem was more – Oh I don't know if I should say this or not, but she had an unhealthy interest in men."

"Are you trying to say that my mother is a prostitute?"

"I don't really know what she is now, but that was one of her problems at school from quite a young age, which of course how she came to have a baby when she was only fifteen."

"I noticed she was very young when I was born."

"She behaved much more like someone ten years older but without the common sense or regard for morals. That was what Rosie couldn't bear."

"But you said she left me when I was a baby yet she was still a child herself."

"I know, but she and her mother were always arguing and I think everyone was much happier when she went. Mind you I was in Ramsgate then so I only heard things second hand. Jennie was always well behaved with me when she came on holiday in the Summer, but I wasn't able to have her once she got to thirteen because she was always talking to strange men. It wasn't her own age she was interested in, more like people who were old enough to be her father. I couldn't have that. Not in my home, not in Ramsgate!"

Andy came back in. "She wasn't answering so I guess she must be out on call so I left a message. If she doesn't ring back I'll pop into the police station and see where she is."

Ellie began to clear the cups away. "I have to go to the Co-op again tomorrow. How silly. It should be Jennie doing all this instead of me. Will you be all right Aunty Flo? Andy and me have to go to a meeting at church tonight. Mum would normally be there too so it's a chance to let many of her friends know what has happened. There's plenty in the fridge and larder for you to eat or we can bring something back with us for you later."

"Don't you worry about me dear. Just tell me what I can do to help and I'll get on with it. Are you sure you don't want me to come with you. All these forms and things can be so confusing."

"We don't have to worry about that tonight."

"Well maybe I can do some ironing or hoovering. I will soon get it sorted out. And don't worry about food, I shall make a sandwich. I can do some for you while you are out. I remember how you used to love my fish-paste sandwiches."

"Don't worry about that Aunty. Just relax after that long journey. I don't actually think we have any fish-paste. Just make yourself at home. We will have a bite to eat after our meeting. See you later."

She almost dragged Andy out of the door. "Leave the car Andy I need to walk. My head is just going round and round and I don't think I could have stood another second of her and – did she say fish-paste sandwiches?"

"I'm afraid so." Andy smiled at her and they both began to laugh.

"Oh Dear!" she sighed, "How can I laugh at a time like this?"

"Thank goodness you can. With all that is happening you either laugh or cry and I never know what to do when you cry. By the way did I tell you that I've got a day off tomorrow so I can help"

She put her arm into his and kissed him on the cheek. "Lovely. That will be good. Come on let's get this next thing done."

They walked to the church in spite of the drizzle. There were still some hardy souls letting off fireworks and there were enough oohs and aaahs to keep them amused in spite of the overhanging sadness. The meeting was about to begin and she was able to let them know what had happened. Their kind response was a bit too much for her to cope with, so they left before things had got started and went to a pub for a light meal.

Andy saw Ellie home and then walked back to his flat leaving his car parked in Hurley Street.

By the time Ellie got in Flo had already gone to bed, much to Ellie's relief and though it was still quite early for her she did feel very weary and this time she did sleep.

Chapter five

Jennie and the mirror

Jennie kept ringing the bell and knocking on the door even after it was obvious that Albert wasn't in. She could see the next door neighbour peering round her orange floral curtains so turned her back and looked across the empty street, pulling her jacket tighter. The lights reflected off the wet road and the loudest sound was the water gurgling at the top of the drain and the steady drone of the cars on the main road. Her old Christmas cracker plastic rain-hat stopped the top of her head from getting wet but only transferred the water down her back. She was not happy.

She muttered to herself. "Where has the daft old bugger gone?" She looked at her mobile and rang his number. She could hear the muffled sound of ringing in the house and knew that he had gone out without the mobile she had persuaded him to buy even though he had protested that it was too modern for him. She had told him to take it with him but he had simply said "If I want people to ring me on the telephone I like to be at home."

It didn't seem to occur to her that Albert still had a life of his own. After all she was only booked twice a week and it wasn't either Tuesday or Friday. But this was urgent for Karl had told her to not to return without money or else. Jennie knew what he meant. She was fed up with Karl and his demands but he still offered her more security than going back on the streets.

Albert was her most regular punter. Twice a week was all he could afford and probably all his heart could stand but Karl needed cash as his last drugs run had failed when Darren Fox was caught with the goods on him. Somehow the blame always fell on Jennie.

The rain had made it impossible to find a punter on the street and the line of dripping terraced houses gave her no invitation. Albert had been her one hope. He was a laugh as well as being quite spritely in spite of being over seventy. He really only wanted to chat with her when she went round though he was happy enough for a bit of hand massage on Fridays.

Once she had offered to give him a blow job. She had to explain what this meant and he had blushed. "Oh my goodness me, Ruth would never have done that." Even though Ruth had been dead for two years, just one month short of their golden wedding, he still couldn't allow himself to do anything she would not have understood.

The rain slackened for a moment allowing Jennie to run from the porch to the cinema round the corner. She sheltered in the doorway between posters for the latest Disney film and 'Walk the Line'. They were doing another refit of the cinema and a large skip covered the entrance to the alleyway. She scanned the contents from the safety of the doorway. There were two old mirrors on top. One was broken but the other was still intact.

It was just drizzling now so she pulled it off the skip and stood it up against the side' It was about half her height and still in a gilt frame. She turned round looking at her skirt to see if Karl was right about saying her bum was falling below her hem line. "Pig" she muttered, thinking of him.

The mirror seemed to have a fault in it which made her seem thinner. "Oh I like that. That is just what I would like at home." As usual she had not thought about her actions or how she could carry the mirror.

She discovered that the frame was easy to hold so she got it balanced and walked down the street. She was in luck. Nobody seemed to be around but the rain began again so she put the mirror over her head and decided to go home.

The smells from the fish and chip shop were too tempting especially as she hadn't eaten all day. She hadn't told Karl about the emergency fiver she had tucked in her shoe.

"Sausage and big portion of chips please Charlie" she said. After all she may not get another chance to eat for some time.

"Chang Lee." corrected the man serving her.

"Yes please, and salt, vinegar, pickled onion and a sachet of tomato sauce."

Chang was used to the ignorance of his customers so he took no notice of them as long as they paid.

"And I'll have a Pepsi" She only just had enough money and had to scrabble about in her purse to find the last two pence.

"Cor! I thought I was going to have to pay you with my body." Chang did not catch the implications of this so he smiled and assumed she was talking about the weather. "Not very nice."

"What, my body?"

Chang smiled. "No weather. Body is O.K."

Jennie laughed. "Do you mind if I eat them here?"

Yes. Fine; Chips no good when wet."

Jennie wondered if he was trying to be funny or whether it was a bit of wisdom from a fortune cookie. She stood by the doorway enjoying every mouthful and forgetting about Karl. The mirror was leaning against the wall. She began to think that the onion was a mistake as Karl would smell it and that would be trouble. Still, it didn't really make a difference. Karl would thump her anyway. She would just have to try and keep away from him.

Just as Jennie was down to her last few chips, she saw the girl from the ticket office running across the road. They had seen each other before at a party and in the pub. She remembered that her name was Joyce. It was too late to move away.

"Hi there Chang, give us cod and chips twice please." She gave her long hair a shake which reminded Jennie of a spaniel that had been her Aunt's pride and joy. Perhaps that was why she had never liked Joyce.

"Don't mind me." she complained as Joyce spattered her.

"Sorry love. I didn't see you there. Oh hello! It's Jen isn't it; from the Pig and Poke?"

"Yes."

"Sorry I didn't see you. I left my glasses in the office and I can't see that well without them. I know Kev but then only because he's big enough for me to see. Good job he moves from time to time otherwise I might lose him as well. Bloody awful day isn't it?" She hardly paused for breath before starting again.

"We've been really busy this afternoon. It's the rain you know. It always brings them in unless there's something good on telly. I mean to say you can't really imagine all those adults would want to watch Disney if it wasn't raining. I blame the telly myself. It drives them out of the house. Ooh I say. Where did you get the mirror? That's good isn't it? I mean it makes me look thinner. "

At last she paused as Chang had Jennie's order ready. Thankfully the rain had eased again. "Right then, it's time to go before the rain sets in again. Bye!"

She was half way through the door when she heard Joyce saying, "We used to have one just like that at the Regal. How much was that? Really! Have the chips gone up again!"

Jennie tried to stroll nonchalantly to the first corner. Once she felt she was out of sight she ran as fast as he could with the mirror, splashing through the surface water. She managed to get about fifty yards before the chips caught up with her and made her stop with a stitch in her side. Puffing and wheezing she leaned the mirror on a wrought iron railing and bane over to try and catch her breath. As she began to breathe more easily she became aware of a small boy in the house pulling faces at her. It was enough to get her moving again so with a two finger salute she picked the mirror up and walked more calmly to the next corner.

When she looked behind her she was relieved to see an empty street. Then she began to think of what she could tell Karl.

45

Chapter six

Consequences.

Jennie was glad to see the house again in spite of Karl's threats. With the railway line behind them and an area due for demolition and redevelopment the house had been empty for some time before squatters had got in. Now there was only her and Karl and Elroy who had the downstairs.

She opened the door quietly and tried to creep up the stairs but the old timbers had too many creaks in them for silence and Karl's called out. "Is that you Jennie?"

"Yes. Who were you expecting; the milkman?" She knew it was a mistake as soon as she said it.

"Come here slag! Where's the money?"

"I couldn't get any love, honest, I did try. Honest, I even went to Albert's but he was out."

"Liar! What would an old git like him be doing going out on a day like this. You're just trying to lie your way out of the thrashing I promised you."

Jennie wasn't quick enough to avoid his grab or the slap on her head that sent her reeling across the room. She was still holding the mirror and raised it above her head to stop him hitting her again.

"What the fuck have you got there?" Karl grabbed the mirror. "What do you think this is? It's not going to bring in any money. It doesn't even give the right reflection. Where did you get it? Nicked it I suppose. Well we need to get rid of it quick. It's almost as bad as advertising nicking something like this. You really are the most stupid slag I have ever known."

"I thought it might be worth a bob or two. You take it and do what you like with it. Look it has a lovely frame." "Yeah, the frame might be worth a fiver."

He looked more closely at the frame and sniffed. "Yeah." He sniffed again. "Chips, fish and fucking chips. You had money for fish and chips."

His backhander took her across her face splitting her lip and sending her crashing to the floor. She was hardly aware of his second and third punches or the kick he gave her for good measure. The painless darkness had already welcomed her.

He stopped as he saw she was no longer suffering and slapped her face to try and bring her round. "Stupid cow! What did you make me do that for? You know I get mad if you don't do what I tell you." He dragged her over to the settee and threw her on to it. She moaned slightly.

"All right bitch, you lie there and moan all you like while I try to get rid of this rubbish." He picked the mirror up and walked out without giving her another glance.

When Jennie came to it was almost dark and the occasional firework banged down the street. Her head was aching and her blouse stained with blood from her lip. Her first thought was to look for her pills to try and take the pain away. Perhaps if she took enough it would all go away forever.

She staggered to and old chest of drawers they had and pulled out the top drawer. Nothing she wanted was there. She found her bag and tipped it out on the floor as her search became more desperate. Kneeling among the lipsticks, keys and condoms she finally found half a dozen unknown pills and a strip of the all-important sleepers.

Karl had promised to get her more after her overdose on Monday but Darren getting nicked had blown that. Among the pills a single photograph lay face down. She picked it up and gazed at the chubby little baby with its gummy smile.

"No bloody good, I've never been any bloody good, so don't look at me like that. You're far better off without me. Just you be a better kid for mum that I ever was."

She reached over to the sink and emptied a cold cup of tea out and filled it with water. She returned to the bed and began to swallow all of them. She lay down and waited for them to take effect in to that far off state where nothing could hurt her anymore and nobody else mattered.

As she lay there her mind began to wander back to her mother telling her she was a wicked girl. Daddy was different. He was kind and cuddly. She was his little Jennie. Then her mother spoiled it by making him go away and making her go and stay in that horrible children's home. Her mother had always spoiled things. Nobody could have any fun.

Ellie was born on the 1st April. How appropriate. She had fooled Jennie right from the word go. Johnny of course didn't want to know. He even refused to think it could be his. He might have been right but he was her boyfriend. Then Ellie was born and her mother had become an angel; nothing was too much for her. But it didn't last long and the pressure soon began to build up again and she began to feel cut off more and more from the baby because she was a wicked child again even though she was nearly sixteen. More and more she yearned for her father and his warmth and affection.

Then there was that last fearful argument. She could still hear her mother shouting at her. "You're just like one of those tarts your father used to see and the sooner you are gone as well the better."

Jennie had hit her mother. She had never done so before though often tempted. This time she had screamed back at her mother. "Where is he, where is my daddy? I WANT MY DAD!"

Her mother had hit her back so hard that she had fallen over. "Dead! That's what he is. And hell is where you'll find him because that is where you are going as well"

Jennie had sat in the middle of the floor screaming until her mother had thrown a bucket of cold water over her.

"You witch! You're an 'orrible witch. You've never loved me. Why do you hate me so much. Is it because Daddy likes me more than you? If he's dead it's because you killed him."

By this time she was standing again and her mother slapped her across the face again.

The lights were fading. From downstairs she could hear the thump, thump, thump of Elroy's music.

That had been the end as her mother screamed at her. "You stupid, stupid child. It's because of you he had to leave. He was a filthy, cruel man and you let him do disgusting things. You are disgusting! You aren't fit to have a child and I am going to make sure you never get close to her again as long as I live. Now get out! Get out! Get out! She had grabbed Jennie by the hair and pushed her out of the front door, slamming it behind her. She had left the house in tears, never to see her precious little Ellie again.

Chapter seven

Shotgun

Elroy had heard the fight. He always did. He had watched Karl leave the house carrying the mirror. It wasn't that Elroy had too many scruples but he had always fancied Jennie and here was a chance for him to see her. Maybe she could work for him like she did for Karl. He waited to be sure Karl didn't turn round and come back because of the rain and rolled a couple of joints as he did so. If he got Jennie in a good mood maybe she would listen to him. He put a rollup behind each ear and strolled upstairs.

The door was slightly ajar so he called "Hi, Jen! It's me Elroy."

There was no answer so he strolled in. Jennie had fallen on to the floor and Elroy had seen too many junkies crashed out to think that he could do anything. He ran downstairs and grabbed one of the mobile phones on his bed. He dialled 999. "Ambulance please, my neighbour has taken an overdose and it looks like a big one. Number 5 Nelson Street. Yes people do still live here."

He paused as they asked him for more information. "Yeah!. Her name is Jennie Burns. I think she has been in before but this one looks real bad. I'll leave the front door open and then try to keep her awake. Right, yes it is upstairs."

He threw the phone back on his bed and pulled the covers over them before going back upstairs. He suddenly remembered the two roll ups and threw them in as well. It was quite an effort getting her off the floor and dumping her in a chair. He went to the kitchen and put the kettle on to make a strong cup of coffee for her. He was just in time to stop her slumping onto the floor again. He tried slapping her face gently and she did roll her head in response. He tried lifting her again but she was a dead weight in his arms and wouldn't move. He thought how he had wanted to get close up and personal with her but this was not what he had planned.

He had just got her upright when he heard someone coming up the stairs. A young policeman stood at the door. "Good evening sir. Can you tell me what is happening? We were told by the ambulance station that there was an incident here and as we were close I thought I might be able to help."

"What do you think I'm doing with an unconscious bird in my arms?"

"Right then, let me give you a hand. What is it? An O.D?"

"I guess so but she hasn't spoken to me since I found her spark out on the floor."

Let's try to get her walking. By the way My name is P.C. Henriques. Who are you?"

"They call me Elroy and that's good enough for me. Bloody hell! She weighs a ton."

Slowly between them they got her moving though her feet were dragging most of the time. The sound of the ambulance arriving was a great relief to them both.

The crew soon made her take notice and she began to struggle when they tried to make her vomit some of the drugs but she soon collapsed again.

The ambulance man spoke to his colleague. "Better pack a bag for her Sue. She's likely to need a change of clothes by the time they've sorted her out. I see a small case under the bed. Better use that."

Sue soon found some clothing to take and the reached under the bed for the case. She pulled it out and as she did so there was a thump as something else fell to the floor. She looked to see what it was. "Oh shit Harry! We've got a gun."

Jeff Henriques came over and carefully pulled the gun out from under the bed. It was a sawn-off shotgun.

"Do you know anything about this?" he asked Elroy but Elroy had already gone. No way was he going to be around for that sort of trouble.

Jeff said "I'll have to call this in. Keep her here until I come back."

He ran down to where his car was parked with Mary still in it. They knew from bitter experience not to leave a police car unattended. "It's an OD Mary but they've only gone and found a shotgun under the bed. Can you ring it in while I go back up and make the place secure.

He went back up the stairs where Harry and Sue were still working on Jennie.

"We're going to have to take her in mate. She will need the good old stomach pump for this lot and we shouldn't wait too long."

A police car drew up outside and the first officer up was Sergeant Forrester who was the station firearms officer. Better known as Timber to his colleagues he guessed immediately that the gun spelt big trouble.

"Who found the gun?

Sue replied. "I guess I did. I was just going to pack some clothes for Miss Burns and pulled out this brown case when the gun fell down from under the bed. We haven't touched it."

"How did it get out here then?"

"I pulled it out Sarge. But I was careful not to touch it."

"Good." Timber prodded it with his foot. "Bloody hell! That's a vicious looking shooter. Who lives here?"

"Miss Burns is here and there was another man when I got here but he scarpered as soon as he saw the gun. A black guy called Elroy but he said he lives downstairs. There does seem to be signs of another man being here."

Harry interrupted. "Sorry to trouble you gents but I need to get this girl to the hospital sharpish otherwise she may not be able to answer any questions and judging by the cuts and bruises you can see she has been badly beaten and she didn't do that to herself."

Timber looked at Jennie. "Yes. You'd better take her but make sure I know where she is and don't let her walk out of the hospital until I have seen her. What are your names?"

"I'm Harry Parr and this is Sue Walinski and we are based at St Georges and that is where she will be going.

They had Jennie on the stretcher and down the stairs as quickly as they dared.

More Police arrived and the gun was safely bagged and taken off to forensic for testing and fingerprints.

Timber wandered downstairs and into the flat but there was no sign of Elroy.

He went back to Jennie's flat. "I want this place completely turned over. We have a gun but now where is the ammo. They made a thorough search of Jennie's flat but found nothing until Jeff Henriques noticed that the flower in a vase was dead. He turned the vase upside down and the ammunition for the gun fell into his hands.

Timber looked at it. "Bloody fool. He's asking to be shot himself. My guess is that others are involved. It takes connections to get a gun and ammunition like that, and they won't be pleased that he's lost it."

After they were satisfied that there was nothing else of interest they left. Elroy watched them go from his car where he had sheltered from the persistent drizzle then drove to his favourite pub hoping nobody had tried to tidy his bed up.

*

As the ambulance raced her to hospital Jennie's half-conscious mind slipped back to her childhood again. She was playing with her father while her mother was at church. He would pick her up and make her laugh. When the social workers had come to the house and asked her lots of questions about her dad she had kept quiet. He had always told her it was a secret and nobody else was to know because it was their private secret. Her mother was even worse after that and always made her go to church as well. Dad had left soon afterwards.

Ellie being born had brought her back to a sense of reality. As she thought of Ellie she began to cry. The one good thing that had happened to her and even that was taken away. Twenty years had not made that pain any the less.

She was still crying when the ambulance stopped outside emergency and she was wheeled in. She knew the routine but just didn't care anymore. They could do what they liked with her, just as everyone else had done.

She woke suddenly as her stomach was being washed out and the retching made her become conscious. After that was over she felt exhausted. The doctor took her pulse. She thought that he looked nice, he wouldn't be cruel to her.

"All right Miss Burns." He had a squeaky voice as if his voice was still breaking.

Jennie began to focus on the present. I could make his balls drop she thought, and giggled at the thought.

"Are you listening Miss Burns?" The squeak sounded annoyed. Perhaps he could read her mind. "You can stay the night and then someone from the psychiatry department will want to see you before we can let you go."

The Sister whispered in his ear. He shrugged his shoulders. "Do you understand?"

Jennie understood perfectly; she even knew the questions off by heart. She looked at him. "Balls" she said and giggled again.

"Bloody useless!" squeaked the doctor. "She'll be back in less than a month."

"Balls" repeated Jennie as she drifted off to sleep.

She slept unaware that they had found the shotgun and that the police would be waiting for her.

As she slept Sergeant Forrester called in to the hospital but soon realised he would get no sense out of her so he got an assurance from the Sister that she would not let Jennie go until one of his officers had spoken with her.

Meanwhile Karl had returned to the flat having got rid of the mirror. He was surprised to see all the police cars and an ambulance there but soon guessed that Jennie had taken another overdose. When he saw them bring out the shotgun he knew he would have a lot of explaining to do. He slipped away quickly. People like Karl always have somewhere else to hide.

Chapter eight

Rude awakening

Jennie was still deeply asleep when the hospital morning began and did not take kindly to being woken up. Her head was still throbbing and her throat was raw from all her treatment. Being subjected to a thermometer being stuck in her ear was one step too much.

"Get away from me!" She yelled, and promptly regretted doing so as the resultant cough seemed to rasp her throat open.

"A drink." She whispered. "Get me a fucking drink."

"There will be a cup of tea coming shortly. Now just relax so I can take your temperature. It isn't going to hurt."

"No! I need a drink."

"Very well then; I will just go and get the rectum thermometer."

Jennie could see that this was not a battle she could win and her throat was just too sore to argue any more. "Ear then."

After the nurse took the temperature she began to plump up the pillows so that Jennie could sit up. As she straightened the sheets Jennie suddenly became aware of a police officer sitting by the door.

She whispered to the nurse. "What's the fuzz doing here?"

"She's come to see you. I think she wants to know why you had a sawn off shotgun under your bed."

Jennie suddenly realised what had happened. She swore loudly.

"Do you mind! We have a lot of patients here who do not want to hear you mouthing off obscenities."

The police officer heard Jennie swear and came over to the bed.

Jennie's mind panicked. What could she say? If she told the truth Karl would kill her. She decided to feign weakness.

"Good morning Miss Burns. My name is Mary Heron and as you can see I am a police officer. We were called to your flat yesterday after you had taken a large overdose. When the ambulance medic took a case from under your bed so that you could have some clean clothes, she discovered a shotgun. I would like you to tell me what it was doing there."

"I'm sorry. I don't know what you are talking about. Please let me rest, my head is very, very tired."

"You weren't very tired a minute ago."

"But I don't know anything about it. It must have been left there by the people before us. We've only been there a week."

"No you haven't. You have been to the hospital three times this year and all at the same address and it was your case that was propping up the gun. "

"It was there when we moved in."

"You said we. So you are not on your own. We didn't think you were especially as it's obvious you've been hit recently. Can you confirm for me that Mr Karl Kuyper is also still living at this address?"

"Jennie realised she was in danger of saying more than was healthy so she went on the offensive. "Piss off and leave me alone. I'm not saying anything else to you."

"In that case I will have to assume that you are responsible for the gun and charge you under the firearms act with having an illegal firearm in your possession."

"So what" I've told you it's not mine and you won't find any of my finger prints on it so you will have a problem proving that I have anything to do with it."

"So you are telling me it belongs to Karl."

"I never said that!"

"There's just you and him there so if it isn't you it must be him."

"And I told you it was there before we moved in."

"Which, I presume, is why it was on top of your suitcase?"

Jennie could feel that she was digging a hole that she could not escape from. "Nurse!" She called out. "Nurse, I'm not feeling well, I think I'm going to faint."

Mary smiled. "That's OK by me. I can wait. If we need to we can charge you with the possession and get you remanded in custody. I must say I think you have a nerve, sleeping on top of a loaded shotgun. Didn't you ever worry about it going off while you were in bed? Tell me, what is Karl going to think when he knows you are here with me? I think you may need protective custody as you are a witness if you are telling me the truth, but Karl must be worried. His gun is gone. You are with the police. I'll give you a rest to think about what to say."

Mary returned to her chair by the door where she could see Jennie but not be overheard. She rang through to the police station and reported on the situation.. Jennie became even more agitated but none of the staff took any notice of her.

Mary returned and sat down but said nothing.

Jennie glared at her. "So you're back again pig. I'm still saying nothing."

Mary stopped the urge to correct her grammar and just sat there saying nothing.

"Do you hear me pig. I'm not saying nothing. I had nothing to do with the gun and I don't know what was going to be done with it either."

Mary spoke. "So Karl had plans to use it had he; perhaps a robbery or worse? If you know that then we could charge you with being an accessory before the fact and that would carry a long prison sentence."

"Go away! Leave me alone! You'll get me killed saying things like that. It's nothing to do with me. "

"All right Jennie. I've spoken to my boss and she agrees with me that we will let you go for now but if you change your mind just ring me on this number. But you know I will want to talk to you again later." She handed a card to Jennie and then left it on the bedside table when Jennie refused to take it. Mary got up slowly and walked out of the door, turning just before she left. "You should think Jennie. We may be your best hope of living."

As soon as Mary was out of sight Jennie was ringing for the nurse to come and demanding her clothes. It was only the opportune arrival of Albert that calmed her down.

"You've taken your bloody time." She yelled at him, ignoring the fact that she wasn't even expecting him. "Where were you yesterday when I needed you?"

Albert was a bit nonplussed at her attack. "I was up town at the funeral of one of my old mates. Then I stopped off at the Pig to try and cheer myself up. That's where I heard about you being in here, so I thought I should bring you some grapes but I had to wait until the shop was open."

"Well I want to get out of here before the shrink comes to bore me with his stupid ideas."

"He's only trying to help you. Did you take too many tablets again? Oh dear. I do get worried about you sometimes. You know you really should look after yourself better and that bloke of yours – well I just don't like him and what he does to you. Just look at your face again. It's not good enough."

"O be quiet you silly man. You don't know what you're talking about. Just get me my clothes from the desk and help me to get out of here."

"I don't think they will give them to me. And the Sister said you had to wait until the doctor said you were fit enough to be discharged.

"Bugger them! I can go when I want to." She got out of the bed and staggered towards the door.

Albert called her back. "You can't go like that. Your gown is all open at the back!"

"Miss Burns!" The Staff Nurse had seen her move. "You've been told you cannot go until the doctor says so."

"Just give me my fucking clothes and let me get out of here. I know what the doctor will say and it's no use him saying it. There's no way I'm staying in now I can move and you can't stop me. Just give me my clothes and I'll sign you bloody paper."

Albert tried to intervene. "Don't be so ungrateful Jennie. They probably saved your life last night and they do have to do things properly."

"I didn't ask them to bring me here. I don't even know how they knew where I was or what I had done. Why don't they let me die in my own way rather than have Karl kick me to death. He's probably waiting for me now."

"He won't be anywhere near with the police being around."

"Don't make it worse Albert. I've got to get out of here now. I'm not waiting any longer. The police have already got my number and if Karl finds out he might think I've grassed him up and you know what he will try to do."

The Staff Nurse beckoned one of the Auxiliary staff. Can you get Miss Burn's case please? As you say, we cannot stop you. Here is the voluntary discharge form. Frankly I think everybody will be glad to see you go after your behaviour this morning. You wouldn't think we had just saved your life."

"I didn't ask you….."

Albert interrupted before she upset the nurse even more. "Thank you. I know what you mean and I'm sure she is just upset by the police. We are grateful, really we are."

The nurse came with the case and Jennie quickly changed into her clothes. She left the case on the bed and grabbed Albert's arm. "Come on you silly old fart. Let's get out of here. If I can get home before Karl it might just be OK. I might be able to make him think I've been there all the time.

Albert stopped to catch his breath. "Slow down Jennie. I don't think that is going to work. You've been here all night and the police have searched your flat already. You don't really think Karl doesn't know what has happened already. Even if he doesn't how will you explain where the gun has gone."

She stopped. "Shit! He really will kill me this time. What can I do? Where can I go?

"You can stay at my place. After all I have a spare room that you can use and you know you don't have to worry about me. There's nobody else there to bother us."

Jennie thought about the offer quietly for a moment as she rested on one of the stone columns outside the hospital. "Yes, that might just work because he doesn't know where you live and he would never expect you to take me in. But I do have to go to the house and get my stuff."

"I'll come with you in case he's there."

"Don't be silly Albert. You would only end up getting hurt as well."

"I am an old soldier you know. I was the regiment's boxing champion at my weight. I fought in Korea until I got shot in the leg and had to come home. That's when I married Ruth."

"Albert! That was over fifty years ago. I have to go in by myself. I will meet you at you gaff later. Just let me have the bus fare and I will see you later."

Albert got his purse out and began to count out some coins."

Jennie saw a fiver and plucked it out. "You've been on a free bus pass for too long. I'll see you later."

Albert watched the bus until it was out of sight. It wasn't really his responsibility, but somehow he couldn't convince himself so he changed his direction and went to the police station instead of going straight home.

Chapter nine

Warnings

Jenny tried her best to get into the house as unobtrusively as possible. The front door was unlocked so she pushed it gently and listened for any noise. There was no reggae music playing so she know Elroy could not be in. Everything was quiet. She crept up the stairs and went into her flat. The room had obviously been thoroughly searched and drawer contents were scattered on the bed. She sat there trying to recapture what had actually happened last night. She didn't hear Elroy until he spoke.

"Hi there babe! Glad to see you still in the land of the living."

The shock of hearing him made her leap to her feet. "You bastard Elroy!"

Don't you ever creep up on me like that again!"

"Hey! Cool it honey. I'm the good guy, well at least as far as you're concerned. I was just glad to see you after all that shit last night."

"Were you there? Oh, I think I remember. Didn't you say something about dancing with me?"

"Well, it was either me or a copper with the biggest feet I've ever seen."

"The police were here? I didn't just imagine it then?"

"'Fraid not, and they found a real wicked looking piece under your bed, so I guess they are out looking for Karl, and in case you ask he has not been seen. I heard he had been stopped last night for trying to sell an old mirror but they let him go before they knew about the shooter."

"Where is he now? Do you know?"

"Don't know and I don't want to know. The filth were here for a long time last night so he wouldn't have come anywhere near and there is a special's car down the road keeping a watch. See down there next to the red Ford. There is a grey Astra with a couple in and they are not having a picnic or anything else."

They must have seen me. O God, what can I do? I've got to get my gear and move out. I need to earn some money fast so's I can get away."

You'll need something warmer than that if you plan to be out in this weather. Have you got anywhere to go?"

"I'll find somewhere. Now just go and let me get my stuff together and then I'm off."

"You know where I am if you need me."

Jennie wasted no time in filling two carrier bags with her clothing but as she turned to leave her way was barred by an older man wearing dark glasses and sporting an Elvis haircut.

"Planning to move on are you Jennie? Me and my friends have a place for you to stop in. After all we don't want your loose lips causing problems for Karl. We would not be happy at all so why don't we just go quietly and have a nice long drive.

Apart from feeling scared, Jennie couldn't help thinking that he was making a bad effort to sound like a Hollywood extra in an old black and white gangster film. The thought gave her a bravery she did not feel.

"Don't you come here trying to scare me! If you want me to keep quiet just leave me alone but if you come any closer I'm going to scream all the way down to the cop car that's been sat out there all morning. Now get out of my way and tell Karl for me that he had better back off or else I could remember a lot more."

She swung her bags at him and to her surprise he backed away and let her through. As she got to the top of the stairs he called out. "You're walking now babe but any talk and you are dead."

Jennie ran down the stairs as fast as she could in her high heels. As she reached the street she saw Elroy leaning on his car.

He pointed to the front seat and without a second thought she got in. "Bastard!" She exclaimed.

Elroy got in and started to drive. He smiled. "Yeah! They never did find my father. I thought you might want some fast wheels when I saw him trying to hide on the landing."

"He might have killed me and you would have just gone and left me."

"Dave wouldn't have done that. He's all muscle on the outside and jelly in his brain. He wouldn't know how to kill you without being told. Still he is in with some nasty stuff now. Karl probably sent him round to scare you. Where are we going?"

"I don't know. Where have I got that will be safe? Let's get a drink somewhere so I can think."

"I can get you some trade if you like. You've been wasted with Karl. He doesn't appreciate your talents. You need to work the older end of the market, a bit of escort like with Albert. I could look after you and give you a fair split of the takings."

Don't be stupid Elroy. Karl would never let me work for anyone else. He would kill us both. Can you imagine him letting you walk in and take his meal ticket because that's what I am. I'm what pays for his keep and he won't give me up. Not even now."

Elroy smiled again. "I don't think he will have much choice soon, not if he's running around without his shotgun. I can just see him trying to explain that to his new friends."

"You let me out Elroy. You hear me! Let me out!"

Jennie grabbed the steering wheel and tried to turn it but just caused it to swerve before Elroy stopped it in the middle of the road. "Go on then Jen, get out. I'll put this down to nerves but my offer stays open and you'll come crawling back to me. Karl is history and the sooner you realise that the better it will be. He's no use to you anymore."

Jennie almost fell out of the car and dropped one of her carrier bags. She slammed the door shut. "Piss off Elroy."

Elroy did so leaving his tyre tracks all over her best knickers. She then had to get out of the way as a lorry demolished the bag and left her laundry all over the road.

Jennie managed to get all her stuff together without further mishap, then sat on the pavement feeling totally lost. Suddenly she realised she was just around the corner from Albert. Perhaps he was her best hope after all. Five minutes later she was ringing his front door bell.

Albert was in but he wasn't alone.

Jennie could see her sitting in the kitchen as he came to the door.

I'm sorry Albert. I didn't know you had company but I do need your help. You are the only person who might be able to tell me what to do."

As she spoke her eyes filled with tears, her voice broke and she began to shake.

Albert had to catch her to prevent her from falling. "Steady girl. I knew you should have stayed in hospital longer but come on in and let's see what we can do. Anyway I have someone here who might be able to help you and she wants to have a chat with you."

Jennie was surprised at how strong Albert was in holding her up and leading her into the house at the same time. She was in the hallway before she realised what he was saying.

"I can't see nobody, not like this. I don't want her to see me, just let me sit in the front room for a while."

By now she was snuffling as she spoke, tears mingling with her running nose. She wiped her sleeve across her face. Albert did as she had asked and helped her in to the room and sat her in his favourite chair. She slumped into it as he went out and brought her bag and other clothes in.

As he put them down he looked at her sprawled like a hastily dumped pile of washing. "You just take it easy lass and get your breath back. Then you can have a chat with me and Mary.

"I can't Albert, I can't see anybody now. It's all too much for me. I just wish it was all over." She used her sleeve again and Albert put his clean handkerchief into her hand.

"Thank you." She whispered and promptly blew her nose very loudly.

Albert was not to be put off. That's why you need to talk with Mary. She's come here especially today and on her day off too."

Jennie was too tired to argue any more. "Just leave me alone for a while please Albert, then I'll talk to her."

Albert walked to the door and then turned to her. "I've brought your bags in Jennie. You can stay if you want to."

She looked up at him not quite believing what he was saying. "What?"

"I said you can stay if you want to."

"You don't really mean that Albert. You don't want the likes of me here. I'd be nothing but trouble for you."

Albert looked at her directly. "There's nobody else in this life to trouble me my dear. You would be doing me a favour as long as Karl stays away."

Before she could say any more he closed the door and returned to the kitchen where Mary was waiting patiently, nursing a large mug of tea. Albert had given up cups a long time ago as being insufficient for him.

She looked up. "Well?"

He went over to the plug and put the kettle on again. "Give her a bit of time to rest. She looks all in and she needs somewhere to stay."

"Do you mean you want her to stay here?" Mary's voice sounded surprised if not actually slightly shocked.

Albert smiled at her. "Have I shocked you dear; life can be very lonely when you're on your own at my age, and Jennie has been the one person to bring me a bit of joy."

"Have you been one of her punters Albert?"

"Oh dear! I see you that you disapprove. Is it because I pay for my little bit of pleasure, or have I just become another dirty old man. Age doesn't stop you wanting company you know."

Mary blushed. "I'm sorry Albert. It's none of my business but I wouldn't like to see you getting hurt. She could take advantage of your kindness."

The kettle began to whistle and Albert poured the boiling water out into his old green tea pot. "We'll see. Somehow I feel that she has had enough of living in chaos. Perhaps I can bring some peace into her life, like being a place of safety. That's why she's here now you know, for safety."

Mary wanted to believe the old man. "I hope so. But it's not just Jennie. It's everything she's tied up with; Karl, shotguns, drugs and her life style. Karl seems to have disappeared for now and I don't think he will be far away."

The front room door opened and Jennie appeared. She gazed into the kitchen and mumbled. "Got to go to the loo."

While she was upstairs Mary asked Albert. "What have you told her about me?"

"Just that you are Mary and that you are here to help her."

"So she doesn't know that I am the police officer that saw her in hospital?"

"No, I didn't want to scare her off and you're in civvies now, not uniform."

"I have to tell her because I will have to arrest her for being aware of the shotgun and that Karl planned to use it."

"Not today you don't because you are off duty"

The sound of flushing warned them that Jenny was on her way back. Albert went and poured out a fresh mug of tea. "Do you want some more dear?"

"No thanks Albert. I still have some."

"It must be stone cold by now."

"You get used to that in the police."

Jennie reappeared and came into the kitchen, looking suspiciously at Mary. She sat down at the other side of the table.

Albert plonked the mug of tea in front of her. "There you are my dear. Not too strong and two sugars. Do you remember meeting Mary before?"

Jennie's face was still blotchy and Albert's handkerchief was clutched in her hand. She studied Mary. "I can't remember, but you do look familiar."

Mary tried to reassure her. "I was wearing my uniform when you saw me before."

Jennie frowned as she tried to think. "Nurse? No." Then she started. "Fuzz! Albert she's fuzz!"

Mary acted quickly. "It's OK Jennie. I was there last night so I know all about you and the hospital and about Karl and the shotgun."

"Karl! What about Karl?" She had pushed her chair back and sat bolt upright when his name was mentioned.

"He was stopped last night when someone saw him carrying a mirror but he was released when they discovered it had been in a skip. That was before we knew about the gun and you."

"Gun? What Gun?" Jennie did her best to sound surprised.

"Come on Jennie. You know what gun; you had some nerve sleeping on top of a shotgun."

Jennie tried to get up but Mary moved over and grabbed her arm. Jennie screamed.

"Albert. What have you done?"

Albert stood by the cooker not knowing what to do. "It's all for the best dear. Drink you tea and listen to the girl."

Mary was still holding Jennie's arm but she relaxed her grip and Jennie pulled away from her and sat down again.

Mary looked her in the eye. "Yes Jennie. Listen to me. I've come here informally to give you a chance to speak off the record. I met Albert this morning and he was worried about you. He though that you might be in danger with Karl. We need to know about him and what he was planning to do with the gun."

"I don't know. I wish I did because he'll kill me if he even thinks I've spoken to you."

"Mary persisted. "Tell me about the gun Jennie and then I'll stop pestering you."

"It wasn't him. He was looking after it for a mate and I don't know who he is. It was only for a week. He was going to take it back this weekend."

"Where was he going to take it?"

"I don't know, I tell you I don't know. Just leave me alone!" She collapsed over Albert's blue rose formica table and began to weep loudly into her arms.

Albert went over and put a protective hand on her back. "You didn't need to be so hard on her especially as she's weak and tired."

Mary looked at them. "Yes. I'm sorry. But it is so important that we find out what the gun was going to be used for and when. I think Jennie has given us some idea if Karl really was taking it back this weekend. Jennie! Are you listening to me? You will have to come in to the police station tomorrow morning and make a statement. It will depend a lot on what you say whether or not you can be charged with an offence in relation to the gun. If you are straight with the interviewing officer he will take that into consideration, but if you try to be silly then he won't like it."

Albert asked. "When does she have to be there?"

"Ten o'clock. I should be around at that time so I can keep an eye on how things are going."

Albert walked with her to the door. "Thank you for coming. She'll be all right with me. I will make sure she is there if I have to carry her.

Mary shook his hand. "Thank you Albert. I am sorry if you found it upsetting but it is so important for us to try and find out about the gun." She called back into the kitchen where Jennie was still slumped over the table. "Goodbye Jennie. I'll see you tomorrow morning." There was no reply.

Albert shut the door and walked slowly back into the kitchen where he sat next to Jennie. Gently he put his arm round her shoulder. "I'm sorry if it upset you dear, but it had to be done. It isn't going to go away all by itself. Not now there is this gun involved. Why don't you go and have a lie down upstairs. Give yourself time to think and have a decent sleep. You don't need to worry about him while you are here."

Jennie put her head into Albert's shoulder. "I'm so scared of him Albert. I don't know what to do."

"Have you no family?"

Jennie snorted. "Family! That's joke. Last I heard of my father he was in nick and my mother hates me. Even Ellie must hate me."

There was a short silence before Albert spoke again. "Ellie? Is that your sister?"

"No Albert. Ellie was my baby but my mother took her away from me and threw me out. I think I will go and lie down. I really do feel very tired."

As she got to the stairs she turned. "Did you really mean I could stay?"

Albert nodded. "Yes, that's what I said, after all it doesn't sound as if either of us has anybody else."

Jennie managed a smile. "You really are a daft old bugger. You sound just like my dad."

Albert made himself comfortable in his armchair and watched the television until his eyes switched off. It was three o'clock when his bladder made him wake up and go to the toilet. He looked in on Jennie and she was fast asleep. Then he returned to his armchair turned off the television and made himself comfortable and on guard.

Chapter ten

Moving the bed.

Andy had his usual light breakfast and walked round to Hurley Road after texting Ellie to make sure he wasn't too early. Flo was busy in the kitchen when he arrived.

She opened the door for him. "Goodness gracious me!" She exclaimed. "What do you think you are doing here at this time of the morning? Ellie is still asleep."

"That's all right. I'll just pop up and let her know I'm here."

"You'll not do any popping up while I am here." Flo barred his way to the stairs with a frying pan, which he assumed had originally been meant for the breakfast.

Ellie's voice came from upstairs. "It's all right Aunty. I'm decent. Do let him come up please."

Flo glared at Andy and did not look is if she was going to yield whatever Ellie said but she did lower the pan and return to the kitchen muttering as she went. "Really! I don't know what the world's coming to."

Ellie was fully dressed as she had read his text. "Thank goodness you're here. I've been sitting here for half an hour. I've had a rotten night's sleep and I don't think I could face Aunty Flo by myself."

They hugged each other and Andy kissed her lightly. "I don't think I could ever cope with her by myself. She is something else!"

The smell of bacon began to waft upstairs.

He smiled. "Looks like you are in for the full English today. None of this nibbling a couple of slices of toast. We'd better go down before she cooks the lot."

They got to the kitchen just in time to stop Flo from cooking the second half of the bacon. She was already tucking into a large bowel of cornflakes while keeping her eye on six rashers of bacon and three frying eggs.

"There you are. Come and sit down here Ellie. I could only find cornflakes I'm afraid. Personally I do prefer All Bran and fruit, especially prunes. They keep me regular as clockwork. Muriel too; we never have to bother the doctor. I didn't know that Andy was going to be here for breakfast as well."

Andy hastily reassured her that he had eaten already but would welcome a cup of tea.

Flo ignored him. "Sit down Ellie. Now do you want three rashers or four?"

"Sorry Aunty, I only eat toast for breakfast."

"What nonsense" You need a good hearty breakfast to set you up for the day. No wonder you have nearly wasted away. We have to book the vicar and let all her friends know don't we?"

Before Ellie had a chance to reply she went on. "We'll make a list after breakfast." As she spoke she plonked a plate in front of Ellie already filled with two eggs and three rashers of bacon. There now eat up. How many slices of bread do you want? Here's two to be getting on with."

To Andy's surprise Ellie did as she was told and began to eat. "Well." He said, "I never thought I would see the day. Do you mind if I make myself a cup of tea?"

As he poured his tea Flo continued to chatter while Ellie ate silently. "Did your mother have any friends Ellie, or shall we just have quiet little service at the crematorium?"

Ellie stopped and even though her mouth was still busy she paused. "Of course mum had lots of friends, both at work and at church. She used to go out with her friends from the factory on Fridays nights." She stopped and swallowed. "Oh Andy it is Friday. I think I have told most of them and I expect Patsy will have told everyone as well. The people at church know but I haven't been able to speak to the minister yet to make sure he can be there next Thursday. She began to get up but Flo stopped her. "You finish your breakfast dear. We can deal with the rest later. Have you really done all that by yourself already?"

Andy replied for Ellie. "Yes she has been very busy. The doctor suggested she make a list. It's next door. You might like to see it in case there are family members that should know. I'll go and get it for you., and I should try to get my sister again."

He went into the front room and tried to contact Mary again but had no luck so he left a text message for her. He tried the police station but was told that Mary had a day off. By the time he got back into the kitchen Ellie was in tears and Flo was trying to console her.

"Now come along dear, I was only trying to help. If you don't want your mother to come to the funeral then that is perfectly all right!"

Her words did nothing to help and Ellie ran out of the kitchen and upstairs to her room where they could hear her sobbing.

Andy looked at Flo. He said nothing in case it would make things worse and he expected Flo to fill in the gap. She did not disappoint him.

"I only asked her if she was planning to find her mother and invite her to the funeral and she looked at me as if I was mad and said that her mum was dead and had to be at the funeral. Then she turned on the tears and – well I mean. I had better go and make sure she is all right."

As she moved towards the door Andy stepped in front of her. "No. I t's me she will want to see." Before she could say anything else he ran upstairs leaving Flo muttering about how she didn't understand young people and how thoughtless they were.

As soon as he got to the door Ellie yelled at him. "Go away Andy, I don't want you to see me like this."

He ignored her and walked in. "Don't be silly Ellie. I'll have to get used to seeing you like this when we are married."

Ellie turned towards him and threw her arms around him burying her face in his chest. "Oh Andy, darling, darling Andy; you won't ever leave me will you? You're the only person I have left." She sobbed deeply into his clean shirt. He held her and stroked her hair.

After a while she pulled away from him and looked into his eyes intently.

"I just don't know what to believe any more; my mums not my mum but my gran; my real mum didn't want me and they don't even know my father's name, and my grandfather died in prison for God knows what and the only member of the family I know is Aunty Flo and she is just so – so – indescribable.

She began to giggle at the thought and pulled him tightly towards her, so close that they could feel each other's hearts beating. Slowly Ellie began to relax but she took Andy's hand and placed it on her breast and kissed him long and passionately.

"Make love to me Andy. Make love to me now."

Ever practical Andy asked. "What about Aunty Flo."

She giggled again. "There's not room for her as well." They both began to laugh.

I thought you wanted us to wait until we were married."

"Somehow that doesn't seem so important anymore. I just know that I want to make love to you so much that it hurts and nothing else matters. You do want me, don't you?"

"Want you! If you only knew how many cold showers I have had since I met you. But are you sure?"

"I've never been so sure of anything in my whole life except that I love you, and I want us to make love now."

As she spoke she rolled off the bed and unbuttoned her pink blouse then unhooked and unzipped her skirt, letting it fall to the floor and leaving her standing there just in her bra and pants. She had no tights on. "Your turn."

Andy felt confused about this turn of events and even less sure about Aunty Flo downstairs but nevertheless he followed suit. Shoes off, shirt vest and trousers tumbling to the ground.

Ellie sat on the bed and slipped out of her underwear and lay there waiting for him. She watched his every move. He looked good, lean and fit. She began to tremble at the thought of what they were about to do.

Andy slipped his pants off and rolled over to her. As their feet touched they discovered that he still had his socks on and this started them laughing again. Andy slipped them off and this time they held each other closely enjoy the touch of their bodies together.

Andy began to caress her, letting his hand stray over her body from her stomach up to her breasts then down to her hips and round to her buttocks. They kissed and moved together slowly and sensually until they were completed. Still they held each other closely as if to hold on to this moment for ever. Gently they stroked each other.

"Are you all right up there?" Aunty Flo's voice cut through the emotions of the moment. Together they replied. "Yes, everything is fine."

Ellie sat on the edge of the bed. "I must get to the bathroom. Can you look to see if Aunty Flo is out of the way?"

He opened the door slightly. After all Flo might not appreciate the sight of him at to moment either. "All clear." He said.

Ellie grabbed her clothes and ran to the bathroom while Andy began to dress himself. He was just zipping his trousers up when there was a knock on the door.

He walked over and opened it. Flo was there looking worried. "Are you sure everything is all right? "

Andy smiled at her. Yes, we are fine now. Ellie has just gone to the bathroom to wash her face. We'll be down very soon. I hope there is some tea still in the pot. I'm gasping."

"I don't know." said Flo looking straight at him. "All that laughing and crying; not to mention some other very strange noises!.."

Andy smiled even more. "Everything is fine now Aunty Flo. Ellie just had a weepy spell but I cheered her up."

"Well, I don't know but it sounded as if you were moving the furniture."

Andy nearly cracked up as he said. "You are right. You could have heard that. Ellie wanted some help moving her bed."

Flo couldn't understand why he thought that was so funny.

Ellie emerged from the bathroom fully dressed but still a bit flushed. Hello Aunty, I'm fine now. Sorry I behaved so stupidly downstairs. I'll try not to do it again but thinking about mum still makes me want to cry. Is there any tea left? I feel very thirsty."

Flo looked even more confused. "What did you want to move your bed for?"

Ellie did not bat an eyelid but carried on. "Perhaps we can check my list in case there are people you know that I have missed off. I'll ring the minister now and arrange a meeting with him and see if we can sort the rest out over a cup of tea. Will that be all right with you Aunty?"

Flo was on the retreat now. This new found confidence was not what she expected. "Why, yes, of course, a pot of tea, good idea, I'll just go and put the kettle on again." As she turned to go she suddenly looked at Andy. "You're not wearing your shoes Andy."

Andy looked down at his feet. One big toe was sticking out of his sock. He felt the colour rush to his cheeks and he and Ellie both began to laugh again.

Suddenly a light seemed to shine in Flo's mind. "Oh! - Oh! – "Then to their surprise she said "I'm not surprised you need another cup of tea."

They all went downstairs and while Flo went to put the kettle on Ellie rang the Rev. Brian Evans, the minister at their church.

"Hello Mr Evans. It's Ellie Burns here. Oh good. You have heard about mum already. That was good of them to let you know. So you will be free on Thursday for the funeral. Oh I am relieved. I know mum wouldn't have wanted anyone else. Oh that would be kind. Oh yes that would be lovely. So the crematorium service would be at two o'clock and then there would be a service of thanksgiving at the church at three followed by tea. Good, oh that is all such a relief to me. Thank you. So I can come to talk to you tomorrow afternoon and is it all right if Andy comes with me. Good. Thank you so much."

She went back into the kitchen and sat down. A fresh cup of tea was there for her.

"What a relief." She said. "The funeral people had already rung him and everything is sorted. I have an appointment with him tomorrow afternoon. The crem will be at two o'clock and then they want a service at the church with tea to follow. Mrs Wagstaff and the catering squad have offered to do it for free in memory of mum. Isn't that good of them!"

Andy gave her a hug. "So all that worrying was for nothing."

Ellie looked around. "Where is Aunty Flo?"

"Even she has to go to the loo sometimes."

"Well before she comes back, can you come with me to see Brian Evans tomorrow."

"Yes of course I will. But won't that upset Flo?"

"Did I hear my name mentioned Ellie?" "

"Oh hello Aunty; yes its very good news. The church has sorted out the funeral for Thursday afternoon as I thought. Two o'clock at the crematorium and then three o'clock at the church for a service of thanksgiving with tea afterwards for those who want to stay."

"My goodness that was quick; I must go and see that the arrangements are all in order. Perhaps I will come with you to church on Sunday and see the vicar so he knows what to do."

"He's a minister Aunty and his name is Brian Evans. Andy and me are going to have a chat with him tomorrow afternoon."

"But I must come as well. You won't know what to tell him."

"He won't need to be told what to do Aunty. He has known mum for years. Anyway I want to ask him what he knows about Jennie. If mum spoke to anyone about her it would be him."

"But you won't know what to ask him?"

"I don't need to know because he will be telling me what is needed. If you come to church on Sunday you will be able to meet him and to meet the lady who is in charge of the catering at the church."

"Someone else in charge of the arrangements! I won't hear of it. I should be responsible for it as her sister."

"I am sure they will be glad of you help but Mrs Wagstaff is a personal friend of mum's and she has all the resources she needs at the church."

It took some time to stop Flo from chuntering on about how she should be doing everything. She was still unsettled when Ellie and Andy had to leave to sort out the last of the paperwork at the Co-op.

Chapter eleven

Bin bags

The visit to the Funeral Director confirmed that mum had indeed had a policy with them which would cover the whole cost of her funeral. Ellie chose a simple coffin as she knew that her mother had always felt it was a waste of money and resources to buy a fancy box when you couldn't see it. She had demurred at the suggestion of a wicker coffin as she knew well that Flo would say it showed a lack of respect.

They had been really helpful and she came away feeling almost redundant. Rosie was in their chapel of rest and available for viewing though Ellie declined the offer as she had already seen mum at the hospital. She and Andy stopped for a sandwich lunch in a nearby park and enjoyed a spot of November sunshine. It made a lot of difference to the previous week of heavy showers and drizzle.

Andy had some things to attend to at his flat so he left Ellie and arranged to come round in the early evening. Ellie went home via her work at Tescos and called in to see her boss Jill. She agreed to go in to work for the morning, which was always one of the busiest times of the week.

As she went through the door she glanced round and could see that Flo had been busy. The house looked tidier than it had ever been. She had not expected the black bin bags filled with mum's clothing. One was for the WRVS or Oxfam, one for the next jumble sale. This was just a bit too efficient for Ellie and she stood there looking at them and began to cry again.

Flo enveloped her with a smothering hug. "Come, come; these things have to be done and I knew it would be difficult for you. After all none of it would fit me, and I can't see a smart young woman like you in any of these styles. They might fit Muriel but I don't think Rosie would approve somehow. She did have some very old fashioned ideas. I blame our parents for that."

It all sounded so logical that Ellie couldn't argue with it and she would have found it hard to do. This time Flo had definitely got it right.

"Thank you Aunty. You are quite right. It would have been ages before I could have done that. What were your parents like? Mum never really said anything about them."

"Well, I don't know what I can say about them. Father had been a soldier in the war and I think he still thought we were his recruits. He never asked me to do anything, he always told me. They were both very religious and we had to go to church every Sunday morning and afternoon. I was eight years older than your mother so when she was born our parents were nearly forty. Father wouldn't allow mother to work, or to have any friends outside the church and then only the ones he approved of."

"How awful!"

"Well, yes it was awful. I think it was my father that put me off men altogether. I was always a bit rebellious and I suffered for it so I left home as soon as I could and never went back. When Muriel came to live with me they cut me off and I never heard from them again. I didn't even know that my mother was dead until my father died and Rosie told me."

"It's no wonder mum didn't say much about them."

"She of course was their ideal child. She was only eight or nine when I left and she just did everything she was told. When she became pregnant with Jennie it was a disaster. She told me that she didn't know anything about sex and wasn't even sure how Jennie was conceived, but that Reg had fooled her somehow. He was probably just fooling around with her but he hadn't reckoned with our Dad.

They were married as soon as he found out and then he had no more to do with her afterwards. He was such an unforgiving man and though it seems awful I find it hard to think of him with any forgiveness for all the bullying and unkindness that he showed. I couldn't even think of going to church until Muriel showed me that there was so much more to it than his hateful ideas."

By this time Flo was looking quite flushed and Ellie had to get her to sit down.

"I'm sorry I asked. It sounds as if I was lucky not to know them. Let me make you a cup of tea. You look quite exhausted."

"Thank you my dear. I think a cup of tea would be very welcome unless you have a sherry. Just thinking of that man still makes me feel ill."

"I am not surprised that mum never said much about him."

"It did affect her though. It was possibly worse than me because she never really loved Jennie. She could never get her father's words out of her head when he said she was the spawn of the devil. Think she was always too hard on the girl but she did turn out to be wicked. I know she should know about Rosie because I would hate for anyone to feel like I did when I discovered that my mother had been dead for five years."

"Rosie was only ten when her mother died and she was on her own with that man for five years before she escaped. It was the one good thing to come out of her time with Reg. He was a no good evil man but compared to our father he was a gift from God. But I am afraid that the wicked streak is in Jennie and Rosie did to her as her father had done to her. She threw her out and shunned her thereafter. If you do find her be careful because she is not the mother that you would want to find."

Ellie poured the tea out and gave Flo a cup. "I suddenly feel that I must find her. I have had such a lot of love and encouragement in the middle of all the family misery that I almost feel guilty that I should have been so privileged when mum, you and Jennie have had such horrible life experiences. Somehow I need to find Jennie to let her know that I know about her and that I can love her just because she is my mother, in spite of anything else she may be."

Flo looked at her. "You are going to be a remarkable young woman Ellie but I am afraid you will get hurt even more by what you find."

Ellie stood looking out of the window. "I am the future and I have heard in the last two days so much sadness and wickedness that I can never be the girl that I was last week. I believe that there can be change and hope and I do believe in love."

Her mobile phone rang. It was Andy. "Hi Andy; where are you?"

She listened for a moment the turned to Flo. "It's Andy; he's going to get a takeaway. Do you want a pizza or a burger."

"Don't they have anything English – like fish and chips? It is Friday you know. We always have fish on Fridays."

"Andy – O you heard, is that all right – it is. Aunty what do you want?"

"Large cod and chips please a pickled onion and a large gherkin."

"Andy – Oh you heard again. Don't be vulgar, you know what I like, no it's not a big gherkin. Right we'll see you soon."

Andy dutifully turned up half an hour later with the order and while Ellie picked her way through her chicken and chips Flo demolished her cod and chips, gherkin, onion, five slices of bread and butter and three cups of tea.

She gazed with scorn at Ellie's chicken. "It's Friday you know. We always have fish on a Friday "

Andy couldn't resist the question. "Why is that then?"

Flo paused to lick her fingers. "Because that is what we have always done and it's a way of helping our brave fishermen make a living, and it's something religious as well."

Andy and Ellie looked at each other and tried not to laugh.

Andy started suddenly. "I was going to ring Mary again. She has been all over the place according to the desk sergeant but was supposed to be off today. I left a text message earlier but haven't even had one of those back. I hope she's OK. She hasn't rung here by any chance."

Flo finished wiping her plate with her last slice of bread. "No, I don't think so."

Ellie sat back. "I wouldn't bother her this evening. She may be out or even have a date. She doesn't get many evenings off. I think I'll have an early night. My head is still full of stuff and I feel very tired. You don't mind, do you love?"

"No, of course not! I might pop by her flat later on the off chance and you can get your beauty sleep. We can't have you going grey and wrinkly yet."

By this time Flo was in action. "I think that's the most sensible thing you've said all day Ellie. You get off to bed and leave the tidying up to me. And you young man can leave her to me. Off you go now. We'll see you tomorrow, but not too early. I want to be sure she has a good sleep and a decent breakfast."

She placed her substantial frame between them and walked Andy ahead of her towards the door, shooing him on his way. Before he could do much he found himself outside.

"You might at least have said thank you for the fish and chips." He said to the closed door. He walked round the corner to the window near Ellie and tapped on it. Ellie turned and saw him as he blew her a kiss.

Ellie smiled and blew one back just as Flo turned round and saw them.

"Really Ellie, I don't know what you see in him. Go away." She shouted and waved at the window. All she got was a big smile and then he blew her a kiss as well.

"You cheeky boy." She moved towards the window but he disappeared as he saw her coming. "Men; they are nothing but trouble!"

Ellie was still looking at the window. "I'm sorry Aunty Flo but I don't want you saying unkind things about Andy. He is really very kind. He took a whole day's leave just to be with me and to help me today. I'm so glad he is around even if he is a bit silly sometimes. I would marry him tomorrow if we had the money to start out on our own."

"You poor girl; just like your mother, completely smitten. I can't understand it. I've never found a man yet who wasn't going to cause more damage than he was worth."

"You haven't been lucky enough to find an Andy. But I will go to bed now. Thank you for your help today and thank you for telling me about your family. I think I can understand you and mum better now. I am going in to work for a while tomorrow to try and take my mind off things so I will be up early."

Good night Ellie. Are you sure you are all right? Do you want any cocoa or a hot water bottle?"

"No thanks. I'm fine, just tired." She walked slowly up the stairs without glancing back just in case she set Flo off again.

It took her longer to get to sleep than she thought because her head was so full of the family horrors and all the secrets she had been uncovering. Finally it all melted into one long dream which she would not remember in the morning light.

Chapter twelve

The shooting.

Andy went directly to Mary's flat but as he had half expected there was no reply. He wrote a short note to her on a piece of scrap paper and pushed it through her letter box. He wandered slowly home thinking what a crazy world he had got into. But Ellie wasn't crazy, anything but.

As he thought of her he cheered up and began to hum one of their favourite songs. He even felt kindly towards Aunty Flo for a moment but the thought made him feel like having a drink so he turned round and headed to the pub where he expected some of his old mates would be.

As he turned into the high street he could see a large crowd gathering half way down and there were police and ambulance sirens. He made his way down to the crowd and could see that most of the street now had been closed off.

He asked a short woman in a headscarf what was happening.

"Don't know love" I can't really see much but it sounds like they've done the night club. Someone got shot and another bloke was run over. What I did see he didn't look too good. Getaway car ran straight over him; didn't give him a chance."

A slight gap opened up in the crowd and the woman shoved her way to the front.

"Look there – what did I tell you, 'Es a gonner."

Andy could see the ambulance men loading the stretcher with the blanket covering the whole body.

"Bloody hell!" Was all that Andy could say.

"Yeah, you can say that again. I heard someone say they had shot a copper down by the railway before they scarpered."

A large policeman came towards them. "Come along everyone, time to break it up and go home. You're not doing any good hanging around here. Just break it up and go home as quick as you can."

Andy recognised him and called to him. "Hey, Les, it's me Andy Heron. Mary hasn't been involved in this has she?"

PC Les Collinson was not a man to move away from his first purpose. "Just wait over there for me Andy and I'll come over when I have this lot moved."

The chatty woman was not amused. "'Ere, who do you think you are then? Lord muck. Got too big for your old neighbours; just this lot now are we?"

Les smiled down at her. "Hello Doris, do you live around here now – come along there please, move away now please; there's nothing else to see."

He turned to her again. "How's Dennis getting on then; still got his pigeons?"

"I expect so. That's why I'm here; moved out a couple of years ago and I doubt if he's noticed yet. Still I'm all right now; got a nice little job at the old candle works and a feller at the weekends if you know what I mean." She cackled to herself and then changed the subject.

"What's gone on here then Les?"

"Looks like a robbery that went wrong. You probably saw the ambulance go off with a body but you'll be able to read all about it tomorrow."

"I saw 'im though. The bloke that was sat in the car what killed the poor sod."

"Do you think you could identify him Doris?"

"Oh yes; he looked at me and gave me such a glare it quite churned me up for a while."

"I'll need you to come down to the station with me and you can tell the inspector exactly what you saw. Are you OK to come down now?"

"Oo! Do you think I can help with your enquiries?"

"If you can identify that man it could help us catch all of them."

She turned to Andy who was still waiting as Les had asked. "Do you hear that love; I might be able to help."

As Les began to lead her off he turned to Andy, "Sorry mate but as you can see I'm a bit busy. I don't know where Mary is but if you see her can you let her know to come in pronto. Young Jeff Henriques caught one in the chase. She would want to know as they were working with each other just yesterday."

Andy drew a breath. He had met Jeff at the pub just two weeks ago and had a long chat with him about the merits of rugby as opposed to soccer. "God! Is he all right? I was speaking to him just recently."

"I don't know. I just heard on the radio that an ambulance was on its way."

"I hope he will be OK. Mary will be really choked if it's anything serious."

"It sounded as if he'd been shot as well so it could be anything. Anyway I must take this young woman in to the police station to make a statement. I'll see you around."

Doris grabbed hold of his arm. "Young woman eh; you're still a cheeky sod Les. I do hope I can be helpful. Do you think there might be a reward?" As she went off she turned towards Andy. "I do hope your friend will be all right."

Andy decided to give Mary's flat another visit just in case she had returned but there was still no answer so he scribbled another note for her and sent a text message for good measure.

He decided to go straight home after that. He got there and sat there watching the television until late. Eventually a news flash came up saying that a man had been killed and two others including a police office had been shot and wounded.

He went to bed but had trouble sleeping as he thought that Mary could have been shot. He wanted to be with Ellie but had to make do with cuddling his pillow.

Chapter 13

Stopped in her tracks.

Jennie had no idea of the time she woke up. She couldn't really believe that she had slept all night without any tablets. Slowly she got up and looked at the sad pile of crumpled clothing she had been able to salvage from her flat. Most of it was her washing. The good stuff had been in the bag Elroy had run over.. His tyre marks were still visible on her best knickers.

"Fucking Elroy!" The sound of her own voice startled her and she realised how quiet it was in the house. It also gave her a chance to remember what had happened and how Albert had come to her rescue.

"Fucking Albert!" but this time it was said with a slight smile. She continued swearing to herself as she walked to the bathroom. "Stupid old git; what does he think? Wanting me to talk to a pig?"

At the top of the stairs the smell of frying bacon hit her. At first she couldn't remember what it was, then she remembered. "God; I haven't smelt bacon cooking like that since my dad was at home."

She stayed in the bathroom a long time trying to think of what she could do. Albert had tricked her into agreeing to go and talk to that woman cop and she couldn't think of how she could get out of it. She carried on thinking as she showered. It was good to have a shower that worked. All her make-up was gone and her age was all too obvious. There was a comb on top of the bathroom cabinet which allowed her to get her hair in some sort of order. Everything else was still in the flat. The thought of returning to the flat filled her with anxiety but she knew she might have to go back again.

Albert heard her trying to slip quietly out of the bathroom and he appeared at the foot of the stairs. "Good morning Jennie. Did you sleep alright? I've done some breakfast for us. I don't know about you but I am starving."

Jennie just nodded and pulled the bath robe she was wearing close then rushed into the bedroom. Everything about her wanted to run away from what was happening but she forced herself to think about the options and the possible consequences.

She had no money so she would have to get some, but if she worked on the street Karl would be sure to find her. Meanwhile she was safe with Albert. He was OK and he would look after her. He reminded her of her father in the way that she felt. She took a deep breath and tied the bath robe securely before going down stairs.

"Good morning Albert."

"Good morning Jennie. Will bacon and eggs be all right or would you like some beans as well? I can't remember you eating at all yesterday so you must be hungry. I'll do some toast as well."

Jennie suddenly realised how hungry she was and began to take full advantage of the meal. As she finished she wiped her mouth with the back of her hand. "Do you know Albert; that is the first proper breakfast I have had since my dad left home. He always cooked breakfast but my mum couldn't be bothered.

Albert paused before he spoke. "It sounds as if you were very fond of your dad. What happened to him?"

"I don't really know. My mum chucked him out and tried to get him nicked. Then she threw me out too and I had three years in and out of crappy children's homes."

Albert thought carefully before he asked the next question. "Was it anything that he did to you? Did he do anything that he shouldn't have done?"

Jennie looked straight back at him. "My dad loved me. We didn't do anything that I didn't want to do. That's all the police and social workers wanted to know but none of them had the balls to ask direct 'did you and your dad screw'? Nasty minds the lot of them. He was really good to me was my dad but my mum hated us both. She never gave me a hug or a kiss and I don't think he got any either. She hated me because she and dad had to marry because she was pregnant with me."

Jennie was surprised at how easily she was talking to Albert. It must be the good night's sleep and the hearty breakfast and the way in which he reminded her of her dad even though he was much older.

Albert tried again. "Do you think that is why you do what you do?"

"No; like I say it was when that witch made my dad go away and I began to run away to try and find him. It wasn't that I meant to do anything wrong but I got hooked up with Johnny Foster and he and my friend Liz told me how to make good money. It wasn't as if I was a virgin or anything, it was just getting paid for what I had been doing for free for a long time. I liked sex and Johnny made sure we both had a good time on what I was able to earn."

She paused to finish her mug of tea. "Trouble was they kept finding me and taking me home or to a children's home. It was always easier to get away from there that at mum's. She used to lock me in my room for weeks. I was really surprised when I found I was six month's pregnant. I thought the extra weight had been down to all that stodge in the children's home."

"Surely your mum took you back when you had the baby. She can't have been that bad."

Jennie didn't like that. "Yes she was. She threw me out and took my dad away from me. She left me to rot in children's homes where everyone was screwing everyone else. Like I said when I found I could get money for it, well it seemed dead easy, especially if I got a bit stoned first. Then you don't mind who's doing it. I wanted the money and they wanted me. Do you know Albert most of them couldn't do it at all?"

Albert's more moral upbringing made him feel that he was getting more information than he had wanted so he decided to change the subject. "What about your baby, your Ellie?"

"Did I tell you about Ellie? God, I must have been stoned. I was only fifteen when she was born. I can't be sure who her father was because I was working by then. It might have been Johnny. He was my bloke at the time. If it was him I hope she never finds out because he is an evil bastard. Karl has got tied up with him. That might even be where he got the gun."

Albert got up. "Talking about Karl, don't forget we have an appointment with Mary Heron this morning."

Jennie had hoped he might forget. "Are you sure we have to go? I still don't want to upset Karl any more than I have done."

Albert smiled. "I'm afraid you don't have an option. Mary only gave you until 10.00 a.m. before she will come to arrest you. If you go in voluntarily then they will let you stay out. If they arrest you they will have to take you to court and that could mean prison."

For a moment Jennie thought that Holloway might be safer than Balham but she had been on remand there before and had no desire to experience it again. She shut her eyes and the long corridor on the remand wing came into mind. She could still hear the screaming and the banging of doors. The thunk of the night lock was the most frightening thing she had ever heard. She ran upstairs and looked at what she might wear.

Albert called up. "We have to go soon."

She called back. "OK Albert, but I haven't any clean clothes since Elroy ran over them yesterday.

Albert paused before replying. "I still have some clothes that belonged to Ruth and there's a box where she used to keep her lipstick and stuff, not that she used much of it. I'll come up and show you where it is."

Jenny wasn't at all sure if she would find anything she would want to use but there was an unused lipstick almost exactly the right shade and a blouse and skirt that fitted, albeit a bit longer than she was accustomed to wearing. She went down to show Albert.

"Oh, I say; what a good fit they are. I bought them for Ruth one Christmas but she never wore them. Too girlish for me she said but they suit you well and its much better than those short things you wear."

"Come on then Albert. If I have to wait I will probably bottle out. If you weren't with me I would probably still try to do a runner. I just hope you are right because I don't want to end up in the nick."

"Don't worry my dear. I booked a taxi."

As if on cue the front door bell rang.

Walking into the police station made her start to sweat and she quickly went to sit in the furthest corner of the waiting area while Albert booked them in.

Mary came out to them. "Well done Jennie. I was quite worried that you would try to do a runner. I see you have smartened yourself up a bit as well. I have some good news and some bad I'm afraid. The bad news is that the Inspector has been called into see the Superintendent about the shot gun. They have heard on the grapevine that a robbery is planned for tonight but they don't know where. It seems likely that Karl is involved. The good news is that he is willing to take your word for what has happened and will deal with you by a caution if you make a full statement. That I'm afraid is going to be tonight; probably not before eight. He is going to be at headquarters all day and I am on a course all day. I will come in this evening to help you."

"Do you mean I have to this all over again? You're just messing me about. You know I can't last that long without my medication."

Albert broke in. "It's all right with me. Jennie needs a restful day and I'll see she goes to the doctor and gets some of her medicine."

Mary smiled at him. "I think that Jennie was talking about something the doctor hasn't prescribed."

"What's that to do with you? You just mind your own business. I'm out of here." Then she stamped out of the station.

Albert made his excuses and went after her. She was already a fair way down the street so he had to hurry to catch up with her. As he caught up with her she suddenly clutched her stomach and doubled up in pain.

"What's wrong Jennie? Are you ill?"

"I can't breathe and my stomach is in agony." The hospital is quite close. Do you think you can get there if I help you?"

Jennie's response was to yell again and collapse on the pavement. As she lay there a police car drew up and a young officer got out.

"Can I help you sir?"

Jennie groaned again.

"I don't know what is wrong. She was just walking down the street when she collapsed. I think she should go to hospital."

"Handy I was here then. Let's get her into the car and I'll run you round to emergency. I don't think she would get that far even with your help. Is she your daughter?"

"No; just a friend."

Between them the managed to get Jennie into the car and they reached the hospital doors in less than five minutes.. They managed to shuffle her into the reception area and sat her down while Albert went to book her in.

The policeman went to the counter and gave some information to the receptionist. Then he returned to them. "I'm sorry to leave you but I have to report. I hope you will be all right Miss. At least you are in the right place now."

The receptionist came and sat next to Jennie. "Can I just have some details please?" Jennie just groaned and bent double.

"Can you help sir?" Albert was suddenly aware that she was talking to him.

"Yes. Of course! What do you want to know? She just collapsed suddenly in the street but I don't know what is wrong."

"Don't worry sir. The triage nurse will be with her soon to assess the problem. Can you tell me her name and address and her date of birth. Her name is Jennie Burns and she is staying at my house at present, number 25 Ballingdon Street, SW12 30T. I don't know her date of birth. She says she is thirty but I think that might be wrong. She was in here just two days ago with an overdose so this might be something to do with that."

"Thank you sir. That will certainly make it much easier to track her records."

It was only about twenty minutes when Jennie's name was called. Albert helped her to the interview room. The nurse got her to lie on a couch. "Hello Miss Burns. My name is Nurse Gwen Jones. Do you mind if I call you Jennie. No what seems to be the problem?"

Albert intervened. "She collapsed very suddenly about forty minutes ago, unable to get her breath and with severe stomach pains."

"Thank you sir!. I gather you are the friend who brought her in. If you would take a seat in the waiting area please! I will have to examine her. We will let you know what happens."

"Oh! Yes, I will go and sit down. Do you have her records?"

"Yes and we know that she was here two days ago."

Albert did what he had been told.

Nurse Jones was joined by a young doctor. "Hello." He said, can you roll your top up for me please so I can check your stomach. Tell me when it hurts.

Jennie let out a yell.

"Sounds like your breathing is back to normal but the pain goes right across your stomach so it isn't localised. It could be drug related. Did you say that you have not had your usual drug regime."

"No!" Whispered Jennie.

"And we had to clear you out the other day because of an overdose. Does this hurt as well?"

Jennie yelled again.

"That is more in the colon area. Have you eaten anything unusual. Jenny thought. "It must have been Albert's full English breakfast. And I've run out of my drugs."

"Yes it could just be a bad attack of the wind. How long since you passed a motion."

"What?"

The doctor sighed. "Did a poo."

"I can't remember."

Well I am going to take a blood test just to be on the safe side and give you a laxative. You will probably feel much better once you have been to the toilet. If you had stayed the other day we could have sorted your tablets out but I will have a word with Doctor High as he had the toxicology reports then. It was him that saw you."

"Is that the one with a squeaky voice?"

Nurse Jones smiled. "He's a very good doctor. Now swallow this and let me take some blood."

Jennie swallowed the liquid she was given and pulled a face. "What was that?"

"That was the laxative. It should work in about two hours. I can see you don't inject."

"No way! Not since my best friend died."

"What happened?"

"She was in Holloway for six months and the day she came out she scored. I wasn't there until the next day and she had drowned in her own vomit."

"Nasty! Now you can go and join your friend. Have a cup of tea but nothing solid. Take this tablet with your tea and that should ease the discomfort then hopefully nature will do the rest. It will be two hours at least before I can get the right prescription for you so please stick around and make sure you know where the ladies is."

"Can I have a sedative now?"

That's all you're getting for now until we know more about what is going on inside you. Now off you go and I will see you later."

Jennie thought about going out but her stomach was still painful and she had no money to try and score on the street. By some miracle she managed to stay and the laxative took only an hour to work and sure enough her stomach cramp had eased.

Albert was surprisingly good company and regaled her with stories of his army adventures and his time in the magic circle. Three cups of tea later and two more visits to the ladies she suddenly realised she had fallen asleep and so had Albert.

She was surprised at how relaxed she was especially when she saw that it was now four o'clock.

Nurse Jones appeared. "Hello Jennie! I thought I should bring these to you personally. It is a prescription for some quite strong tablets so there is only enough for three days. Then you must come to the Drug clinic for a full assessment of your addiction. I gather that the laxative has worked its wicked way."

Jennie grimaced. "Yes; almost too much!"

"Try to eat regularly but not too much at a time and you must drink a lot of water with the tablets. Try to look after yourself a bit better. Some exercise wouldn't come amiss."

Jennie just nodded and grunted. Albert was still snoozing. Briefly she wondered how to escape but somehow she couldn't. "Wakey,wakey. It's time to go at last. I'm hungry so let's get a burger on the way back."

Albert grunted and nearly fell of his chair. "What's the time? Are you all right?"

"Yes I'm OK now. It was your blooming fry up gave me the gips. Come on, let's get out of here. It was nearly five by the time they got back and Albert was feeling exhausted in spite of his snoozing.

Chapter fourteen

Putting on the pressure.

It wasn't for long as at seven there was a loud knocking at the door. Albert went to open it and Jennie ran upstairs and hid behind the bathroom door.

She heard Albert saying, "Hello Mary, I thought we were coming to see you at eight o'clock. I think that's what you said wasn't it? Come on in. We've been at the hospital most of the day as Jennie had a funny turn just after we left you but she is all right now."

As Mary came in Jennie could see she was escorted by two male officers. "I' m sorry Albert but we can't wait until eight. We think Jennie can help us over a murder and robbery which took place an hour ago. Can we see her now please?"

Although he felt a bit taken aback Albert regained his composure and called up to Jennie.

"Jennie, can you come down please, it's Mary and she needs to talk to you very urgently."

Jennie's response was to slam the door shut and lock it. "Go away. Go away. Leave me alone. I'm dead if they even think you've spoken to me."

Mary went up the stairs and spoke through the door. "Come on out Jennie. You can still make it easy for yourself. We have an eye witness who has identified

 Karl so we know it's him we want but you can save a lot of time if you help. It's murder now not just knowing about a gun."

"Bugger off!"

"If you want we can break this door down and take you without your consent. You are now a material witness to a major crime and if you don't help then we may have to charge you as an accessory to the robbery. That will mean holding you in custody."

A much quieter Jennie spoke again. "They really will kill me if I say anything at all to you."

"They won't be around if you come out now and help us to catch them."

The door opened and Jennie came out. "I'll come but you can stick your protection. How do you think I could operate with you lot around. Anyway, what's so important about me? You have the gun that was in our place."

"We know that which is why we might be able to go easy on you. But you did know about the gun and you were living with Karl who we now know is involved for sure."

"You can't blame me for the gun. It was Karl put it there. It scared the shit out of me especially being under the bed. The fucking thing might have gone off at any time."

113

Mary held Jennie's arm and headed her towards the front door. I can't make any promises Jennie but if you do help us it will be noted by the Crown Prosecution and we could support them giving you a caution."

"What's that mean?"

"Apart from an ear-wigging from a senior officer you would be free."

Albert was standing there with his coat already on. "I'll come with you Jennie."

Mary stopped him. "Sorry Albert but this will take most of the night. If you are still willing we can bail her back to this address in the morning."

"Of course she can stay here. Do you think I would give up on her now?"

"No Albert, I didn't think you would. But it will be very important for her to have a secure place to stay. This case may take several months before it is sorted finally. I just wanted to be sure you know what you would be taking on and of course, she has to agree as well."

"I do understand that Mary, but if she is willing to stay with me then I will be glad to give her a home. You know I have grown very fond of her. Silly isn't it for an old codger like me to think she might care about me to stay."

"I don't think that's silly. I think it is a wonderful opportunity for her and she may welcome being cared for. It could be quite a change for her.

I'm so glad you said that. I was just saying to her before you came that she needed someone to look after her. Maybe she can change if she knows that someone cares about her?"

"I hope so too Albert, but be careful. She may be in some danger and she will soon get restless again. Anyway we must go. I'll see you soon." She waved to him as she got into the car.

Jennie looked alarmed at the thought of losing her main support. "Isn't Albert coming with me?"

Mary calmed her. "Don't worry. He'll come down later to bring you back to his home as long as you want to go back. He can't do any good sat around the police station half the night, can he?"

Jennie sat back in the car and grudgingly agreed.

None of them spoke much after that until a message came over the car radio that Jeff Henriques was out of danger.

"Thank God for that!" said Mary. "You probably owe your life to him you know. It was him who found you the other day thanks to your friend Elroy."

"He's no fucking friend of mine. He just wants me to work for him instead of Karl, and he ran over my kit."

"All the same you owe them your life. We don't think it was Karl who shot Jeff, but it was certainly one of his friends. We will want to know who they are."

"Karl doesn't have any friends except for those who would kill me just because I know about them. In fact I am probably dead already and this is the way to hell."

They arrived at the police station and booked her in at the desk. The clerk there looked at his list. "Room two is free and Inspector Crawford is on his way over from Lavender Hill for the interview. Good news about Jeff though."

"Yes "said Mary, "now we just need to catch the man who did it. Come on Jennie let's get out of this madhouse."

As they were half way through the door he called after them. "And your brother has been looking for you." Mary checked her mobile and saw that there were about four texts from Andy. She sighed. He would have to wait until the morning.

The interview room was bleak and Mary sat on one side of a table with Jennie on the other. Both chair and table were well bolted to the floor. One of the other officers stood by the doorway.

"What's going to happen?" asked Jennie.

Mary looked at the papers she had collected at the desk. "Two things, first I have to charge you with possession of a firearm and take a statement from you about that."

"But you said I wouldn't get done for that."

"No Jennie I aid that we would have a word with the prosecution service in your favour. But first we do have to charge you. After that you will be interviewed by Inspector Crawford. He will want to know anything you can tell him about Karl and why he had the gun and about his associates."

"Why can't you do that?"

Because it's a major crime and that has to be done by a senior officer. Our serious crime squad is based at Lavender Hill so it has to be one of their senior officers who sees you. He will want proper answers to his questions and he won't stand for any messing around. The sooner we know who we are looking for the better it will be for everyone and the safer you will be."

Jennie looked down at the table. "What have I got to lose? I'm as good as dead already."

"Don't talk rubbish. Albert is willing to stand by you and help you. You're really lucky to have someone like him to care about you."

Jennie kept looking at the table. "Silly old bugger. What does he know about me apart from twice a week? He'll only end up getting hurt as well."

Mary couldn't help smiling at the frank way in which Jennie had spoken about her relationship with Albert. "I don't know about that, but I do know that he's a very lonely old man who likes your company and is willing to go out on a limb to help you."

"Oh yeah! Then that's what we are. Just two lonely gits together. Anyway, you said you had to charge me so why don't you get on with it."

"OK Jennie, just let me switch our recording machine on and then I'll caution you. She leaned over to the switch and turned the recording on then spoke into it giving her name and rank and said that she was interviewing Jennifer Burns at 1920 hours on Friday 7th November about being in possession of a shotgun. She then asked Jennie to speak as well so that her voice could be identified. She cautioned Jennie and advised her that she could have a solicitor present.

"Not likely, there's enough people know about this already."

"Can you confirm that when we were called to your rooms at 5 Nelson Street on Thursday 6th November this year that there was a loaded shotgun under your bed."

"I was unconscious, wasn't I so I don't know how you found it."

"But you knew that it was there."

"Yes. It was scaring the shit out of me having to sleep on top of it."

"Keep it simple Jennie. Was this your gun?"

"Of course it fucking wasn't. What do you think I would want with something like that?"

"Can I confirm that you share the rooms with Karl Kuyper?"

Jennie remained quiet for a moment then shrugged her shoulders. "You know that I did."

"Can you tell me in your own words how it got there?"

"I don't know. It was just there two nights ago when Karl told me not to shake the bed in case it went off. I was bloody scared and slept on our sofa that night. He must have brought it in when I was out."

"Why didn't you report it?"

"Are you joking? Karl would have killed me. He will probably still do so."

"Now tell me about the evening we found the gun."

"Well it all began really when Darren Fox got nicked. That meant Karl didn't have any money so he sent me out to get some but I couldn't get any because it was peeing down with rain and even Albert was out. I found an old mirror in the skip outside the cinema and took that home in case it was worth a bob or two. But when I got back Karl was in a foul mood and he smelt that I'd had some fish and chips. So he beat me up and went off with the mirror and left me on the floor. When I came too I was so miserable that I took every pill I could find. Next thing I knew was being hauled around the room by Elroy and some copper and then the ambulance people came and found the gun. "

"Why did you take the mirror?"

"Promise you won't laugh."

"I looked at it and it made me look thinner. I was looking to see if my skirt was caught in my knickers."

Mary couldn't resist a smile.

"There I told you, I knew you would laugh at me."

"So you took the mirror home and Karl beat you up and took the mirror away"

"Yes. But it was my fault really because I should have given Karl my money and not had the fish and chips. It was the pickled onion that gave me away."

"Is that why you tried to kill yourself?"

Jennie stopped for a while. "I guess so."

The door opened and a Police officer looked round.

"Sorry to interrupt but I though you would want to know that Inspector Crawford is here and would like to speak to you."

She turned to the officer. "Tell him I will be with him straight away." Then she looked at Jennie. "You've made a good start Jennie but the tricky bit is now when Inspector Crawford comes in. Just remember what I said. Keep your answers simple and for heaven's sake don't lie."

Jennie pulled a face. "What does it matter/ He can't kill me but Karl can."

As Mary left she turned. "Remember Jennie, it is your choice, but we are the only people who can keep you alive if what you say is true."

Chapter fifteen

The inspector.

It was almost half an hour before Mary returned with Inspector Graham, a tall dark haired man with a military type moustache. He looked as if he had been poured into his uniform. With him was a woman sergeant.

Mary introduced them as Inspector Graham and Sergeant Jane Marriner.. I have to go now Jennie. I will see you tomorrow. Just answer their questions sensibly and you will be OK."

They sat opposite Jennie. She was already unnerved by his steady stare. He switched on the tape. "It is now 2045 on Friday the 7th November and the interview with Jennifer Burns is continuing with Inspector William Graham and Sergeant Jane Marriner."

Jane spoke to confirm her name and voice.

"Thank you for agreeing to speak to us Miss Burns. As you know we are investigating the death of a Mr Nigel Ashton and the shooting of P.C.Henriques and Mr Dick Watson during the course of an armed robbery earlier this evening."

He paused briefly as if to let his words sink in properly. I am glad to say that Mr Watson was only superficially wounded and that P.C.Henriques is going to make a full recovery. We have an eye witness who has identified Karl Kuyper as the man driving the car that killed Mr Ashton. We understand that Mr Kuyper is a close friend of yours.

He stopped and looked directly at her and Jennie nodded slightly. "Please say so for the tape."

Jennie whispered yes.

"It is very important that we find him and his friends before they do any more damage to anyone. I gather you may be at some risk yourself."

Jennie nodded again but added "Yes."

"I would appreciate any information you can give me about him or his associates."

Jennie sat back. "What do you want to know?"

For the best part of twenty minutes she tried to give monosyllabic and superficial answers then Jane said "I thought you had been threatened by one of his friends recently."

Jennie remembered the Elvis haircut at her flat and decided she had no loyalty to him. "Yes, I went back to the house this morning and there was this idiot pretending to look like Elvis and sound like a gangster."

The Inspector and the sergeant looked at each other. "I think that sounds like our old friend Dave Morris."

The Inspector agreed with her. "Does that name ring any bells with you?"

Jennie remembered Elroy calling him Dave and Karl had mentioned a Dave who thought he could drive. "Karl does know a Dave who thinks he can drive, but I don't know his second name. I try to keep out of Karl's affairs as much as possible because I just get a beating if I ask too much."

Sergeant Marriner sat back. "I'm sure that's one of them guv', Elvis haircut, pretend drawl and he's a driver. It's just the sort of thing he would get into. I can't see him with a gun though." She turned to Jennie. "How about Mick Earnshaw, or Johnny Foster?"

"Jennie began to feel uneasy. The mention of Johnny was not good news. "I was at school with a Johnny Foster. I don't see him now though. He's an evil bastard."

As she spoke she suddenly remembered Karl talking about Johnny getting the gear. She hadn't realised what he was talking about but now she realised it was the guns for the raid. Now was the time to clam up.

She looked at Sergeant Marriner. "Don't I know you from somewhere?"

Jane ignored the question. "Do you know anything else about them?"

Jennie shook her head.

"Please speak so that your answer can be recorded.

Jennie looked down at the table again to avoid the Inspector's eyes. "Sorry but I don't know nothing about any of them."

The Inspector banged the table making her jump. "Don't lie to me Miss Burns. You do know a damn sight more than you are telling us and you are wasting precious time."

Jennie sat up straight and yelled. "I don't know any more."

"Very well Miss Burns. I know when people start to lie to me and that's what you are doing now. As far as I am concerned you knew about the gun and about the plans and that puts you in the frame for a conspiracy charge. If I can prove it you will be going down with the rest of them. Meantime we will check what you have said and it had better be right. In the meantime I am going to give you bail. Jane will you deal with that and make sure she gets back to her lodgings with a condition of residence and to report here at 14.00 each day to be ready for further questioning."

Jennie suddenly realised what was happening. "Here ! You promised to give me protection. What about my protection?"

The Inspector stood up. "You haven't told us anything that would put you in danger. There is nothing that would make you a good witness; in fact the very opposite. The fact you came to the police station is not enough for you to be put under protection."

Jennie exploded. "You bastards; you promised you would protect me if I spoke to you. You know they will kill me if they even think I've been talking."

"That would mean you have something to say but you haven't so there is no reason for you to be protected. If you think you can provide useful information then tell us now."

"You're setting me up. You think that if I'm out there they will come to kill me and then you can catch them."

"Not at all Miss Burns. That would be very unethical. I can only provide protection to a material witness. That is someone whose information is vital to a successful prosecution and whose life could genuinely be at risk. Your evidence would be more likely to get them off and you are still in my mind just as likely to be standing there with them in the dock because that is where they will be."

"You're trying to blackmail me into saying what you want to hear. They will kill me and you won't care a damn."

"You have a choice Miss Burns. I am giving you a chance to think while free or you can think about it in Holloway."

"Bastard" shouted Jennie at the top of her voice as he opened the door and walked away. Jane Marriner spoke into the microphone. "Inspector Crawford has left the room. Interview suspended at 2137." She switched it off.

Jennie looked at her. "Have you recorded all that?"

Jane Marriner stood up and took Jennie by the arm leading her to the door. "I guess you would prefer to go back to Albert's."

"Let me go you bitch."

"Come on Jennie. I am sure Albert is waiting for you to get back. We'll do what we can in the meantime but you really are going to have to come clean about everything, and not just tell us the bits you want us to have."

"I knew it was a mistake trusting you lot. It'll serve you right if I get done in, then you won't get anything from me at all."

125

"Come on Jennie. You can't stay here now. Let's find Albert."

"I need to see my doctor. I need a proper prescription. I need my pills to keep me calm and help me sleep."

"I believe you got a prescription this afternoon so that is all you will get."

Jennie got up still swearing and complaining all the way back to Albert's. He had been warned she was on the way and sure enough the kettle was on. She went straight into her room and took some of the pills she had been prescribed.

Downstairs she could hear Albert trying to persuade Jane to stay for a cup of tea and a sandwich. She went down slowly.

"Thank you Mr Smith. It is very kind of you but I have a very long day again tomorrow. Jennie has given us a lead to follow but she has to report at the station again tomorrow at 1400."

"Not if I can help it." Jennie muttered.

As she was leaving Jane said, "She may be in some danger so if you have any anxiety at all then ring us straight away."

"Of course my dear; but she'll be safe here. I'm an old soldier you know."

"Yes sir. That's why you should ring through straight away. We wouldn't want anyone to get hurt."

Jennie sat at the table and began to nibble one of the sandwiches. Albert came back. "Cup of tea then Jennie?"

"No I want coffee." She wondered why she had said that just to be perverse. After all she didn't even like coffee.

Chapter sixteen

More revelations

Andy was quite relieved that it was Saturday as he had the day off anyway. Normally he would be getting ready to go to the sports club where he played football but he had already spoken to the captain and cried off.

He had tried to contact Mary again at the police station but at least this time they had told him she had his message but was up to her eyes in work at present. He went round to Ellie as soon as he dared having forgotten she planned to work that morning. He was just in time to walk with her. They walked down the road holding each other as if it was springtime in Paris and oblivious to the crowds of Saturday shoppers. He went in to the shop with her as she went to report to Jill, her supervisor.

Jill Moore had lived in the area all her life and survived two marriages and five children. She had a soft spot for Ellie, probably because she was one of the few youngsters she could trust to babysit. Not that Darren appreciated being looked after now he was twelve. Her eldest daughter had been at school with Ellie and they were still good friends even though Sharon was a year younger. She was relieved to see Ellie and to know she was all right.

"Hello Ellie; I'm so glad to see you. Is everything sorted OK? I bet you have been busy with all the organising. Has Andy been a help?"

As she said that she gave Andy a hug. "I bet he has, haven't you Andy? Not like my Mark and Matt. Useless buggers they are when it comes to anything that might make them think. Just like their father."

Andy blushed slightly. Jill's familiarity always made him feel slightly uneasy. He thought of the reputation she had of chasing her last husband three miles round Tooting Bec with a butcher's knife before he got away.

Ellie had no worries about her. After all she knew the full story and could understand why Jill had been so angry, and it had only been half a mile. "I'm all right now Jill, but every now and then something just sets me off. One minute I'm fine and then suddenly I'm crying my eyes out again. I still can't really believe it. Andy has been brilliant and my Aunty Flo has come to help."

"Not your mad aunt from Ramsgate? Are you sure you 're coping? She was a real nut case when I last met her."

Andy smiled. "That's her."

Jill put her arm round Ellie's shoulders. "So that's why you want to come back to work as soon as possible?"

Ellie laughed at the idea but recognised some of the truth in it. "Yes, I suppose you could look at it like that. I wonder if I could work today through to two so I cover the lunch hour.

Then I am meeting Brian Evans in the afternoon to talk about the funeral service. Then I can be in on Monday, Tuesday and Wednesday and then I need to be off on Thursday for the funeral."

Jill took a note of what Ellie had said. "That's fine dear but if you do need more time just let me know. You might be trying to do too much too soon. You can always do extra in the run up to Christmas. You will need all you can earn now without your mum's money coming in."

Ellie gasped at the import of what Jill had said. "I hadn't even thought about that at all. Not with everything else. I don't even know what bills she paid or how much they are. She never discussed things like that with me. I just gave her some money for my keep and she did all the rest."

Andy took her arm. "Let's not panic yet. You know how meticulous your mum was. It won't take long for us to work out what needs to be paid. I'm sure she probably had some money tucked away for a rainy day. I don't recall her spending much while she was alive. She probably has another life insurance policy with the Co-op like she had for her funeral. If you have any problems Jim from the accounts would be glad to help sort it out."

Ellie's eyes began to fill and Jill pulled up a chair for her to sit on. "I don't know if the council will let me stay or if mum left a will and even if she did she's not even my real mother."

Jill was by nature inquisitive and immediately picked up on Ellie's comment. "What do you mean that she wasn't your mum."

Andy answered for Ellie. "It's a long story Jill. We found some birth certificates that showed Ellie that her mum was in fact her gran and that her real mum was called Jennie and that she was mum's daughter, not Ellie."

"Hang on!" Jill pulled up another chair to sit on herself. "Are you telling me that Ellie was Jennie's kid? Goodness me! And to think that all this time I was wondering what had happened to Jen. I was at school with her you know, just a year ahead but you couldn't miss Jennie even at that age. She got expelled or something and went to a home. That must have been at least twenty years ago. That must have been when you were born!"

Ellie and Andy looked at her in surprise. "You knew my mother"

"Well I knew of her but I was a bit older but it was hard not to know Jennie."

"What do you know of her? Don't worry about the truth because it's already bad enough. Why was she expelled?"

"Well I declare. You are Jennie's daughter and you have only just found this out since your mum died. You poor thing! It must have been one shock after another."

"You can say that again."

"I remember the head saying that she was not going to tolerate such behaviour in her school but she never said what it was but we all knew it was because she and Johnny, um, forget his name, were at it in the library when she walked in. I'm afraid she was one for the boys was your mother and she was only fourteen at the time."

Andy asked, "You've not heard of her since have you? She really ought to know about her mother."

"Funnily enough I did hear the other day when I was with some of the other girls, that she had been seen in one of the pubs in Tooting."

Ellie stopped crying and sat up. "Are you saying that she may still be around this area?"

"Oh yes! But I don't think you will do yourself any favours finding her. I'm afraid she is still interested in the boys, if you know what I mean. Apparently she was in a bad way recently and in hospital. Thank goodness you haven't taken after her."

"Have you any idea where she might be?"

"Not really. I know she was with Wendy Price for a time but Wendy died from an overdose five years ago and Jennie moved on. She is probably with some nasty bloke. Like I say you won't do yourself any favours by finding her."

Andy put his hand on Ellie's shoulder. "I think Ellie is quite sincere in wanting to find her and at least to let her know about Rosie. And she is all the family she knows about except for Flo."

"I'm sorry. As I said they saw her around the Tooting area and that was over a month ago when we had a reunion. She doesn't keep in touch with anyone herself. I can't say I blame her really."

She paused and then took a long look at Ellie. "God; it's really strange to think that you are Jennie's girl. She was younger than me! I don't feel old enough to be the same age as your mother. I don't know if I like that. It's bad enough with the lot I have."

Ellie stood up and gave her a hug. "Thank you Jill, thanks for telling me,; I just needed to know what is true and not. My whole world has turned upside down in the last two days and if it hadn't been for Andy I really don't know what I would have done, would I Andy?"

Andy always got embarrassed when people said nice things about him and this was no exception so he just mumbled and looked down. "Don't be silly Ellie."

Jill put her arm around Ellie. "You know, I do believe he's blushing. He's gone all tongue-tied."

Andy felt his face warming so he coughed and blustered. "I'd better get going then and I'll see you at two. We can get a bite to eat and then go to the church."

Ellie gave him a kiss on the cheek. "I'll come with you to the corner." Then she turned to Jill with a big smile. "I won't tell anyone you are old enough to be my mother."

Jill pretended to throw an onion at her.

Andy and Ellie walked out of the door. "You don't have to say things like that Ellie. It just makes me feel embarrassed."

Ellie just held his arm tightly and buried her head in his shoulder. "Let's get married."

"Married!"

"You don't have to sound so shocked at the idea. Anyway, I don't mean straight away, but as soon after the funeral as is decent. I don't think I could wait another two years. Could you?"

She paused and so did he. "I mean that I don't think I could bear to be without you for another two years, especially after yesterday morning; I mean – " She paused again. "Could you wait another two years?"

And y looked down at her. "No I don't think I could. But where could we live? I can't get a bank loan for another year and then it wouldn't be enough to buy anywhere here."

"We could stay at Mum's and do it up. The council might let us stay, especially if we are married. After all she has lived there for over thirty five years. Surely they will help if I've lived there all my life. If they don't then I will be homeless and we would have to share anyway."

Andy was trying to introduce caution into the conversation without sounding unhelpful. "What about all the changes you have had to cope with in the last few days? Don't you think we need time to sort them out?"

Ellie backed off a bit. "I can't do it without you Andy. You're the only bit of my life that makes any sense at present. Anyway, I don't think I could keep my hands off you now."

Andy smiled. "Does that mean you won't keep my hands off you either?"

Ellie smiled even more. "You just keep trying lover."

It was Andy who walked into a lamp post and made them conscious of everyone looking at them. They moved on quickly to a quieter spot where they stopped and kissed each other passionately.

Andy pulled himself free. "I need to go and have a shower."

"And I must get back to work. See you later."

The time went quickly for Ellie but was more exhausting than she had expected. So many of the customers seemed to know about her mum's death and wanted to give their condolences that she had to stop work on the till and go to the back of the store to do a bit of stock taking. She longed for the afternoon to come when Andy would be with her again.

Chapter seventeen

Good news

Ellie was rather glad that Andy was early. The weather was still dull and drizzly so they share a pizza in a little Italian restaurant where they were regular customers. It didn't take them long to get to the church. Brian's house was next door.

The door was opened by Molly Evans. "Come in; come in out of this wretched weather. Here let me take your coats. We'll just leave your umbrella in the porch so don't forget it. Come into the front room where it's warm. Brian is at the church at the moment but he will be back soon. I was so sorry to hear about your mother Ellie. It must be such a shock for you. Can I get you a cup of tea?"

"Thank you Molly. That would be very welcome."

They sat in the front room while she went into the kitchen. They could hear her   clattering the cups around. She was still in there when the door opened and Brian came in. He was dressed casually.

"Sorry if I have kept you waiting. I had to see a young couple about a wedding this morning and they were a bit late. Still it's better now than on the day. Molly is getting you a cup of tea I presume."

He called into the kitchen. "Can you make one for me as well please dear."

"Now how are you both, especially you Ellie. It must have been such a shock for you. It has been for all of us because she wasn't very old at all, was she? It is such a tragedy for you. I have booked the organist for Thursday and Mrs Wagstaff has got her committee on alert so it's just finding out what you will want us to do in the service."

"Thank you Brian. We don't really know what we are supposed to do."

"Well, let's look at the service shall we. There is a standard order but you should choose any hymns or readings that you think might be appropriate for Rosie and obviously if you or anyone else in your family or friends would like to say anything that would be great. I gather that your aunt has come to help. Perhaps she would like to be involved?"

Ellie immediately thought that Flo would not only help but try to take over the whole service. "I am sure she would like to be involved but she is a very determined lady and she may try to take over altogether."

"Ah, yes; I remember Rosie telling me about her. Does she still live in Ramsgate/"

"Yes. She lives there with her friend Muriel. She's very nice. I don't know about the hymns and readings so it would be better if you could choose them."

"I will pick a reading but why don't you think about the hymns. There's no rush. And have a think about saying something."

"I wouldn't know what to say after what I have found out this week. In fact you should know that she wasn't my mother at all but my gran. I also know some of the truth about my real mother. Do you know anything about her? After all we have been coming here since I was a baby."

Brian sat back in his chair. "I am glad you have found out, but so sorry that you have done so in this way. The number of times I told Rosie that she should tell you the truth, but she wouldn't risk it. I hate keeping secrets especially like this. How did you find out?"

Ellie then told him all about the last two days and the mystery of what had happened

He went quiet before he replied. Rosie told me the whole story two years ago but made me promise to keep it secret. I think you have probably learned most of it. You never knew her parents did you? They were very strict chapel folk and Rosie was their favourite child. I think your Aunt Flo is older than Rosie was and she had left home at quite an early age. Apparently she was very rebellious. I guess that Rosie was very naïve and badly brain-washed."

"Aunty Flo told me that yesterday and that mum had to get married."

Yes, it was a great shock to them all when they discovered that she was going to have a baby especially as she swore she had never had sex with anyone. I don't think she knew what sex was even though she was sixteen, and we had just had the so-called swinging sixties, but she did remember that Reg had tried to do something dirty to her – that's the way she described it. Well they made sure he married her but they never spoke to poor Rosie again."

Ellie was almost in tears. "Poor mum; how could any parent treat their child like that?"

"I am afraid that there were some people who clung to Victorian concepts even though they hadn't even been born then. It was a form of behaviour which I could not consider Christian, but to them it was how things had to be done and it was frighteningly narrow-minded. The worst thing about it for Rosie was that she had been imbued with the same principles and that made her see the child as being evil and I doubt if Reg was ever allowed to do anything to her again even if they were married."

Andy couldn't keep quiet. "How could they do that to a daughter they were supposed to love?"

"It was a very extremist view. I sometimes wonder if they have ever read the gospels and they would never have listened to anyone like me. They were right. They had to be right. The amazing thing is that Rosie did eventually break free from that way of thinking, though she still could not find any love for her child."

"But what about her night's out at bingo and the pub. Surely she wouldn't have been allowed to do that?"

"Until Ellie was born Rosie worked at the factory but never went out at all and that continued until Ellie was old enough to have a friend in to look after her on Fridays. It was I think her final rebellion because she knew it would have made her father furious."

He stopped to drink some of his tea. "The way things worked out she thought she was still being punished and it was easy to see why the child was pushed more and more to her father. Nobody ever proved that they had a physical relationship but certainly Jennie became very promiscuous at an early age. Rosie quite simply could not understand this or even bring herself to accept it. She certainly thought that Reg was abusing her but even blamed Jennie for that. Certainly Reg Burns was not a good man."

Andy could see that Ellie was hardly able to speak now because of her tears. "We know that he died in prison."

Ellie did manage to speak." I never knew how awful it was for her, but she was so good to me. I couldn't have had any more love than she gave me."

"I agree and the way she described it was that she suddenly saw in you her chance for redemption. Jennie could never have looked after you by herself; after all she was little more than a child herself with a totally chaotic lifestyle. She walked out one day after an argument with her mother and never returned. Rosie took one look at you and her whole life seemed to change and she became as good a mum as you could have had in spite of her unhappy past."

Ellie blew her nose and wiped her eyes. "She was a wonderful mum to me and I'll never forget that."

"She also left you well provided for. I don't know if you are aware but I am the executor of her will and I know that she has left everything to you. You may not think that she had much but her parents were very wealthy and died without making a will so Rosie and Flo inherited everything. Because she hated what they had done to her Rosie refused to touch the money at all until the chance came to buy her council house. The rest was put into a trust fund for you. There must be over a hundred thousand pounds in there plus the life insurance policy she had."

Ellie knew it was wrong to leave your mouth open but she could hardly believe what he was saying. Andy too could not believe what he had heard. "How much?"

Brian smiled. "At least one hundred and fifty thousand pounds."

Ellie and Andy looked at each other with amazement. She began to smile. "You did say we should wait until we were financially secure. Now thanks to mum we are, though I would still rather have her here to enjoy seeing us get married. You will still marry me now that I am a wealthy woman won't you?"

Andy squeezed her hand. "I was only worried about how we could afford to marry and whether I could look after you the way I want to, but it looks now that you can look after me."

Brian looked at them. "I can't say it's a surprise, but did you say marry?"

"Yes, we agreed to get married as soon as was decent after the funeral."

Brian smiled. "Of course my dear, I full understand. You can be sure that nothing would give me greater pleasure than to arrange a wedding for you so just let me know when you are ready. Rosie would be glad to know you are going to be settled."

Ellie suddenly realised that she had promised Flo they would be back for tea. "I am sorry, but we need to go as my aunt is making tea for us. I am glad we have had this talk even though some of it has been very upsetting and sad. I hope I never feel so angry with anyone. It just leaves such misery behind. One last thing though is that I do want to find Jennie. I think she should know about her mother and me."

Brian shook his head. "I'm afraid I have no idea where she might be,"

Ellie stood up and added. "I know she is still living in this area and I do want to find her even though I have heard some terrible thing s about her. After what you have told me I feel so sorry for her as well. I must try to find her, whatever has become of her. I feel that I have had all the love that she ought to have had as well. Perhaps I can love her just because she is my mother and never had the chances I have had?"

Brian held out his hand to take hers. "I know you Ellie, and if anyone can do what you want to do, it will be you. You know that I will do anything I can to help. You will always have my prayers and my blessing."

"Thank you Brian. We will see you tomorrow."

"Don't come if you think it will be too much. I will call on you at seven this Monday if that is convenient and we can have a bit more thought about the service. Look after her Andy."

"That is my pleasure."

As they walked out of the church and along the road they were glad they had brought the umbrella. They huddled underneath it. Andy held the umbrella in one hand and had his other arm over her shoulder. "I don't think he should have said so much about your mum, it really upset you."

"Don't be silly Andy. It helped me understand how she must have felt about me. I just hope that I can live up to all that hope and love and perhaps make some amends for the pain she suffered."

They walked on in silence until she suddenly stopped and looked up at him. "Another thing; I do want to find my real mum now, whatever she's like, because I had all the love and she had none. That's not fair, is it?"

"No, love, it's not fair at all. But she does sound a bit of a nightmare. Doesn't she?"

"What; worse than Aunty Flo?"

Andy laughed. "Perhaps she's not worse but certainly different. But can you believe it when he said about the house and all that money. That was truly mind boggling. But you do still want to marry me? After all I am just a poor struggling bank clerk and now you are a woman of property."

Ellie hit him. "You can't get away from me now. After all we need your sister to help us find Jennie."

Chapter eighteen

At last – Mary.

They were still in a good mood as they reached the house but Ellie's mood changed very quickly when she saw the large bunch of flowers in the hallway. The card was from the owner of the factory where mum had worked. Her sadness came back like an unexpected wave crushing a sand castle.

"There you are." Flo's voice bellowed from the kitchen and cut through her thoughts. "Are you ready for some tea? Aren't the flowers nice? He brought them round himself. Wasn't that kind of him?"

What had been the magic of their own intimate world was swept aside by Flo's exuberance. "Come on, take off your coats and come and have some tea. What's the weather out there in the dark. It sounds like world war two with all the bangs and flashes."

Andy noticed the change in Ellie as she looked at the flowers and he could see the start of a tear in the corner of her eye. He felt it was time to do something else to try and divert Ellie's mind so he turned the television on just in time to see the football results.

That was enough for Flo to nod off for a while though she was just as loud asleep as she was awake. When it ended Ellie crept out to make the promised cup of tea and the news came on.

As Ellie came back in with the tray Flo's eyes shot open and she sprang to life. "Really Ellie you don't have to do this I would have done it. Now what about some cake? Muriel and I always have some cake now on a Saturday but I don't suppose you have any cake, but biscuits will do at a pinch."

Then question sounded almost like an accusation. Ellie however knew that her mum had always kept a packet of cakes in the cupboard in case of visitors. She just hoped they were still fresh. Fortunately the packet was still just in date.

"Here you are aunty, a tasty bit of ginger cake."

Flo eyed it with suspicion. "How long has it been there Ellie?"

"I think that Mum bought it the day before she died." She sat down and gazed at the cake flattened by the thought that this was probably the last thing that Mum had ever bought.

Flo failed to notice the change but Andy grabbed her hand. "Come on Ellie. Drink your tea and try not to think too much about your mum. She's OK now and I am sure she wouldn't want you to be so unhappy."

Flo, having examined the cake nibbled the corner. "I think I prefer fruit cake, but this will do. Muriel will be scoffing a slice of Dundee at the moment. I hope she doesn't eat it all."

She then took a mouthful that demolished half the cake in one go.

Ellie put her plate down. "I've lost my appetite."

Andy put his arm round her shoulder and she rested her head on him.

Flo soon finished her cake and washed it down with a couple of slurps. "Not bad, not bad at all. You make quite a nice cup of tea my dear but you must let the pot get warm first and the water must be absolutely boiling. Remember, boiling for tea and simmering for coffee." She poured herself another cup and looked at Ellie's cake. "Are you sure you don't want that dear? It would be such a shame to waste it."

Ellie pushed the cake towards her and no other invitation was needed to transfer it. Before all the crumbs had been swallowed she suddenly remembered. "By the way," she spluttered, brushing the crumbs off her dress and diving down her cleavage to retrieve one that had dared to invade her privacy, "you had a phone call this morning from a strange woman."

Ellie looked at her. "A call, who was it from?"

"Not you dear, him. Any way I told her that he doesn't live here, that you were out and I was not a secretary."

Andy got up. "That must have been Mary at long last, I'd better call back. I'll make it next door. He went into the front room and rang. There was still no answer so he left yet another text. He sat there for a while listening to Flo nattering away to Ellie about her latest diet and how she should eat lots of fruit to keep herself regular. Ellie was right. He couldn't leave her on her own. Giving a sigh of resignation he returned to the kitchen. "She's still not there."

Flo ignored him and carried on speaking to Ellie. "And the other call I had this morning was from Muriel. And I am afraid I may have to go home for a short while because she is getting behind on our orders and business does have to go on, doesn't it? Apart from that my poor little babies are missing me I shall possibly leave after breakfast. It is such a shame that I won't be able to get to church and tell the vicar what we want done."

Andy had to suppress his reaction. "That is so unfortunate. I am sure Ellie will miss you enormously but I shall take her to church tomorrow and see she gets a good lunch. But Ellie has had some good news today, haven't you dear?"

Ellie was looking at him and hoping that Flo would not hear the irony in his voice. "Have I?"

"Come on Ellie, what did Brian say about the house?"

"Oh yes! Mum, or should I call her gran now? Anyway she has left me the house. I didn't even know that she had bought it but she did and she left a lot of money so I don't have to worry about my future."

"That's lovely dear, but you must make sure you invest it wisely."

Flo was off on a new topic and it took some time before Andy was able to interrupt and suggest they might go out and have a meal at a local pub. As he had hoped Flo immediately said that she wouldn't be seen dead in a pub, local or not and that she would make a healthy omelette.

"I must check the train times for tomorrow as it is a Sunday. You can't trust British Railways with travel during the week, never mind on a Sunday. My poor little babies will be so pleased to see me."

Andy had to ask. "Babies?"

"Our little puppies, Snowdrop and Crocus. The poor dears are missing me so much. But don't worry dear. I shall be back in good time for the funeral."

Ellie nudged Andy before he said anything else. "If it's all right with you Aunty we will go and have a meal out. As it's a Saturday we might meet some of our friends. I feel in need of being cheered up a bit."

"That's all right my dear. I will have my omelette and some beans and have an early night so I can start early tomorrow if I can."

Ellie and Andy made their farewells and left.

"Let's take the car' I would like to try the new Indian restaurant in Tooting. Mary was saying how nice it is, but are you all right with Indian food?"

Andy had wanted to go there for some time but Ellie's mum would never go anywhere that wasn't English so Ellie had never been either.

"Of course I am Andy. I've wanted to try it for ages but it would have upset mum too much if I had done something she didn't want to do."

"You do know that you will have to learn how to cook don't you?"

"I could say the same to you. We're not in the middle ages now."

As they got into the car Andy's phone rang. "Hello – oh there you are at last. I've been trying to get in touch for a couple of days."

147

Mary was back in her flat and had just taken her shoes off and got out of her uniform. "Yes, so I gather. Sorry I haven't got back to you but it has been very hectic here. I've only just got off duty. What's been the matter?"

"Well it's quite a long story but Ellie's mum has died and we are planning to get married and all sorts of other strange things have happened that we would really like to have a long chat with you. We are going to the Indian restaurant you told me about last week. Can you join us?"

"It certainly sounds very dramatic and unhappy for poor Ellie. And I haven't had a square meal for two days with everything that's going on here. I just need to change and have a shower and I can be with you in forty minutes."

"That's great. I will look forward to seeing you and telling you the whole story."

"God, Andy; you are making it sound like work. I don't know if I want any more of that just now. But I shall be there once refreshed."

They were at the restaurant quite quickly and were surprised at how full it was. They had to wait half an hour for a table and by the time they had read the menu Mary arrived and ordered straight away.

It was nearly two hours later that they finished the story.

She sat back in her chair. "Well I must say that I am quite stunned by it all. Ellie's mum has died, which is awful by itself; then you say that you discovered that she isn't your mother after all but your gran; and you mother is called Jennie

148

and everyone says she is terrible; and you have had your Aunty Flo to cope with as well. It's too shocking for words."

Andy smiled. "At least she is out of the way for a couple of days."

Mary looked at him. "I'm not sure if that is for the best. Will you be all right Ellie on your own, bearing in mind all that has happened?"

"Ellie looked at Andy. I think Andy could stay with me. Just for the next two evenings. After all we are going to get married as soon as we can."

Andy paused before saying anything. Mary saw his hesitation. "I think that is between you and Andy. But I do know that I would want someone around in these circumstances, especially someone I loved."

Andy felt a slight blush. "I've slept on the settee before, it's no problem."

Mary began to laugh and Ellie joined in.

"What are you two laughing at?"

Mary leaned over and pinched his cheek. "You little brother! Sofa indeed."

This time Andy felt the full rosiness of embarrassment but was saved by the waiter arriving to ask if there was anything else they wanted. "No thanks," he said, "just the bill."

They left the restaurant and Mary invited them back to her flat for coffee. Ellie began to talk about wanting to find Jennie. "I told you about my real mum as well didn't I? Her name is

Jennie. She still lives in this area but she works as a prostitute which is why we thought you might have come across her."

Mary thought about the Jennie who she was dealing with but decided to say nothing yet. "You know I have feeling I might know something but I can't say yet because I wouldn't want to raise your expectations so let's sleep on it. It could all tie in with something we are working on at present."

"I thought you were tied up with the shooting last night."

"What shooting?" asked Ellie.

"Well I didn't want to talk about it when there was so much going on in your life to worry about that, but there was a shooting yesterday evening in the High Street when a robbery turned nasty and one of Mary's friends got hurt."

"Mary was quick to calm Ellie. "Thankfully he is OK now, but another man was killed and we are still looking for the gang. He was actually hit by the getaway car and not shot.. We have made some good progress today though and might even have an arrest tomorrow."

"How could I be involved in that?"

"You aren't but one of the witnesses is called Jennie, but so are lots of people. So I need to check a few things out and see what I come up with."

"I do hope you can help because whatever Jennie is like I must find her. She needs to know that her mother is dead and that I want to meet her."

"Have you thought that she may not want to see you?"

"Oh! No I haven't thought that but yes, if she is as awful as everyone says she might well not want to know. But at least I have to try."

Andy drove Ellie home. Flo was asleep in front of the television. She woke when they arrived. Andy stayed for a short while but when Flo began to yawn it was an obvious hint for him to move.

They stood in the porch and kissed. Andy stepped back. "I think you are right Ellie. I can't wait two years. Let's have a chat about getting married with Brian when he comes round on Monday."

She squealed and threw her arms around him kissing him until they both had to stop for breath regardless of Aunty Flo's shadow behind them. As Andy made his way down the road she looked at Ellie. "Men, they are nothing but trouble."

"Yes, I know, but it's the sort of trouble I want."

Chapter nineteen

Fireworks

Mary couldn't settle after they had gone as her mind raced over what they had been saying and how it could be Jennie that she was working with. Her work day had been very active as two of the gang had been picked up and were in custody at the police station. Neither of them was very communicative but there was enough forensic evidence to charge them especially as Dave had left prints all over the second getaway car.

Jennie had been brought to the police station by Albert to sign on but nobody wanted to interview her then so she was bailed again to return on Monday morning. Mary had made sure that Albert was aware of Jennie's bail conditions as they included a curfew.

Jennie was still very surly after her interview of the previous day but the medication the hospital had given her was clearly very strong and sufficient. Mary had promised to call on them later and with her evening spent at the restaurant with Ellie and Andy she had completely forgotten about her promise.

She was feeling very tired but her conscience made her get up and put her coat on. They were only a twenty minute walk away and it was only half past nine. The cold and smoky atmosphere nearly made her change her mind.

Somehow Jennie had managed to stay a whole day at Albert's. He was a surprisingly good cook and she had been well fed, though after yesterday she had been more careful in what she was doing. Albert tried to do what he could to keep her at ease, even showing her some of the old tricks he had learned in his days as a magician. He had eventually nodded off. At the back of his mind was the fact that Mary might call in but age and so much activity were too much.

Jenny was feeling very agitated by now and was anxious to get out. She had persuaded Albert to lend her some money to go and buy some personal 'things' from the overnight chemist in the High Street. He was too tired to argue so made her promise to be back within an hour.

She was glad of the dark, feeling that it gave her more protection. The smell of the smoke in the air and the small explosions from the garden next door reminded her it was a party night for some.

The slightly drier day had obviously encouraged a large number of gardeners to ignore the recycling opportunities and to get rid of their rubbish in their traditional manner. She went straight to the chemist as she had promised and bought her goods. She still had some clothing at the squat and it wasn't far. She walked slowly to the corner of Nelson Street and looked down to number 5. It was at the far end. Much of the road was already being demolished and was a building site.

She thought that this would be the last place that Karl would think of. She walked carefully as the street lights were no longer working but nearly fell over when a rocket burst above her head, its red and yellow stars reminding her of her childhood. "Aaah" she said and then as the light faded "Ooh".

Suddenly it was as if her head had exploded. Vaguely she heard someone say bitch and she felt her body diving into a pit. She felt her body screaming with another pain and then there was nothing.

*

Karl had patiently stalked her. The building site was littered with old bricks. As the rocket had lit the sky he had picked one up and struck. He struck her again as she fell and when she fell into the rubble he kicked and hit her viciously.

Another rocket enabled him to see her. He bent over and tried to heave her body further into the site so he could cover it with the rubble. He was breathing heavily now from his exertion. Somehow she wouldn't move and it was only when another rocket lit the sky that he saw her skirt was caught on a nail. He wrenched her free, ripping the skirt off in the process, and rolled her body down a slight incline. He could feel his hands were sticky with her blood so he used the skirt to wipe them and then cleaned his shoes with it as well in case they had been spattered.

As he was wiping his shoes he heard her give a moan so he picked up another brick to complete the job. The light had gone, so he had to feel for where she was. He had just found her again when he saw a light coming towards him. A voice called out "Jennie!"

Karl decided it was time to go so he found the pavement and ran to the end of the road and into the lit up area where he could see where his escape could be.

*

When Mary reached Albert's she was horrified to find that Jennie had gone out. Albert tried to explain that Jennie was a bit claustrophobic and just had to go out.

"Do you know where she might have gone Albert?"

Albert thought for a moment. "Well I gave her some money to get some stuff from the chemist so she must have gone there and I think she said that she might go and get the rest of her clothing from the house she was in. I wouldn't have let her go but she was getting panicky so I thought it was better to let her go rather than have her run away."

"No, you were probably right Albert. But I don't like her being out there on her own. We still haven't found Karl and if she is right he could be out there looking for her."

"Perhaps I had better stay here in case she comes back."

"No, I think she will respond better to you. I don't think she's too keen on me at the moment."

Although he wasn't entirely convinced Albert obediently put on his coat and followed Mary out into the street. They hurried to the chemist and were told that she had left there about five minutes ago. They hurried towards Nelson Street and Mary was glad that she had brought her torch with her.

She shone her torch down the road and called out Jennie's name. There was no reply so she called again and could hear somebody running. The torch light was not sufficient for her to see who it was but a rocket light showed her it was a man.

"Did you see that Albert?"

Albert had only just caught up with her and was breathing heavily. "I'm sorry my dear, but I can't hear anything with all my puffing. I'm not as fit as I used to be."

Mary turned to him. "Sorry Albert. I was so worried about finding Jennie that I forgot you may have trouble keeping up."

Slowly they walked down the street. They looked at the old house. There were no lights. "Surely she can't have gone in there in the dark."

Albert took a step forward and caught his foot in a plastic bag. Mary shone her torch on it and they recognised it as the chemist's bag. He picked it up. "I think this must be Jennie's bag. "

"I'm afraid it might be. "Mary shone her light around the area. As the beam reached the pile of rubble it revealed the torn skirt.

"Oh no. That is the skirt she was wearing. I know because it was Mavis' skirt."

Mary shone the torch over the rubble and saw Jennie's bare legs on the other side. She shone the beam up to her face and saw Jennie's blood soaked head.

"Stand back Albert. I must ring for an ambulance and someone from the police station."

She rang the emergency number.

Albert tried to see over her shoulder but she held him back. "Is she all right?"

"I can't tell at the moment so can you hold the torch so I can check."

As Mary checked for Jennie's pulse, Albert could see her battered body. He felt ill.

"Why, Oh why did I let her go?"

Meanwhile Mary had found a slight pulse. Jennie had fallen into a natural recovery position and did not seem to be losing too much blood so Mary left her to be checked by the experts. She took some photos for future evidence in case it became a more serious offence.

The ambulance arrived swiftly followed by a police car. The police also took pictures of the scene before the ambulance put Jennie on a stretcher and into the ambulance. As they did so she moaned.

Albert grabbed Mary's arm. "Thank God! She must still be alive."

Mary took him back to his house and made a strong cup of tea with rum instead of milk as per Albert's suggestion. "It's the best thing I know for shock. Even Ruth used to have a drop of rum in her tea when she was upset."

"He kept saying, "If only I had stopped her from going out."

Mary tried to reassure him but to little avail. Eventually he agreed to go to bed as there was nothing else he could do until tomorrow.

Once she was sure Albert would be all right Mary made her own way home. She went straight to her bedroom and crashed out as she was. It was just midnight.

*

At the hospital they had to take Jennie into theatre and operate on her head. Surprisingly the fracture was not serious and they were able to patch her up quite quickly.

Her other injuries were three broken ribs and heavy bruising though they were concerned about her spleen and one of her kidneys. Her left arm was broken so they reset that and her hand. There were numerous cuts and scratches where she had been thrown into the rubble. It was well into the morning before they had checked and dealt with all her injuries. They made sure she was well sedated so that she would not exacerbate any of her wounds.

Chapter twenty

Sunday revolution.

Neither Andy nor Ellie slept very well that night and he was already up when she rang him at 7.00 a.m. They were still talking at eight when Flo appeared ready to do battle with the kitchen for a cup of tea and half a loaf of toast. Morning was normally faced in a strict pattern which she found difficult to follow in London.

She knew exactly what Muriel would be doing now. 8.00 was a cup of tea, 8.15 wash and dress, 8.30 take Snowdrop and Crocus for a short walk and back for 9.00 and have something to eat with another cup of tea. Here not even the newspaper arrived. Still it was only for one week and she would go home for two or three days. Such sacrifice was worth it for her poor sister. Ellie must need her and she was not one to shrink from her duty.

She was surprised to see Ellie downstairs already. "Are you all right dear?"

Ellie jumped as if hiding a secret. "Fine Aunty, I was just talking to Andy."

As she walked past Ellie and into the kitchen she scowled. "Well don't be long will you? It's time for a cup of tea."

Ellie chuckled into the phone. "I think I have just been summoned to breakfast. I will see you at the church later. After all I have to face them sometime and you will be there with me."

There was a pause as she listened to Andy. She smiled "I love you too. See you later."

"What on earth were you talking about at this time of the morning?"

"Oh nothing much. Just this and that." She smiled. Aunty Flo couldn't possibly understand. Two hours later she was at the church and glad to get away from Aunty Flo's sermonising.

They had forgotten it was Remembrance Sunday, which made it even harder for Ellie to hold back her tears but with Andy next to her she was able to put a brave face on and cope with the many sympathetic comments from members of the congregation. Her own personal friends were the most difficult as she had a lot of hugs and kisses from them.

She even coped with Mrs Wagstaff assuring her that the catering was all in hand and she wasn't to worry about anything. It was only when they were half way home that she remembered that she had not warned Mrs Wagstaff about Flo.

When they got home they found that Flo had found the chicken in the fridge and cooked it for lunch for them. She managed to eat most of it herself as Ellie was still not very hungry. Andy managed well enough though with Flo glowering at him across the table he began to feel guilty with each mouthful he took. Suddenly Flo spoke. "That woman rang again"

He sat up. "Oh dear, I was meant to ring Mary this morning She said she would be in touch today. Why didn't she ring?"

He looked at it. "Shit. I didn't turn it off last night and the battery is flat. I'd better ring her. He walked towards the house telephone.

Flo sat upright in her chair. "Excuse me young man. We don't use language like that here and who gave you permission to use our telephone."

That was too much for Ellie. "Aunty Flo, it's my telephone and Andy is my fiancé and he is always welcome here and to share whatever I have. Anyway, I thought you said you were going back to Ramsgate today."

Flo huffed and stood up "So I noticed yesterday. I am now going to my room for a rest. I know when I'm not wanted."

She swept up the stairs looking very hurt then turned half way. "I had decided to stay with you in your hour of need but now I shall go home this afternoon after my lunch time nap."

Ellie was on the way to following her but Andy stepped in and stopped her. "Leave it Ellie. You won't ever change her. She's a one off thank goodness, and she will only be here until the funeral."

Ellie's eyes were watering and she was trembling with her anger, "I never thought I would want mum buried so soon, but that woman is impossible. She is greedy, arrogant, thoughtless and she used to terrify mum. As for her fish Paste sandwiches I would like to tell her where to stick them!"

Her eyes were moist and Andy could see she was on the verge of bursting into tears again.

"Come on Ellie dear. It's not like you to get so mad. It will only get you crying again and you know I never know what to say or do when you are like that." He held her closely and then felt her arms going round his waist and squeezing him tightly.

After a pause she looked up at him and reached up to kiss him. "Oh Andy; I do love you so much. I wish we could go and move the furniture again."

This time her tears had gone and were replaced by a mischievous gleam as she gave him an even tighter hug.to hold their bodies together for as long as possible. Andy smiled and kissed her forehead. "I must stop thinking of Flo with the fish paste sandwiches. But first let me ring Mary."

He rang but there was no answer. He left a message for her.

"Let's go for a walk to my place. I think my bed needs moving."

Ellie almost blushed but eagerly went with him. They returned two hours later feeling a bit guilty at leaving Flo in such a state but the house was strangely quiet.

Andy found a note on the table which briefly said that Muriel had rung and said she should go home. She would return on Tuesday to make sure everything was all right for the funeral.

Initially the relief was considerable but Flo's absence brought home the emptiness of the house to Ellie. Without her mum there it was never going to be like home again.

Chapter twenty-one

Waking up

Mary slept in on Sunday morning even though her mind was tossing about with all that had been happening. She didn't know whether she should admit to Ellie that she knew where Jennie was. It certainly wouldn't do her any favours to know Jennie. She couldn't think of two people who could be so different.

She had a leisurely breakfast before ringing Andy. His phone was out of action so she rang the house and had a very brusque response from what she guessed was Flo. At least she didn't have to go in today but she was concerned about Jennie and Albert so she waited for a while and then drove to the hospital. Even on a Sunday morning it was a problem finding a parking place.

The morning mist still held the acridity if last night's bonfires and fireworks and made her cough as she stepped from the car park to walk round the corner to the main entrance. Jennie was sound asleep but she was alarmed that nobody was there to keep an eye on the situation. She found the duty staff nurse and was assured that while Jennie was still under sedation she was not likely to cause any problems.

She decided to see why there was still nobody keeping watch and rang. Jane Marriner was on duty.

"Good morning Jane. I'm at the hospital and there is no sign of anyone keeping an eye on Jenny. I am sure that if Karl knows she is still alive he will try again."

Jane was not sympathetic. "Why are you there? You are off duty."

"I've only just arrived. I do think she needs to have a watch on her in case he tries to get at her in the hospital."

"Well I'm sorry Mary but we don't have the resources to do that and our overtime budget has been cut so don't think you can volunteer to work today."

"That's not what I was suggesting Jane but I promised that we would keep an eye on her before and we failed in that with the result that she is in here and lucky to be alive."

"I can't help that Mary. You can't make promises we can't keep. All I can say is that you are on your own time and what you do with it is your own business. She should be all right in the hospital and be sure that they have been alerted to the possibility of an intrusion. Just make sure she has no visitors until tomorrow."

"I really don't feel that I can leave her."

"As I said that's up to you, but there is no help available here. It's Sunday remember and it was a busy Saturday night so we are on skeleton staff. I'll see you tomorrow and we can discuss the case then."

"I would actually like to have a word with you now if possible because there has been an unexpected twist in the situation."

"Is it important? I am due to go shortly and we are up to our eyes with the arrests we made yesterday."

"Oh good; Have you got them all?"

"Not yet but we had an anonymous call naming the gang and saying that Jennie might be in danger. Only Karl and Johnny Foster are still on the loose. It looks like it was Foster who did the shooting."

"So Jennie's information was helpful."

"Yes, but we don't need her as a witness now unless she can come up with a statement of some real value. The Inspector still wants to charge her with complicity but she is pretty low on his priorities. Catching Johnny Foster is our prime target."

"What about Karl? He has tried to kill her already."

"Foster is the prime target and Jennie is probably in greater danger from him that from Karl. They used to be together you know."

"Who?"

Jennie and Foster. I knew them both at school. That's why she thought she recognised me yesterday. I was older than them but Foster caused mayhem while he was there before he was sent to prison. He was dealing drugs in a big way when he was only fifteen and was responsible for the death of one of my friends. Nothing will give me greater pleasure than to see him going down for life."

"Jennie had a daughter when she was fifteen. You don't think that he could be the father do you?"

"I know she left suddenly but she was very promiscuous. It could have been anyone. It's probably better for her child not to know about Foster."

Mary paused.

"Are you still there Mary? Look I must get on with the work here,"

"Right; Thank you Jane; that has been useful. I will see you tomorrow all being well"

Mary put the phone back in her bag. The sister had come on duty so she explained what was happening to her. She was assured that nobody would be allowed to visit apart from Albert but as a precaution Jennie was moved into a side room.

Albert arrived soon afterwards and came up as soon as they would let him in. Mary let him know what was happening and he offered to stay around to keep an eye on Jennie.

Jennie was still sleeping under the effects of the injection she had been given but she was showing signs of waking and it was only a matter of time before the pain hit her again.

The staff nurse did not seem too happy about her ward to be so full of non-casualties hovering around at that time of the morning and kept looking at Albert to make sure he wasn't doing anything untidy.

They knew when Jennie was awake by the sudden stream of obscenities from behind the curtains. The nurses moved into action swiftly and Jennie's vocabulary was mixed with reassurance. The staff nurse moved in with a large needle and there was a slap, squeal and even more foul language which slowly began to fade as the effects of the injection began to take effect.

The staff nurse emerged looking pleased with herself and told them that Jennie would soon be able to see them but only for a short time.

The curtains were drawn back and two slightly dishevelled nurses reappeared.

Jennie was wrapped in bandages and plaster and well supported on the bed to protect her ribs. The injection had obviously been quite strong as she was sitting still and gazing ahead of her as if she couldn't focus.

Albert went over and gently kissed her on the forehead. "Hello my dear. I'm glad you are still with us. You gave us a real fright last night."

Jennie looked at him and a slight gleam of fight came into her eyes. "What the fuck do you think it's done to me?

The effort of being angry made her wince.

Albert was not put off. "Do you remember what happened last night?"

Jennie stopped for a moment. "I can't really remember much. One minute I was watching the fireworks and then I woke up here. Oh yes, I think I heard Karl saying bitch but I can't be sure. It feels like his work but I'm still alive. That's not like him."

Then she spotted Mary. "You satisfied now. You can tell your friends that I don't care anymore. I'd be better off dead."

"Don't be like that dear. You would probably be dead if it hadn't been for Mary."

Mary touched him on the arm and started to move away. "Don't worry about me Albert. I am off duty today but I just wanted to be sure you had pulled through."

"No thanks to you, you bitch. You left me on my own and now look at what's happened. If they think I'm talking they will kill me for sure. I won't be so lucky next time."

Mary spoke softly but firmly. "I am sorry about last night Jennie but you went out when you knew it was dangerous.. If Albert and I hadn't interrupted Karl I am sure you would be dead."

"Albert leaned forward and took Jennies good hand. "Listen Jennie. They are already after you. Mary tells me they have had an anonymous call telling them all about the raid and saying you were in danger."

Jennie winced again as she tried to breathe. "I bet I know who that was. I'm not saying anything but if you tell me who they are, and if I like what you say I might talk. He can't do this to me and expect to get away with it."

Mary ignored the confused message she was getting from Jennie and thought about what she should say. Perhaps it was worth taking a risk. "Johnny Foster, Mick Earnshaw, Dave Morris and Karl. They raided the club on Friday. Karl drove the car that killed a passer-by and Johnny did the shootings. We know it but we need more evidence to prove it."

"What about Paul at the Crown, he's the banker." The words were out of Jennie's mouth before she realised. "That's where they would have gone afterwards."

"Johnny has been knocking off the barmaid there, Maggie. She will know all about it and I bet she will give you all the information you want. Why don't you go and shake her up? Stuck up cow that she is, it was probably her that rang."

Mary gasped at the unexpected information. "That's something we need to know. Hang on while I go and phone my boss."

Jennie watched her as she left the ward. "Where does she think I could go trussed up like this?" She tried to laugh but only hurt herself even more.

Albert held her hand again but only made her wince more. "Sorry dear! I am glad we got to you before he could do any more damage. You really must tell the police all that you know. You won't be in any more danger than you are now and it might mean they get caught and put away for a long time."

"For Johnny and Karl there is no time long enough."

"I guess they will want to keep you here for some time so you should be safe. When you come out I want you to come and live with me. I know that I'm an old fool but I want to help you and you know I have a house all to myself. You could help me to look after it and I wouldn't expect anything in return except your friendship. You would have your own room and I wouldn't interfere in your life as long as you are all right. What do you say?"

Jennie tried to reach out to him but her ribs wouldn't let her bend. After she had got her breath back she lay there for a moment. "I don't know what to say to you Albert. I really do like you and not just as a punter. You've become a really good friend."

She felt like crying but even that hurt. "I haven't had many good friends in my life; only Wendy who died and my dad. Everyone else hates me or just wanted to fuck me or beat me up. I really am no good. I would only end up hurting you and I don't want to do that. But I'm no good and never have been."

She turned as far away from him as she could and tears began to trickle down her cheek. "My mother told me I was the spawn of the devil and she hated me. I didn't know why unless she was right. Your mother's always right isn't she? Only my dad understood me and in the end even he left. It really hurt me then because I loved him so much. I loved to make him happy but he wouldn't, or couldn't take me with him. He left me with her so I never had a chance to be good. She even took my baby away from me. My only chance to show that I could love and be loved and she took her away."

By now the tears were pouring down her cheek and Albert suddenly became aware of a nurse standing behind him.

"I hope you haven't been upsetting her. She's been through great deal already. Perhaps you could come back when she's a bit more rested. Come on Jennie. Let's make you a bit more comfortable. Your friends can come again a bit later."

As she patted the pillows with one hand she wave Albert away with the other and obedient as ever he obeyed and quietly slipped away to the WRVS bar.

Mary was just returning when he was leaving so he told her what the nurse had said. She went with him and they talked over a cup of coffee.

Albert as always tried to be tactful but he couldn't help asking if Jennie's information had been helpful.

Mary held her hand up. "Sorry Albert but I can't say anything at this stage but shall we say it is a good start."

"Oh that's good. What do your family think of you being in the police?"

Her response wasn't quite what he expected.

"Oh thank you Albert. You've reminded me that I have to talk to my brother. Hang on please. It won't take me long."

Five minutes later she returned. "Missed him again but I guess he and Ellie have gone to church. He hasn't recharged his phone and I had to ring the house again much to Ellie's aunt's annoyance."

When they returned to the ward the doctor had just finished his rounds and had ordered her complete rest for the day. She was already asleep again and he had given orders that she should not be disturbed again until tomorrow.

Mary went home to try and get some rest and do some housework but she couldn't concentrate on what she was doing. She decided she would ask Albert about seeing Ellie and she knew where to find him.

Albert had gone back by the local cenotaph and was just in time for the closing hymn. Once that had finished he had a brief chat with some of his old friends and then strolled round to the 'Pig and Poke' for a relaxed Sunday lunch. A cold drizzle still hung in the air but it had cleared the effects of last night's bonfires. He had just ordered his Sunday roast when Mary came in and joined him.

Chapter twenty-two

Lunch and mayhem

Mary sat down next to Albert. "Hello Albert. I thought I would find you here."

He was surprised to see her again so soon. "Oh! I was just having some lunch before going back to keep an eye on Jennie."

"I know, and it is good of you to do that."

"I should have gone with her last night, I should. It wouldn't have happened if I had been there. I've met that bloke of hers, Karl; a really nasty piece of work. She never had any money in spite of all the things he got her to do. He took it all to spend on his own nasty habits. It would serve him right if they locked him up and threw away the key."

Mary couldn't help smiling. "The whole of the Met is out there looking for him and his friend Johnny. I doubt if he will get away. We already have most of the gang. There's nowhere they can go because nobody wants to be involved in the shooting of a policeman."

"What? Do you think it was Karl that shot him then?"

"No we know it wasn't Karl. If you remember we got his gun, but we know he drove the car that killed the pedestrian. Karl is going away for a very long time. I think Jennie will be all right as well. She will be charged but probably just given a caution, and she won't need to give evidence as we already have enough already."

"Will she be safe now?"

"I don't know. If it was Karl that tried to kill her yesterday she won't be truly safe until we catch him. If he knows he bungled the job yesterday he might try again. It just depends how sick he is."

"Are you going to put a guard on her?"

"Not at the moment because we just haven't got enough staff. The priority is catching Karl and Johnny and the two that Jennie mentioned this morning. That's why it's so helpful if you are at the hospital even if you can't talk to her. The hospital staff know you and they won't let anyone else in without you knowing."

"Shall I go now?"

"No, no; wait until you've had your dinner and there is something else I want to talk to you about."

"Oh, all right then, you just ask away."

"Well Albert, it looks as if we have found Jennie's daughter."

"What! Little Ellie? How did you find her and what about Jennie's mother, have you found her as well?"

"Not exactly, but it's because of her that I found out about Ellie's relationship with Jennie."

"Albert wiped the last bit of gravy with a slice of bread. "What do you mean?"

"Well, Mrs Burns died this week and Ellie had to find all the certificates for the registrar. When she found her own birth certificate she discovered for the first time that Mrs Burns wasn't her mother and that Jennie is."

"Goodness me! That must have been a shock for a little girl. But how do you know all this?"

I only discovered all this yesterday when I met Ellie and my brother Andy. The strange thing is that they are planning to get married so Jennie could become my brother's mother-in-law."

"Bloody hell! Sorry my dear, I forgot myself. That is such a surprise. I thought Ellie was still a child."

"I guess she has never got older in Jennie's mid but she is twenty now and at work. She's a very nice young woman; very kind and thoughtful, and anxious to meet her mother so that she can get her to the funeral."

"Does she know about Jennie? I mean to say, I'm very fond of the girl but I would be a bit shocked if she was my mother."

"That's why I would like you to meet her Albert. You know the good side of Jennie. I think she already knows the kind of life Jennie has been living but she still wants to find her. Like I say she is a very kind young woman, totally different from Jennie."

"Jennie's all right you know; just messed up with all that's happened to her and with this bloke Karl. She's always been good to me."

"But you have only really known her through her visits."

Albert felt uncomfortable at being reminded of his professional relationship with Jennie and he leaned over and lowered his voice. "We don't do it you know. I'm not past it but I like her company and she does make me feel as if I'm in the land of the living, even if I do have to pay for it."

Mary had to laugh a bit and Albert felt nonplussed at her reaction. "Just because I'm seventy four doesn't mean I like being on my own."

"Sorry Albert. I shouldn't have laughed. I'm just saying that you see Jennie at her best. But she is also heavily dependent on drugs, mostly non prescribed and prone to considerable mood swings and as we know even suicidal behaviour. She is so unreliable. Even if she agrees to stay with you she will eventually have to get out and her life style is so well established and her own self-image so damaged that with all the best will in the world she won't be able to help herself or you for any length of time."

"Perhaps if she knows that her mother is gone and that her daughter wants to see her it will help her to be more positive."

"I must say Albert, you are an eternal optimist. I just hope she doesn't hurt you too much. What I would like to do is to bring Ellie and Andy to meet you and for you to tell them about Jennie. If she still wants to meet Jennie after that then at least she will be better prepared."

"Of course I will do that for you dear. I will look forward to meeting young Ellie after all you have said about her. She sounds a lovely young woman and I think Jennie would be very proud of her."

"I don't want you to say anything about this to Jennie until I say you can. Is that all right with you Albert?"

"Oh yes. Of course it is. And you say she is going to marry your brother. Well I never, what a small world it is. What a turn up."

"Thank you Albert. I'll talk to Ellie and let you know about where and when we can meet. Now, you have my mobile telephone number so give me a ring if you have any worries whatever. I shall be at home today with any luck. Don't do anything to put yourself at risk will you?"

"No, I will ring you if there is anything out of order. I will get back there now and I will do my best to stay awake and on guard. I'm an old soldier you know."

"Yes Albert I know that which is why I am telling you to be careful and not to take any risks."

He stood up and saluted her. "Right then! Back to duty ma'am!"

Mary watched as he left. It was against all regulations to do this and she would no doubt get into a lot of trouble if it went wrong. She finished her meal and then went home.

Albert made himself known to the staff and then got comfortable in an armchair in the side ward where Jennie was. Someone had rung them to see how she was but nobody came. He was quite exhausted by the end of visiting hours when even he had to leave. The sister assured him that she was aware of the situation and that she would ensure that someone would look in every ten minutes or so. Jennie was deeply asleep so he knew that she would be no trouble. He was glad to get home and have a nap but first of all he rang Mary to let her know he had finished his vigil. She was not available at the time so he left a message.

Unknown to him Karl was waiting outside the hospital. He knew where Jennie was. He had been in already and seen Albert was there so he had waited until the end of visiting time. It wasn't too difficult for him to find an orderly's white coat. He walked to the ward as if he worked there. The nurses were busy tidying up after the disruption of visiting time.

It was so easy to slip into Jennie's room without being seen. Her plaster and bandages were pleasing to him but he knew that only her death would make him feel easy and keep her quiet.

She lay there breathing slowly under the effects of the medication. He leaned over her and wondered what on earth he had ever seen in her other than a means of income. He fingered the heroin in his pocket. Initially he had thought of overdosing her but it would be difficult to make her swallow as she was. The pillow was hardly an original idea but it was handy and it took no time to put it over her face and push down.

The choking caused Jennie to come to and she began to struggle but not for long as she lost consciousness. Suddenly the door opened and the Sister stood there. She saw what was happening and stepped back to shout for help. As she did so Karl pushed past her and punched her sending her sprawling into the room. He heard others coming in response to her call and ran, discarding the gown as he did so. He got out of the hospital before security had time to try and stop him. A bus was coming so he jumped aboard and made good his escape.

Back in the hospital they were trying to revive Jennie and to treat the Sister who had a nasty cut to her head. Slowly their efforts with Jennie began to work and she started to breathe on her own again. The duty doctor was there as she began to come round. In the mist of her medication she was vaguely conscious of the squeaky voice. Balls she thought and drifted off again.

The Sister had a bad gash to the back of her head and need to get it stitched. To be on the safe side they sent her to x ray to be sure no other damage had been done.

The police were called and Jane Warriner came herself and interviewed the staff. In spite of her injury Sister Harris was able to describe Karl.

Chapter twenty-three

Aftermath

After she had taken all the statements Jane rang Mary. "Hi Mary! It's Jane. You were right and I'm at the hospital. Karl has been here and had another go at Jennie. He tried to suffocate her and it was touch and go but she is OK now. It was only because the Sister popped in to see her that it wasn't worse. She was injured as well when Karl made his escape."

She paused as Mary asked if they had caught Karl. "No, I'm afraid he got away again. I can't understand how he knew where she was. – No there's no reason for you to come in. I shall leave someone here but I doubt if he'll be back tonight. – Yes I know you told me. I'll see you tomorrow."

Mary put the phone down though she felt more like throwing it. She had just got out of the bath and the thought of returning to the hospital was just too much for her. Now there was somebody there she could relax a bit. She left a message for Andy as his phone was charged up again. Then she rang Albert to let him know what had happened.

It took her a long time to try and calm him down.

Eventually she curled up on her settee with a book she had been trying to read all week, but her mind couldn't concentrate so she checked her computer for emails and then turned the television on and sat her way through most of a bottle of red wine.

Tonight was an oasis in the chaos of the week and there was nothing she could do. She thought about how Albert had asked her about whether she had any boy-friends. Perhaps she was in the wrong job. It would be nice to have someone else to rely on, someone who cared. The wine soon became stronger in its influence than her worries and she fell asleep where she was.

*

The medication began to wear off and slowly Jennie began to show signs of activity. In her mind there was a deep pit and she kept falling down into it. Each time she landed every bone in her body wanted to scream then there was silence and she could smell clean sheets and polish. She moaned and a nurse who was sitting nearby came over to her. "Sister, I think she is coming round."

The sister then rang through to the doctor and five minutes later they were all there as one eye flicked open. "Well done Miss Burns. I didn't think you would make it. You must have a head made of granite."

Jennie couldn't quite hear what he was saying as everything was blurred, sound , sight, feeling. She did however recognise his voice. From the depths of her parched throat they vaguely heard her say "Balls."

The doctor looked at the Sister. "Doesn't she know any other words?"

The Sister smiled. "It's a miracle she can say anything after that attack. Nurse! Will you ring Sergeant Marriner at the police station and let her know that Miss Burns has come to and while you are at it please give Mr Smith a call to set his mind at rest.

"Yes Sister."

Jennie could hear a ringing tone. "What happened?"

The doctor looked at the Sister. "You had better tell her. She only says balls to me."

The Sister leaned closed to Jennie. "Can you hear me all right Jennie?"

That ringing tone was persistent. "Yes, but can you turn that bell off."

The Sister knew what she meant. "It's all right Jennie. The ringing is just in your head at present. It will wear off soon. You have been attacked again I'm afraid. That is why your face feels puffy and you can't hear or focus properly but you are going to be all right now. For your own sake we gave you an injection to help you sleep so you should be going back to sleep soon."

Jennie struggled to hear above the ringing but the word attack got through to her. "It was him again wasn't it? It was that bloody Karl!"

The effort of such a long sentence made her cough and her head reeled with the pain it caused. The Sister helped her to sit up to prevent her choking but that caused even more pain.

The doctor helped get her pillows in position. "I will give her something for the pain but she should sleep soundly soon. She should have some nourishment and if she can't manage that herself then keep her on the drip feed."

"Thank you doctor; I am sure we can manage fine now."

She plumped the pillows up again. "I have told the police that you won't be able to talk to them until tomorrow but they have left a young lady here to keep an eye on you."

The nurse returned with a tray which held a kidney tray on one side and a cup with a straw sticking out of it. "I thought the straw might help. Here you are. If you take a drink it will make your throat feel easier."

Their calm and efficient approach helped Jennie to relax. "I hate hospitals. When can I get out of here?"

"You will need to be able to stand up first."

"When will that be?"

"Well it all depends on how you behave yourself. If you try to rush things you could be here for another week but if you do exactly as you are told and don't try to be silly, then you may be able to go in three or four days. You haven't broken your leg though it is very badly bruised. Your face swelling should die down in a couple of days. You do have three broken ribs and you will have to be careful for a few weeks to let them and your hand and arm heal. You won't be able to go to work for some time, and you won't be able to enter any beauty contests for at least a month. That's because you nose and cheek bone are broken. Still, considering what you looked like when you came in that is an improvement. By rights you should be dead from the injuries you had."

Jennie found it difficult to take it all in and it was the last words that stuck in her mind. "Did you say I ought to be dead?"

"Yes; both from the first attack and from today."

"Why? What happened then and what day is it now?"

"Today is Sunday and it is now eight o'clock in the evening. You were brought in last night but you have been unconscious most of today. Then this late afternoon a man got in here and tried to suffocate you but Sister Harris scared him off."

Jennie began to cough but soon stopped when her ribs objected. She wheezed instead. "Was that you? What did he look like?"

"No dear. I'm Sister Mackay. Sister Harris had to go off work because she was injured in trying to stop him. All I know is that he was a stocky man with very short blonde hair."

"Karl!" Jennie gasped. "It was Karl. It was him tried to kill me on Saturday. I knew he would have another go but the fucking police wouldn't believe me."

The Sister held her down. "Don't even think of trying to get up. You will only fall on the floor. There is a police lady here now over by the door and there was another one in civvies this morning and Mr Smith sat here for ages to keep an eye on you. They will be in tomorrow to have a chat with you. Now have a sip of your drink and relax. You are perfectly safe now."

She slipped the straw into Jennie's mouth and was relieved to see that she could suck at the contents. I have a ward round to do now Jennie but Staff Nurse Maguire is on duty all night. If you need her just press the button on this lead. OK." She took the cup from Jennie and put it where she could reach it with her good hand.

Jennie tried to nod her head. "Yes. I'll behave. I have some thinking to do."

"You will fall asleep very soon and we will see then what tomorrow brings."

For once in her life Jennie actually said "Thanks."

Chapter twenty-four

The dam burst

As soon as the rounds had been made on the ward Mary came back to see Jennie having ben detailed by Inspector Crawford to take a statement from her whenever she could. Sister Mackay had waited to see her before going off duty so Mary knew that Jennie was improved after a good night's sleep.

Jennie appeared to be asleep but as soon as Mary made a sound her eyes shot open. "What are you creeping around for?"

Mary smiled. "Making sure there's enough of you to make a statement."

Jennie looked at her. "I think I want to talk to him, that posh copper, Inspector something. I want to tell him everything. But you've got to be careful because one of Johnny's mates is a copper and he tells Johnny everything that's going on. That's why you can't find him."

"Are you telling me there's a bent copper in the police station?"

"How would I know where he is? All I know is that he supports Chelsea and has a funny name."

Mary thought for a while then realised that it had to be handled at a senior level.

"Just wait here. I'm just popping out side to ring and see if he can come to see you."

"You said that last time. Where do you think I can go like this?"

Mary ignored the outburst and went outside to use her phone. Inspector Graham was going to be free this afternoon.

She returned to the ward and told Jennie. She was about to leave when Jennie stopped her. "I want you to be there as well."

Mary stopped. "That has to be up to the inspector."

"No it isn't. It's what I want. If you're not there I won't talk and I want you to take down some notes in case I forget them this afternoon."

"Really Jennie; you're not in a position to boss people around like that."

"Oh yes I am" she said with as much of a smile as she could muster. "You want to know what I know and I am only going to tell you because I don't trust these other coppers. I bet it's because of his mate that he knew where I was."

"That's a very serious accusation to make Jennie."

"Don't try to bullshit me out of saying what I want to. If you don't believe it that's up to you but I tell you one of Karl's friends has a mate in the force."

Mary got her notebook out and a pen. "All right Jennie. Just tell me what is on your mind. Do you know the name of the police officer who rings Johnny?"

"He's not an ordinary cop. I think he's a sergeant or something. I don't know his name because they just call him timber."

Mary stifled her gasp. Timber was on the serious crime squad.

"What evidence do you have?"

"I don't have evidence. That's for you to find. I'm only telling you where to look, like upstairs in the sweet shop down the Camberwell Road. That's where they do all their filming. That's what your blokes into, especially kid's stuff. The sweet shop's a good front for kids going in and out. I was doing it when I was thirteen and they are still going. They always did have loads of protection like some of the posh parties that I got to go to. Good pay but some very weird stuff especially with the kids."

Mary stopped. "Look you're giving me all sorts of new stuff and I can't take this down by myself."

Jennie ignored her. "I used to work them with Wendy but when she died I packed it in. It was too dangerous to do it on your own. Then Johnny Morris, we were at school together and he got me into all this. He's really gone bad but I think he has had it this time. He's tied in with some real wicked people. They make him look very small. Anyone who threatens their safety disappears like when the Krays were in business. I think they put the money up for this robbery and they provide the guns. They won't be pleased at Karl losing his shot gun."

Mary coughed and tried to stop Jennie again. "Jennie, I can't use any of this without another witness."

Jennie was breathing heavily by now and it was clear she might not be able to go on much more. "That's why I want you to take it down now so's I don't forget. Then Karl was deep into drugs. Not taking them but shifting them from place to place. You have Darren Fox in custody at present. He was Karl's runner. The other bloke you want there is Steve. I think his name sounds Irish but I'm not sure. He supplies Karl with all the drugs to sell and it might be the sort of place Karl would go to hide out. It's over in Tulse Hill but I'm not sure of the address."

She stopped and her eyes began to close and her breathing became shallow.

Mary waited for a while then quietly got up and left the room. The Staff Nurse saw her. "I hope you haven't been wearing her out. She's not strong enough for too much talking yet."

Mary nodded. "I know. She's just gone to sleep again."

The Staff Nurse looked into the room to make sure Jennie was comfortable while Mary took the opportunity to call the office and report on the situation.

She was put through to Sergeant Forrester who wanted to know if she had said anything. Mary decided not to tell him but rang back straight away and asked for Jane Marriner. She repeated what Jennie had said about Timber Forrester and was surprised when Jane did not seem shocked.

Jane told her, "We have begun an investigation into how Johnny seems to know what we are doing. We thought we had him cornered but he moved just before we got there. It seems apparent that he is getting information. Leave it with me and I will have a chat with the boss."

Mary went downstairs to get a cup of coffee and found Albert there already on his second having been there since before the canteen was even open. He had been waiting to get permission to see Jennie.

Mary explained that Jennie was still very tired. Then she reminded Albert that he had agreed to meet Ellie tonight as long as Ellie was willing.

"Yes of course I will. I just hope that I can be of some help to her."

"I'm sure you can. Do you have any family at all." That was just the button to press for Albert and for the next hour she heard the story of how he and Ruth had lived there since 1970.

Albert gazed into the bottom of his cup swirling his memories around. 1956 they had got hitched when he came back from the Korean War. He was still hobbling from his injuries but still fit enough to do the right thing as she was already six months pregnant.

He and Ruth had grown up together, neighbours in the old Lewis Buildings in Chelsea. It had sounded posh living in Chelsea but the truth was quite different. He had been called up when he was eighteen, just in time for Korea. He had only been there six months when he was shot in the leg.

He got a post at Aldershot when he came back which is where he met Fred Gibbons. Fred was forever doing magic tricks and when they were discharged they set up as the Gibboni Brothers and got a regular slot with a travelling Circus. Ruth never liked him being away but the money was reasonable and the work steady until television killed off most of his opportunities.

Fred had moved to Cornwall with his parents and he had become a milk man. He still had his Magic Circle card and performed whenever he had the chance, Not much now because he had arthritis in his hands.

He had been out the night young Albert died. It was so silly and he had always blamed himself for it as he had taught the lad the tricks from the circus, juggling, tumbling and balancing.

The lads had been celebrating as Al had joined the Army that night and on the way home he had tried to walk the narrow parapet of the railway bridge. Even now the thought of such sad waste of life made him emotional.

They had a sandwich from the bar and time passed quickly. Inspector Crawford and Jane Marriner were earlier than she had expected. Mary was quite glad of their company by then as Albert seemed to have an inexhaustible supply of reminiscences.

Mary had a private talk with them before they Interviewed Jennie showing them her notes from the morning. Jane told her they had already begun checking her allegations about Timber. Mary told them how fragile Jennie was so the Inspector went up to the ward to talk with the Doctor while Jane joined Mary and Albert.

Albert took to Jane straight away and soon got back into his stride talking about Jennie and what he could do for her once she came out of hospital. Jane tried to calm him down and be more realistic but he wasn't really listening to anyone else.

Without really thinking she let slip that she knew Jennie. "I remember Jennie when she was at school. She was wild then and if I remember rightly she left at the end of year 9. I believe she went to a children's home."

Albert looked at her in surprise. "You knew Jennie?"

Jane felt a bit uncomfortable at this level of incredulity.

"Well, yes; I grew up in this area and went to school in Balham. I was older than Jennie but she was hard not to notice. One of the men we are looking for was in my class as well; Johnny Foster. Jenny used to follow him around. He was a nasty piece of work even as a kid but it looks like he has gone right over the top now what with the robbery and other things that are coming to light."

Mary looked down. "You mean like Timber being bent."

"We don't know that for sure yet, but he is being questioned."

"Jennie was quite clear about it. She has mass of information as long as she is still willing to talk. I shall have to talk with you on your own before we see her."

Albert waved his hand. "Don't worry about me dearies; I'm just amazed at how everything is happening at the same time. This time last week Jennie was just a welcome visitor, now she has become the most important person in my life. She's been attacked twice, she's told me about her abusive childhood and now her daughter turns up. It's a bit hard for an old man to keep pace with it all."

Mary put a hand on his shoulder. "Don't you worry about it Albert. We should have it sorted out soon."

Jane looked at them. "It's going to take a long time to take her statement. It might be an idea for you to go home and have a rest Albert."

Albert gave a sniff, got out his handkerchief and blew his nose, then wiped a tear away. "I think I'll do that you know. I'm no use sat here and I can't drink any more of that stuff they call coffee. I'll come back this evening when you've done with her. She's a good girl under all that muck you know. She's been really good to me. Made my life worth living again she has."

He got up slowly and wandered towards the door then he paused and looked round at them. "She's a good one and she could be a real good one." The he gave them a little wave and left.

Chapter twenty-five

The Interview

Jane looked at Mary. "Right! Now what were you going to say?"

Mary explained how Jennie had spoken of Timber being involved in a child pornography ring as well as actively giving Johnny information that would help him with robberies and burglary. The group all had links going back and based on a common support of Chelsea.

By the time she had filled Jane in with all the details the nurse came to let them know that Jennie was awake and had been treated. Jennie was in fact now sitting up for the first time since the attack though her face was still puffy and discoloured. Her arm was in a plaster cast and a cage protected her bruised leg.

Mary smiled as she came in. "Glad to see you sitting up again Jennie. That must be a good sign."

She was greeted with a stream of abuse but continued to smile. "You really are on the road to recovery. This is Sergeant Marriner, though I think you met her the other day. She tells me that she used to be at school with you. She is here to take the statement that we talked about earlier."

Jane sat down beside the bed, Hello Jennie. I doubt if you remember me. I was in the same year as Johnny Foster when you left school. I am a sergeant in CID now and it's my job to help you to make a statement that will enable us to protect you in the future. We have set up a recording machine for you to speak into and I'm just going to switch it on so I would be grateful if you wouldn't swear too much in the next few minutes. One of our clerks will have to type it up and she gets quite embarrassed when she has rude words to type."

Jennie was about to speak but Jane put a finger across her mouth and went "shush" as she switched the machine on. She spoke into it. "This is Sergeant Jane Warriner speaking from St George's Hospital where I and Police Woman Mary Heron are about to interview Jennifer Burns about the robbery at the Rialto Night Club on Friday evening and other associated matters."

She passed the microphone to Mary and she spoke into it stating her name. Jane then handed the mike to Jennie. "Can you speak in here and say who you are so they recognise your voice."

"You've already said who I am."

Jane took the mike back and spoke into it again. "That was the voice of Jennifer Burns, better known as Jennie."

She switched the mike off. "Mary tells me you have a lot to say and this is the best way we have of making sure we get it right. When we get it typed up we will give you a copy to read and to sign as a correct copy. I won't ask any more questions than I

195

need to because I think you will be able to talk better without us interrupting you. Don't think about the mike, I will make sure it can pick your voice up. Is that OK?"

"Was you really at school with me?"

"Yes, but you probably won't remember me. I had really long hair then and glasses."

"You must have been one of those swotty ones that went to college."

"I guess that was me and look where it got me."

That made Jennie smile, then she winced. "Don't make me laugh, my ribs are killing me. I suppose you were going to say look where what I did got me."

Jane smiled. "Are you OK to begin?"

"Yes; let's get this done but where's the bloke I spoke to yesterday? I thought he was going to be here."

"He's talking to the doctor at present but he is happy for us to take your statement."

"I'm trusting you lot with my life so if I get done again I'll forget everything I'm telling you." It was nearly forty minutes later when she stopped talking. As Jane gathered the machine together she put her hand on Jennie's.

"Thanks Jennie. This is really going to help. We will do our best to use this information discretely. We are well aware now of how much danger you are in because we found Maggie Cross at the Crown this morning. She had been shot. Paul has been picked up in North London with the money. It looks as if he was getting away with the money and had left Maggie. I don't think he killed her."

"I told you I was going to get killed."

"We are keeping a twenty-four hour watch on you from now on so nobody is going to get close to you."

Mary had been patiently waiting for the interview to finish. "How are you feeling Jennie because I have something else to tell you."

Jennie leaned back on her pillows. "Go on, hit me with it. Things can't get any worse."

"I don't know if this will be better or worse Jennie but I met your daughter yesterday. She's been looking for you."

Jennie's eyes opened wide and her mouth dropped. "My daughter!"

"Yes Jennie; your daughter Ellie. She's twenty now and engaged and she wants to meet you."

"My mum would never allow that. She swore on the Bible that I would never get a chance to corrupt my daughter, and she has kept me away all these years."

"Mary touched Jennie slightly on the shoulder. "She can't stop her any more. Your mother died last week. It was all very sudden and Ellie had no idea until then that you even existed."

"You must be having a terrible joke on me. You can't be telling the truth. My mum can't die. She's not old enough. Who's going to look after my baby?"

"You're not listening Jennie; she isn't a baby any longer. She is a twenty year old young woman and she is at work and engaged to be married. You mum has done a really good job in bringing her up but she never told her about you. It's a shame you were not involved."

"No I'm glad she didn't know me. She would be ashamed to know me and she mustn't. I would only spoil it all for her."

"She knows about you already Jennie. She knows what you do and how you have been living."

"You didn't tell her did you?"

"I didn't need to. She had found out before I saw her."

"And she still wants to see me?"

"Yes; she is quite determined to meet you. She is very clear in her mind about that."

She pause while Jennie buried her head in her hands. "Mind you, I don't know what she wants to say to you, but she definitely wants to know you and to talk to you. I think that she needs to try and understand how it all happened. She loved your mother and is very shocked at her death. I think she would like you to be at the funeral as if that might start to make things better."

"Oh God no!! I couldn't do that. Not after all these years. Any way I can't go while I am stuck in here."

"I spoke to the sister and she says that you should be able to move by Thursday and they could let you go by wheelchair and ambulance car."

"Oh, no, no, no. Everyone would be looking at me if I came like that. She would get out of her coffin if I went. "

"It's not for your mother, it's for Ellie."

"What if she hates me, and doesn't want me. I would die if she hated me. I only left her because I loved her so much that I knew I couldn't be any good for her. I've tried so hard to forget her all these years but I still have her photograph in my purse and when I get really down I look at her picture and pray that I got at least one thing right in my miserable life. But I can't risk meeting her in case she hates me."

 "She might hate you for not seeing her."

Jennie was weeping in spite of the pain it was causing her. "Stop it. You're torturing me when I can't fight back. Oh God; I do want to see her but I am afraid of her seeing me."

"She will be proud of what you have done today. It has taken a lot of courage for you to speak out the way you have."

"That isn't courage; that is spite; they just got me so angry and if they are going to kill me then at least I can take them down as well. You see that's me, spiteful and vicious. I'm a whore, a thief, a druggie, name it and I've probably done it. My friends are killers and robbers, they don't care for anyone except themselves and neither did I."

"What about Ellie and Albert?"

"I thought Ellie was safely away from me so I couldn't damage her and Albert is really just one of my punters. He has been good to me but he only knows me from Tuesday and Friday at seven o'clock for one hour at thirty quid. I know he only wants to talk but there is a lot of difference between two hours a week and living with someone. It would do my head in. It's so sad that I can't help feeling for the daft old bugger. He wants me to go and live there you know. But I can't do that to him. I'd kill him in a month. I told him and do you know what he said? He said at least he would die happy knowing that I had somewhere safe to live. That is so sad. How can I be loved?"

"I don't know Jennie, but he is sincere and Ellie is sincere, and whatever you have done, however terrible it may be, they both love you; Ellie because you are her family, Albert because you have brought a little bit of light into his life."

"Don't! Don't say things like that. It will make me cry and I can't cry because it hurts."

"I'm going to leave you now Jennie. Have a think about what I have said.. Albert may be in to see you tonight and if you are willing I will bring Ellie in to see you tomorrow."

Mary rose to leave and suddenly realised that Jane was still there standing by the doorway. They were both quiet for some time as they walked out of the hospital. Jane had to go to Battersea with the tape but as she left she turned to Mary. "That was really good of you. I don't think I could have done that but you did. God! She nearly had me in tears."

Chapter twenty-six

Washing day

Monday morning at Hurley Street promised a degree of normality as both Andy and Elle had to return to work. Andy rose early as he had to go back to his flat to change into his suit. First however he made a cup of tea and took it up to Ellie. Ellie was asleep but all the covers were on the floor. He put the cups down and gently drew a sheet over her before coughing gently. She woke with a start.

"Andy! What's the matter?"

"Nothing love; I just brought up a cup of tea. I have to get back to my flat and dress for work."

"Oh, is it that time already? I had better get a move on as well"

She paused, took a sip of her tea. "I keep thinking how awful everything is in my family and I wouldn't blame you if you didn't want any more to do with me. I seem to be completely cursed and it won't do your career any good to be mixed up with me and my awful family,"

Andy put his cup down, sat on the bed and pulled her towards him hugging her. "What has brought that on after last night? Nothing in the world is going to break us up."

Then he kissed her.

Ellie hung on to him, weeping gently. Almost by accident his hand fell on her bare flesh and he began to run his hands over her body. It was not long before they were both naked and oblivious of the time.

Their passion was rudely shaken by her alarm clock reminding them that there was a world outside that was waiting for them. Andy got dressed but Ellie lay there a bit longer. He gazed at her still naked body. "I think your tea's gone cold."

"Mmmmm. Can you wake me like that every morning?"

By now Andy was focussed on what he had to do. "I must go and you had better move too or you'll be late for work."

"Beast, haven't I moved enough for you already?"

Andy paused trying to think of a suitable reply. In the end he just blew her a kiss. "See you at 5.00, usual place."

Ellie took her time getting dressed. Somehow reality seemed less important.

She began the day at work with some enthusiasm. It was a relief to be busy and so forced to think of other things than the last few days. There was however no escape as it was just as bad as Saturday with so many of the customers who seemed to know about mum.

She took an early lunch break but it was no better in the afternoon and she had to escape to the back of the store. Jill found her there and tried to console her. "I guess you've hit another weepy time." She said. "I'll get your till covered, after all Monday's aren't that busy. You look as though you need a rest my girl. Why don't you go home while it's nice and quiet and put your feet up for a while."

Ellie was ready for the idea but the thought that Aunty Flo might have returned filled her with dread. Then she felt guilty for feeling that way.

"I think I'll stay on, at least until Andy is free. It's only another hour today and we have to see his sister later and the minister is coming round as well."

"I expect his sister has been busy with all the palaver up at the cop shop." As usual Jill knew most of what was going on in the area.

"It gets a bit frightening when people start shooting off guns in the street. Thank goodness that poor copper is going to be all right. They got most of the gang except for a couple but they know who they are after this time."

"Oh, I hadn't realised it was that bad. Mary did say there was a flap on but I'm afraid I wasn't really taking it in. Anyway I feel a bit better now that I've had a weepy time. I'll go back to my till and leave at five tonight if that's OK."

The next hour flew by and she was soon outside waiting for Andy. They went back to his flat so he could change out of his suit and be more casual.

Mary called while they were there. She took Ellie's arm and asked her to sit down.

"Ellie, I need to tell you about your mother. Then you might understand how strange everything is. I do know her and in fact I am going to see her soon."

"Did you say you know my mother?"

"Yes, and I have had a chance to tell her about you and how her mother has died."

"How did she take it? What was she like? How did you find her?"

"Hang on Ellie. I can only answer one question at a time. I think it's better if I tell you how first. You know I said that I thought it might all tie up with the case we are working on at present. Well it was last Thursday night when I was called to a flat where someone had taken an overdose. Well her name was Jennie Burns. She had been living there with a man called Karl Kuyper. He is one of the men involved in the robbery so we wanted to ask her about him but she was very reluctant to tell us anything. It seems that Karl doesn't know that and on Saturday evening he attacked her and left her seriously injured.

Ellie gasped. Is she all right?"

"Fortunately I was out with a friend of hers looking for her and when we found her she had just been attacked by Karl and had quite a few injuries. We got her into hospital where she was made as comfortable as possible but even though she is in hospital he slipped in and attacked her again even in there. Thankfully he was disturbed and failed in his attempt, but it is clear that Jennie is in serious danger at present and we are keeping her under guard. We have interviewed her again today and she has been much more helpful. At the end of the interview I was able to tell her about you and how her mother had died."

"What did she say? Did you tell her that I want to see her?"

"Be patient. I have told her and she is frightened to see you because she is in such a mess. Also it will be difficult for you to see her before tomorrow evening. I have told her about the funeral. She didn't think her mother would want her there but I told her that you would want her there so she is thinking about it."

"What about all her injuries?"

"Well, as long as she does what the doctor tells her she could be able to do it but she will need a lot of persuading. You do know that she is a very strange lady and her language leaves a lot to be desired. A bit like her life really."

"I know what she does, like she is a prostitute and that I will be shocked when I meet her, but I can cope with that. I just feel so sorry for her because I had so much love shown to me by my gran whereas her own child had no love and was so rejected. My friend Jill tells me that I will be shocked when I see her and that I wouldn't want to meet her if I did know her, but everything I believe in tells me that I can't reject her."

Mary smiled. "I think she described her quite well. She is so totally different from anyone else you have ever met and entirely different from you. I can understand how she can be pitied because she has lost so much in not knowing you and seen how well you have grown up. Just seeing you will be quite a boost for her, but it will be a shock for you however good your intentions are."

"You lost your mum and dad as well didn't you? How did you manage?"

"Well we hardly knew our dad because he was in the army and was killed when Andy was just a baby. Then mum had cancer when I was sixteen so I had to help our a lot. She died just over a year later and I was able to look after Andy because he was a teenager and able to do a lot by himself, But it was tough."

Andy piped in. "What she means Ellie is that she left school to look after me rather than doing her A levels and go to university so she never had a chance to mix with people of her own age until I was able to fend for myself. That's when she joined the police. I thought it was because she fancied blokes in a uniform, but it hasn't worked yet."

"Hey little brother! I am only twenty seven. There's plenty of life left though this week has been really exhausting."

"I pity the bloke who does end up with her!"

Ellie leapt to Mary's defence. "Andy, that's not a nice thing to say about your sister after all she has done for you."

Andy held his hands up in mock surrender. "Sorry; believe me I know better than anyone what a great sister I do have and you will have the most wonderful sister-in-law going. Between the two of you I don't have a snowballs chance in hell."

Mary held her hand out to stop them. "Anyway we have a date with Jennie's friend, Albert later and I am starving so who is cooking?"

Ellie realised that in spite of being in the supermarket all day she hadn't bought any food. "Well, I don't have anything here except breakfast stuff and Aunty Flo has eaten most of that, so it's probably pizza."

Ellie suddenly remembered that Brian Evans was due to call in half an hour. "Oh; I forgot that the minister is coming round to talk with me about the funeral service. He will be here soon. "

"Don't worry Ellie. I'll get a take away and Mary can buy the drinks when we get to the pub. All right sis?"

"All right indeed! I had better get out of your way then and see you at the pub in about a couple of hours. Will that be time enough?"

Andy looked at Ellie and guessed that it would be pushing her too much. "Better make it two and a half. You won't be too drunk by then, will you?"

"Don't push it Andy. Just because you're my brother you can't malign me."

"I just remember someone telling me about the sore head she had this morning."

"OK, so I did have a bad head this morning but yesterday was worth a bottle of wine before I could stop thinking about it. It doesn't mean I need one today. Anyway I'm off. I might as well pop into the hospital and check up on Jennie and make sure she is OK to see you tomorrow. Meanwhile we are meeting her friend Albert this evening. Mind you I wouldn't put it past Jennie to have crawled out of the hospital and tried to escape. See you both later."

Andy got up as well. "I have to change out of my office clobber so I will pop back later to get you. You will be all right with the minister on your own won't you?"

"Yes; I'll be fine with Brian. He just wants to talk about the order of service for the funeral and I have thought about a couple of hymns that mum liked for the service. See you back here at eight then."

"No problem." He blew her a kiss as he went out.

Chapter twenty-seven

The old soldier

Having had a good rest in the afternoon and a couple of sandwiches for tea, Albert went back to the hospital to see if he could have some time with Jenny on his own in the evening visiting. The staff nurse recognised him and told the police officer on watch that he was safe.

Jennie was awake again and sucking a liquefied meal through a straw. He could tell she was getting better by the amount of complaint she was making but she did seem pleased to see him.

"There you are you old goat. I thought you had given up on me at last. This woman says she is going to give me a bed bath but I was trying to tell her that I am covered in so many bloody bandages that she would be wasting her time and my patience." She glowered at the nurse who was standing nearby. The nurse smiled back and left them to talk.

Albert pulled a seat up beside her bed. "I'm glad to hear you sounding so much better my dear. I've been in before but you were asleep and then with the police that I didn't get to see you much. I was so filled to the brim with the stuff they call coffee so I've been home and had my Sunday nap. The police seem very pleased with what you have told them."

"Keep it quiet Albert. I don't want anyone else to know that I've grassed to the police even if Karl and Johnny deserve it. I warned Karl that if he ever laid a finger on me again I would see him done for it. Well he did, didn't he and then he had another go when I was in here. By the time I've finished with him he'll wish he was on a boat back to Africa."

Albert took hold of her good arm. "Don't get too excited dear. They will get him and his friends. Did you know his picture was in the papers and there's a reward for their capture."

"Did you say a reward? Here, do you think I might get something if what I have said helps catch them? I could do with a little nest egg. I've had time to think in here as I can't do anything else and I reckon I'm not really up for this anymore. Mary told me that my mother is dead and that my little Ellie wants to see me. Do you think that she would really want to know me?"

"I know and I am supposed to be meeting Ellie tonight. Mary wants her to meet me so I can answer some of her questions before she sees you. Isn't it strange how things work out? Mary tells me she is a lovely young woman and I am sure she would want to know you and to see you. Mary tells me she is getting married soon to her brother. Can you imagine that? All this time Mary has been helping you her brother has been helping Ellie."

He suddenly became aware that Jennie was looking angry. "It's all right Jennie. He is a nice young man who works in a bank. You could have knocked me down with a feather when I heard. It seems that Ellie has been looking all over the place for you."

Jennie mellowed as he said that. "She hasn't has she? Been looking for me? She does want to see me then. She wants to know me in spite of all these awful years." She began to cry even though it was still painful to do so.. "But she can't get married, she's only a baby, she can't be old enough, isn't she still at school?"

"I will tell you when I see her but she has left school and is working. Mary tells me she has a job at Tesco's. You never know, you might have seen her and didn't know it."

"Oh God! I'm longing to see her and yet I'm so scared as well. Look at me; I'm a complete mess. How on earth would she want to meet me like this?"

"She knows what has been happening. Mary says that the poor girl was really upset about what has happened to you. I think she really cares. She even knows about you and me and she is coming to see me this evening so I can tell her more about you. Mary tells me that she is a lovely young woman. I am sure you will be proud of her."

So my mother got her perfect child after all?"

Albert couldn't readily think of an answer to that so he just mumbled. "She is your child, and yes I think she has been brought up well but she is kind and caring and she wants to know you. Do you know it was only last week when your mother died that she even knew you existed. Up to that time she had always thought your mother was hers. Isn't that awful? You and her have a lot of catching up to do."

Jennie was looking less happy. "What about after, she won't want to know about me after when she finds out how I live for real. I don't know if I can change now. I've never been any good and I don't want to ruin her life as well as my own."

Albert made her wince by squeezing her hand. "My offer still stands. I don't have anybody at all except you. I know that makes me a sad and stupid old man but my only friends are either dead or dying and you are the only reason I have for enjoying a bit of life."

He paused for breath. "I will look after you and you can live your own life, but it is a chance for you to get off the street and to live decent. I know that I ain't much but I can offer you love in spite of what you've done in the past because I know about it and I know you. You are just as sad and lonely as I am but you can also be kind and thoughtful. You ain't never had a chance before now, and when I'm gone you can have the house because I have nobody else to have it except the tax man."

Jennie just about managed to turn to face him. "Albert, you don't know what you're asking. I'm less than half your age but I've seen ten times as much as you will ever see. You had nearly fifty years with one woman and I've had more men in twenty years than anyone can remember. I do like you and because I like you I can't do what you ask. I am no good. I doubt if I can ever be any good. I only get by with the drugs and I couldn't stop them because I get so bloody depressed without them. I'm OK here because I am so drugged up anyway but outside I can't cope which is why I end up with creeps like Karl. You could offer me all the love in the world but I couldn't believe it was real, even if I wanted to. Even if Ellie wants me it won't make a difference to how I am."

Tears were rolling down her face. "The damage has been done for me. I don't know what I will do or where I can go, but if I came with you it would be to use you and I care too much for you to do that."

Albert got a tissue out of a box on the table and wiped her face. "I know what you are like and I don't mind if you just use me. I ain't much use for anything else. Anyway you just told me that you cared about me so what else would I want. I know about your drugs and we can work on them together in your own time. I won't expect miracles. And what else are you going to do? If you try to stay on the game without protection, you will have to go back on the streets and how long would you last. No my dear I think we are stuck with each other."

As they looked at each other the nurse came in armed with a bowl of water, a wash cloth and a towel. "I'm sorry Mr Smith, but we have our ablutions to do."

Albert got up, leaned over and kissed the top of her head. "I aint heard that word since I was in the army. You just give what I said some thought. You know it's the best thing. I'm off home to tidy up before I see that girl of yours."

As he left Jennie managed a small wave before she collapsed back onto the pillow and wept quietly to herself.

The nurse washing her was surprisingly gentle. "He seems a nice old gent. Is he your dad?"

Jenny grimaced. "No, but I think he would like to be."

The Staff Nurse was standing near the door when Albert left. He stopped for a while. "Are you all right Mr Smith?"

"Yes my dear. I'm as right as I can be and I can't say or do any more than I have done and said, but she won't get rid of me that easy. I'm an old soldier you know."

Chapter twenty-eight

Next steps

Mary arrived at the hospital just as Albert was walking down the road. She was glad that he would not be there as she wanted a private chat with Jennie. She was surprised to find that Jennie actually seemed pleased to see her.

She was almost friendly. "I had Albert in just now and he is still going on about me going to live there when I get out. I don't really know if I could do it but he is so persistent. He needs much more than I could ever give him. I mean, I can't imagine not having sex and he, poor bloke is a bit past anything too energetic."

Mary laughed at Jennie's frankness. "He can give you security and safety and a great deal of affection. He really does care about you, and strange though that may seem to you Jennie, Albert has no illusions about you."

"Yeah; he does seem genuine, doesn't he? But I can't let him own me. I can't be like a pet dog or nothing like that. I would still need my freedom and he might not like that. Here! He tells me he's seeing my Ellie tonight and that you fixed it up."

"Yes, that's right. I thought it would be good if Ellie met someone who knows you better than I do and she was happy with that."

What about me then? When can I see her? Albert tells me she's getting married and I thought she was still at school."

"That's right; she is twenty now and working at Tesco's in the High Street and she is engaged to a nice young man called Andy who has a steady job in a bank."

Jennie could not resist a smile. "Albert told me that he is your brother. That means you and me's going to be related."

Mary quietly wished that Albert had kept his mouth shut about that. But thought it was bound to come out sometime anyway. "Yes and that probably means I will know what you get up to in the future."

"Bloody hell!!"

"I was planning to bring her to see you tomorrow afternoon if she can get the time off work. You know she wants you to go to the funeral."

"Yeah, but I don't think that would be good idea. Not like I am, all trussed up. She would enjoy that. Probably think I deserved everything that has happened."

"Ellie would never think anything like that"

"Not Ellie, my mother."

"You would be coming to support Ellie. I think you owe her that at least."

"Anyway, how would I get there like this?"

The hospital will lend you a wheelchair and send a nurse with you. They have some volunteer drivers as well. It will be difficult but not impossible."

"What if Karl is still out there waiting for me. I would be like a sitting duck."

"I will be there and so will some of my colleagues. He would be mad to try anything."

"But he is mad. He once killed a bloke in a police station and got away with it. That's when he came to this country from South Africa. He promised to kill me and I know he will if he can."

"We will be there to protect you and there are not many places to hide in a cemetery."

"When did you say Ellie was coming?"

"After lunch tomorrow; the funeral is on Thursday afternoon.

"I don't know what I can say to her. I'm scared to let her see me like this."

"She isn't short of words. You will soon be chatting easily. Just concentrate on her and try not to scare her too much.

"You are going to be there tonight as well aren't you? Keep Albert in check. He doesn't know when to stop talking sometimes. At least I get paid for it."

"I'm glad you reminded me. I need to get going otherwise they will be there before me. I will come and see you before Ellie

216

gets here tomorrow but I will have to go in to the office tomorrow morning."

"Jennie relaxed. "That's good. I think I can trust you to see she is OK. It's just as well that you are going now because I am beginning to feel knackered. I will try to be on my best behaviour tomorrow. It's odd how you can want something so much that it scares the wits out of you when it might happen."

"I guess I can understand that Jennie. I don't know how I would feel if I was in your shoes."

"That's all right the 'cos I can't get my shoes on just now."

Mary gave her a wave as she left and Jennie slumped into her bed.

*

Brian Evans was on time much to Ellie's relief. She explained about her meeting with Albert later and that she needed to be away by eight.

"Goodness me! I don't expect to be that long. Everything seems to be in order and it just needs your opinion on what you want included and if you or someone else would like to contribute to the service, like read something or talk about your grandmother."

 Ellie had not even thought about taking part in the service apart from being there "I haven't even thought about doing anything. I really don't think I could without bursting into tears."

"Is there anyone else in the family who might want to say something?"

Ellie thought about Aunty Flo and gave a little shudder.

Brian noticed it. "I think I know what you were thinking and you are right, she would be a bit of a risk."

"The only other person is my real mum, but I haven't even met her yet though I am seeing her tomorrow."

"You have actually found her then. I know you were very keen to do so."

"Yes, but she is in hospital and I don't think she is too keen on coming. I don't know what to think until I have seen her and I must say I am getting worried."

"Would you like me to visit her to see how she is? The thought of coming where people like Florence might take offence could be a challenge too far for her, and quite honestly it may be a bit too much for you to handle as well at this time."

Ellie thought for a while. "No, I think that Andy's sister has already done that. She is the police officer looking after my mother because she is a witness who is in danger. Strange what a small world it has become isn't it? I do want to see her but I don't know what I can say or do when I meet her. From everything I have heard about her she is the last person I would ever want to know, but she is my real mother and she has had a terrible time."

There was a pause before she could continue. "I just can't leave her now that I have found her, whatever happens. I know mum would have stopped me. Not that she would do anything to hurt me deliberately. But this is too important; it's about me and my life, my real mother; it's not about how hurt she was. She was so good to me you know and I loved her for it, and I always will, but I had all that love and care while Jennie has had nothing except rejection and anger. I think I owe it to both of them to mend that gap, however confusing and frightening it is."

Brian looked at her with admiration. "You know Ellie I think you are a very brave and caring young woman. You will have my blessing and support it there is anything you think I can do for you or your mother. Do you think she will come if you want her to?"

Ellie thought about that for a while. "It depends on whether she can get out of the hospital and if she cares enough to come. If she is willing to come that would be a good start, wouldn't it?"

Brian nodded. "Yes, I think that would be a very good start. The healing process always begins with forgiveness and if your mother came it would give her a chance to say goodbye to the hurts of the past. I don't know if it would make much change to her life though."

"What do you mean?"

"Well, I'm afraid she might find that a very difficult thing to do now however much you might want her to change. She will find it hard to break away from everything she has, and all the way of life she knows."

Ellie went quiet again and Brian waited for her. "Isn't it a bit like what you say about how God always loves us in spite of what we do? I want to love her because she is my mother, even though I don't know her. What I know of her scares me, but I can't let that stop me from trying, can I?"

Brian looked at her with a great sense of warmth. If only the rest of his congregation could understand half as well as this young girl he would be a happy man. "The important thing Ellie is that your life is different. You have chance your mother never had, and opportunities your grandmother never had because of the way things were in those days. You are what they only hoped to be."

Ellie felt her eyes filling at his words. She had so much for which to be thankful. She knew now that she was right to want to see her mother because if nothing else it might help Jennie to know she was not alone any more. All the fear of what might happen by getting involved was nothing in comparison to the need to meet her mother.

"Thank you so much Brian. It means a great deal to know that you know and will be there for me whatever happens."

"Well I had better not keep you from your visit. I hope it goes well. As for the service I will say a few words about Rosie. After all I have known her for some time. Oh, I nearly forgot about the hymns. Do you have any thoughts?"

Ellie thought for a while. "I know she was always humming 'Rock of ages'. Would that do? Oh yes, and she liked 'What a friend'."

"Those will be fine. A nice change from Jerusalem and you missed my pet hate which is 'My way'. It might be alright if they sang 'God's way' but the last time I suggested that I was told that nobody would know the tune. I will be at the church from lunch time so if there is anything else ring home and ask my wife to nip round to the church. The ladies will be there on Wednesday evening to get some preparations done for the tea afterwards. Perhaps your Aunt would like to be involved?"

220

"She is away at the moment but I expect her back tomorrow and I am sure she will down there like a shot. You had better warn Mrs Wagstaff."

"Good point Ellie, but I am sure they won't want anything to go wrong. You will be in my prayers for tomorrow as you meet your mother. Give me a ring later to tell me how things went."

Chapter twenty-nine

The Pig and Poke

Andy was back as promised and they decided to walk round to the Pig. The rain of the last few days had stopped and the evening was dry and clear with the first signs of a frost.

They had a more relaxed chat about anything that took their minds off the day and got to the pub just before eight thirty. Mary was by the door waiting for them. She led them over to where Albert was sitting in his usual corner.

"Hello Albert, can we join you. This is my brother Andy and this is his fiancée Ellie. Andy is just going to buy some drinks, what would you like?"

Albert beamed. "That's just what I like to hear Mary; company and another drink; a pint of the best for me please and to hell with the bladder control."

Mary smiled. "Don't you think it's time for a coffee?"

"Coffee!!" choked Albert, "I'm swimming in the stuff. I need beer to wash it out of my system. I spend half the day in that canteen and it got worse the more I drank and then I only got to see her for a short time."

Mary and Ellie sat across the table from him while Andy obediently got the drinks. Ellie was a bit unsure about this strange old man with his long grey hair and whiskers, but she still leaned forward. "Are you the Albert who knows my mother?"

"My goodness! Mary told me she was bringing Jennie's daughter to see me tonight but you are all grown up. Jennie thinks you are still at school." Albert put his glass down and peered at her. "Are you Ellie?"

Andy arrived back at the table with the drinks. "Here we are! A pint of best for Albert and me, half a cider for Mary and a coke for Ellie."

"Well I never!" Albert sat back in his chair and stared at Ellie. "Jennie will never believe this. Then he turned to Mary. "Does she know about Jennie?"

"She knows some of it. I think she should hear it from you as well as me."

Albert repeated himself. "Well I never! She doesn't look at all like Jennie."

"In the circumstances Albert, that is probably just as well."

"What do you mean?" asked Ellie.

Mary realised she had opened up too much information but it was too late to avoid being truthful. "Well, you know how you said it couldn't get any worse."

Andy butted in. "Easy Mary, Ellie has already had a really bad time over this."

"Yes I know but there is no easy way to tell this. As you know Jennie is in hospital at present as a result of a serious assault. We are now certain that it was an attempt to kill her."

"Kill her!" gasped Ellie.

"Yes I'm afraid so. You already know that your mother has been working as a prostitute and for the last two years she has been with a man called Karl. He and some of his friends raided a night club the other night and a man was killed, probably by accident, but Karl was driving. Two other people were shot and wounded, including one of our officers. Jennie knew what was going on and she is one of our main witnesses."

"Jennie is a witness to a murder!"

"Not to the actual killing, but she was aware that her partner was in possession of a shotgun which we found the night she first came in here. He and another man called Johnny are both still at large. They are both killers and because Jennie can be a witness they want her dead so she cannot talk. One of them, probably Karl attacked her and nearly killed her the other evening. I told you this morning that if Albert and I hadn't been out looking for her he might have succeeded then. But to make it worse he broke into the hospital last night and nearly finished the job." "One of the nurses was injured when she interrupted him but he got away. As you can gather we are worried about the fact that they are still at large."

Ellie sat there in silence trying to take it all in. Albert broke the silence. Your mum had run away from Karl and was staying at my house. We've been sort of friends for over a year now."

He suddenly felt a bit embarrassed so he took a long drink of his beer as he felt their eyes asking him what he meant by friend.

He put his beer down and turned to Ellie. "She was just telling me about you last week end. She's not a bad person you know. She's been very good to me." That didn't seem the right thing to say either so he took refuge behind his beer again.

Mary leaned over and took hold of Ellie's left hand. I am sorry Ellie, this must all seem like one horrible nightmare."

Ellie was looking straight ahead with a light mist in her eyes which slowly slipped down her cheek as a tear. "No, I never had a dream as bad as this."

Andy moved his chair closer and put his arm around her, easing her gently into his shoulder. She responded without any resistance. All the raucousness of the pub seemed to have faded into a background hum as she tried to add this information into her already overloaded brain.

"Albert put down his now empty glass and burped. "I beg your pardon. I think I've drunk too much today. I'm not used to all this excitement and I don't think I want to be either, but I can't give up on her now, can I?"

Ellie sat up straight. "I still want to meet her, I want to know what the hell she meant by leaving me and never letting me know she was my mother, what was so wrong with me that she left me behind, never knowing, no letters, no cards, nothing, and what she did to mum was awful. How could anyone do all that?"

Albert replied before he thought of what he was saying. "She got chucked out by her mum. They had never got on with each other because of her father.........."

His sentence was cut short by Ellie screaming. "Stop it, stop it. I don't want to hear any more!" Then she buried her head in her arms and began to sob loudly. The rest of the pub suddenly went quiet as all eyes turned to see what was happening.

Albert sat back. "Oh Lord! Me and my big mouth. I am sorry love, I really am. You shouldn't take any notice of me. I'm just a sad old man who has drunk more than my tongue can cope with."

Mary looked across at him. "Really Albert, I thought you would have had more sense. I wanted you to make things easier not worse."

Andy was holding Ellie as tightly as the table allowed.

"Andy, Andy." Mary tried to catch his attention.

"He snapped back at her and she could see that his face was also tear streaked. "What? I thought this was supposed to help and now look at what you've done. You should have told us before we came here what was happening."

Ellie suddenly pulled herself free and rushed towards the ladies toilet, still crying but now also trying not to vomit. Mary followed her.

"Albert was still numbed by her reaction and sat in his chair looking sheepishly into his glass. "I'm sorry!" he kept repeating.

Andy's normally calm nature boiled over. "Oh, just shut up you drunken old bastard. I suppose you are one of her dirty old men, aren't you? Aren't you?"

He went to get up but was stopped by a large hand on his shoulder.

"Are you looking for a beating mate? Albert's a friend of mine and nobody talks to him like that when I'm around. Now either you apologise to him or I'll start rearranging your face."

There was a ripple of support for this suggestion and a woman's voice shouted. "Go on Kev you give him one, let him have it." A woman behind him was fumbling with her glasses and urging him on at the same time.

Albert held his hand up as Andy was about to be hauled out of his chair. "No lad put him back down, it is my fault. He had every right to be angry with me."

"Nobody has that right." The woman was standing over him peering through her glasses. "You aint got no right to speak to an old man like that. I can't see that he's done you any harm. I've a good mind to belt you one myself or report you to the police. Go on Kev you just give him one."

Albert began to laugh and they looked at him in surprise.

"Oh dear, I've done enough damage already. I don't want you to have a split lip as well. Please Kevin put him down. I promise it's all right. I just made his girl-friend sick and he was giving me a right good telling off, and I deserved it because I 've drunk too much and spoken too much, that's all."

Andy shook himself free of Kevin's hold and stood up. He wasn't afraid to defend himself if necessary. At the same time

227

he knew he had gone too far. "All right, I'm sorry. I got angry and said more than I should have done."

Albert stood up as well. "You don't need to be sorry, it was all true. These are friends of mine as you probably gathered. Kevin and Joyce and this is," He paused. "Oh dear I've forgotten your name."

"It's Andy Heron; Mary is my sister."

Albert sat down again. "Oh yes that's right. Mary is your sister and Ellie is your girl-friend.

"She's my fiancee."

"Fiancee! Yes I remember now. Mary told me all about it this morning and I was talking about it with Jennie earlier. You are going to marry Ellie and Ellie is Jennie's daughter, and you are Mary's brother and she is the police officer. Goodness me this is getting too complicated for me."

Joyce sat down next to Andy, "What? Do you mean Jenny who took our old mirror and lives in the squat. They're looking for her bloke for the shooting aren't they?"

Albert nodded. "And for trying to kill her yesterday."

Kevin pulled up a seat and sat down as well. "I thought I saw him today up in Waterloo. I didn't know they are after him. I just kept out of his way. Then I went to the Regal to see an old film called the 'Wild Bunch'. It's on all this week, all about a gang on the run and a final shoot out like I've never seen before. Then me and Joyce came straight here so I haven't heard much else."

Joyce grimaced. "I think it was a horrible film, really nasty and violent. Not like a real cowboy film at all. Do you think Kev should tell someone?"

Andy asked. "What, about the film?"

"No stupid, about seeing that bloke Karl."

Andy saw Mary and Ellie coming back. "Well now's your chance. My sister is part of the investigating team."

As he saw Mary Kevin stood up and pulled another chair up next to his. "Hello, I'm Kev." He sat down suddenly as Joyce pulled hard on the back of his jacket.

Ellie was looking very pale and she went to Andy. "I want to go home Andy. I don't think I can take any more today."

Albert stood up. "I am so sorry my dear. I didn't mean to upset you." Ellie managed a weak smile. "Thank you Albert. It is probably best to know it all. I just can't believe it can get any worse and I just hadn't realised how angry I was feeling."

Joyce joined in. "It does you good to let rip sometimes."

"Maybe, but I'm not used to it. I am sorry I made such a fool of myself."

Andy stood up. "I had better get her home while she has enough energy."

Ellie needed no further invitation and they made their farewells.

"Give me a ring first thing to let me know if you still want to come. I will be at the hospital on watch from eleven tomorrow."

Ellie paused. "You said three o'clock didn't you. I will be there."

They were quiet as they walked home.

When they reached the house Andy paused. "It will be tough tomorrow and you will need a good night's sleep. I will sleep on the sofa if you want me to stay."

"No, Andy. I want you with me. I don't want to be on my own. But I just want you to hold me tonight. I haven't enough energy for anything else."

Andy kissed her. "Sounds like an old married couple already. You'll be telling me you have a headache next."

"But I do have a headache. Could you get me an aspirin from the bathroom cabinet and a glass of water."

By the time Andy had done so she was fast asleep on the bed still fully clothed. She barely noticed him rolling her on to the bed properly and covering her with the duvet. He slipped downstairs and made himself comfortable on the sofa.

Back at the pub Joyce had told Mary about Kev seeing Karl in Waterloo and after some persuasion she had got them to go with her to the police station to make a formal statement. As she was leaving the duty officer called her. "I just thought you would like to know that there is a contract out on them. With any luck someone else will sort them out."

Chapter thirty

On the run

Karl was desperate now. Having failed to kill Jennie he knew that he would have to find somewhere to lie low. He made his way over to Camberwell where Steve lived in a flat on the tenth floor. He had plenty on Steve so he knew that he would be safe there. Steve was one of the main suppliers in the area and had some protection so it could be a safe place.

Karl knocked on the door with the usual code for a friend but there was no reply. He went back to the pub where Steve did a lot of trade but again there was no sign of him.

Nonetheless Karl decided to stay there and wait. If anyone did recognise him they were not going to say anything. Closing time came and there was still no sign of Steve so he went back to the flat and knocked again. He waited on the stairs when there was still no answer. Two hours later and Steve arrived, clearly the worse for drink and drugs. Karl had to help him into the flat and even then he was so drunk that he fell on the floor of the hall and lay there.

Karl decided to leave him there and made himself at home though Steve had only a very basic larder. At least there was plenty of alcohol. He poured himself a large whisky and watched the television for a while before checking on Steve.

He was still lying on the floor and had been sick so Karl decided to leave him there and to use his bed for the night.

It was late morning when he woke to the telephone ringing. The answer phone cut in and it was clear that the caller was not happy. Steve had a delivery which was overdue and they were coming this afternoon to collect it or else.

Steve was still where he had left him in the passage way. Karl turned him over and could see by his colour that he was dead. He checked for a pulse but there was none.

"Idiot. Why do you choose now to kill yourself?"

He dragged the body into the front room and perched him on the settee. It was obvious that he couldn't stay any more, especially with the heavy brigade coming this afternoon. He checked Steve's pockets for cash. He had about three hundred pounds on him. "Trust you; you make a sale then kill yourself on the profits. Where is the rest?"

Karl was now thinking of himself. What could he steal? He scoured the flat and found more money. He picked up a tin with sugar written on the side and looked in. There was sugar but when he tipped the tin out it had been hiding fifty small bags. This must be what Steve's visitors were after. He filled his pockets and left half a dozen packets back in the sugar tin.

There was a large flour tin as well and Karl tipped that up as well. A large packet fell out well wrapped in plastic. Karl opened it and caressed the barrel of a revolver. He smiled. "Just what I need" It was fully loaded.

The telephone rang again and he waited to hear the message. To his relief it was Johnny He picked the receiver up.

"Hi, Johnny! It's Karl. I came here last night but that sill sod Steve has done himself in with an overdose. What do you mean they tried to do a runner. What? Paul and Maggie tried to get away with the money. They got them you say and Paul is inside.

"What about Maggie? She is out but you will see to her. No I haven't been able to get rid of Jennie yet. I thought I had done her the other evening but somehow she survived. I shall be all right this time though. I found a gun in Steve's place. Leave it did you say? Why? I want to kill her."

He listened for a while. "Can we trust them? A boat that will take us to Belgium and new passports! It seems too good to be true. OK! I'll see you by the docks at seven. It should be dark enough by then. I'll have Steve's gun in case of any double cross. I'll wait here until two and then get out before Steve's friends arrive. I'll bring his stash with me. It should pay for the trip. Yeah; see you later."

He relaxed for a while. Shame about Maggie.

At two he left the flat and left the door slightly open. From a safe distance he waited until he saw two men going in and then he rang the police and threw the phone away.

Chapter thirty-one

The morning after.

Andy was up early as he had to go back to his flat to change for work. He made Ellie a cup of tea and took it up to her. He had to waken her.

"What's the time?"

"Seven thirty. I have to be at work by quarter to nine today and I won't finish before six. Will meet you after work to see how you got on with your meeting."

"Meeting? What meeting?"

"Three o'clock; you and Jennie and Mary and if you remember you are going in to work early today to try and make up some of the time you have had to miss."

Ellie sat up. "Why didn't you wake me earlier?"

"You looked like you needed as much rest as you could get. Anyway there's a cup of tea for you. I must be off. Ring me later."

It didn't take Ellie long to get ready and she was on her way to Tescos just in time to catch her bus. She was able to help set up the tills before Jill arrived. She was surprised to see Ellie there.

As Ellie came over to her she guessed what she wanted. "Don't tell me, you want some time off today and you will make it up next weekend. How did yesterday go?"

Ellie gave an embarrassed laugh. "You're getting to know me too well Jill. Yes please, but the reason is that I am going to meet Jennie today. I am going to see my mother for the first time. Brian Evans was really helpful yesterday and Jennie knows about me now and she wants to see me. Isn't it wonderful? She wants to see me!"

"I think what is wonderful is that you want to see her! After all we have told you about her, and all the rest you have found out, you still want to see her. She's the lucky one."

"But can't you see Jill. Now I know she exists I just have to see her even if it never happens again. I know our lives are totally different, but maybe if she knows that I care and forgive her for leaving it might just make a little difference to her life."

"Like I say, she's the lucky one. I just wish one of my kids wanted to see me half as much as you do her. They all disappear when I want to talk to them. Anyway I can't see that I'll get much work out of you until this is out of your system and the funeral is over. What do you want?"

"Well, I think I have it worked out that if I work until lunch then I can go home, get ready and then get to the hospital by three to meet her. I can do all tomorrow but then I have Thursday off for the funeral so that means I will just owe you for three hours today and six for the last two days and I can make that up next week."

Jill stopped her. "I sent you home the last two days because of sickness so the only time you will owe is for today. That makes my book-keeping easier and the manager has already agreed to it. How about that?"

"Oh Jill you are an angel. You have been so kind and helpful this week I could kiss you."

"Not in the store you don't; .anyway a couple of gins will do later. Now you get back to work and after work on Friday we can go down to the pub and you can tell me how everything went."

"It's a deal. Shall I come back after seeing Jennie?"

"No. I can't see you being in any fit state of mind after meeting her so keep you mind occupied with the small basket counter until twelve and then go home."

As the lunch break came Ellie was putting her coat on and going home as quickly as she could.

As she walked through the door she could smell cooking and knew that Flo must have returned. She called out and was quite surprised when Aunt Muriel popped out of the kitchen. Muriel wasn't really an aunt but they had always called her that because she and Flo had been together for as long as Ellie could remember. Muriel was the very opposite of Flo. A small slightly built woman, she was very shy and rarely had too much to say for herself.

She came over to Ellie and kissed her on the cheek. "Hello my dear, you must be surprised to see me, but next door offered to look after our dogs for a few days so Flo and I thought we would come to give you a hand with things. Flo is upstairs unpacking. She will be glad to see you. Oh dear you do look wet. You must have been caught in that nasty shower. Let me help you with these wet things."

She was a busy natured woman and Ellie's coat was off in no time and Muriel went off to hang it up. As she did so Flo came downstairs.

Ellie managed to raise a smile. "Hello Aunty. It's good to see you back. I've seen Muriel already; she's just hanging my coat up somewhere.

Flo beamed at her. "Come in my dear, you are just in time for some lunch. I just did some sandwiches and cake. Muriel did some shopping on the way but she forgot the fish paste so we have to do with a tin of tuna that I found in your cupboard."

It was all set out in the sitting room on the coffee table. Ellie excused herself for a moment while she sent a text message to Andy to warn him that Flo had returned. She went up to her room to change and as she did so she began to wonder what she and Jennie could talk about. She was fairly sure now that mum had made it difficult for Jennie to stay. Albert had suggested to Andy that she had gone because she thought it would be better for Ellie.

Ellie had already realised that Jennie was still only a child herself, not even sixteen when she was born, much younger that she was now.

"Are you coming to join us?" Flo's voice snapped her out of her thoughts.

"Yes, I'm just changing, I'll be down in a moment." She waited for a minute then went downstairs.

Flo started straight away. "There you are. I thought I should pop down to the church and make sure they have the catering properly arranged."

"Mrs Wagstaff is the lady in charge of the church catering and she will be down at the church tomorrow evening to sort it out."

"Well I am sure they won't mind me giving them some ideas. After all she was my sister and I really ought to have a say in the arrangements."

"I am sure Mrs Wagstaff will be glad of your help, but she will have everything she needs there."

"When can I see the vicar about the hymns? I hope you are singing 'the Old Rugged Cross'. It's one of my favourites. We sang it when we were children."

Brian Evans has already sorted out the hymns and the order of service with me."

"Oh; perhaps I'll give him a ring. I'm sure he won't mind changing a hymn or two."

This was too much for Ellie. "Don't you dare ring him. He has more than enough to think about than for you to take over the service as well as the catering. The service has been agreed with me and that's the way it will stay."

Flo sat down heavily in what had been mum's old armchair. "Well I never. How dare you speak to me like that! I am only trying to help."

Ellie was now in full flow. "Help; what you try to do is take over. This is my life and it's my mum, whatever else may have happened, and I have already sorted things out and they don't need changing just because it's one of your favourites."

Muriel moved quickly to Flo's side. "Now, now Flo, don't take on so."

To Ellie's surprise tears began to appear in Flo's eyes and Muriel put a consoling arm on her back and gave Ellie a slight smile.

"She does mean well my dear, but she gets so involved it's hard for her to know when to stop." She looked down at Flo. "Never mind Flo. Muriel is here."

Ellie felt guilty at how harshly she had spoken. "I am sorry Aunty Flo. I didn't mean to be so rude. It's just I have had to grow up so quickly in the last few days that I am not a child any more. I do appreciate your help, but please try to understand a bit more what is happening to me."

Flo blew her nose loudly and gave her eyes a wipe. "No you are right my dear. I'm just an interfering old busybody. You were quite right to tell me off. Of course the vicar is too busy to change things around just because of me and as its Rosie's funeral she shall have proper fish in the sandwiches."

Muriel patted her back and winked at Ellie. For the first time Ellie appreciated how important the relationship was between the two women. Even though Flo seemed ordered and overpowering it was really Muriel who kept her going. Suddenly she was no longer the shadow in Flo's light but a real solid presence.

Ellie decided to tell them what was happening. "One of the reasons I am back so early is that I am going to the hospital this afternoon. I'm going to meet my mother for the first time. She is in hospital at the moment but I am hoping she will come to the funeral. I will see you later and tell you what has happened."

Both Flo and Muriel were too surprised to say much as Ellie walked out. As she was putting her coat on she heard Flo saying "I don't think that is a good idea."

Muriel's quiet voice replied. "It is Ellie's idea and she had to find it one day. We will pray for her, won't we Flo?" "Oh yes, yes, as you say Muriel, yes we will pray for her."

Chapter thirty-two

Sitting up.

By a combined effort, Mary, Albert and the nurses had persuaded Jennie to get out of the bed and to sit in a chair. Once she was there she was there she was surprised that it actually was more comfortable though her language during the transfer had caused much giggling in the younger staff. The Sister was not so amused. Fortunately Mrs Matthews in the room next door had turned her hearing aid off.

Jennie was brought a bowl of hot water so she could wash herself and start to feel in control of her own life. They helped her wash her hair and get rid of the last knots of dried blood and mud that had resisted their previous care. By the time she had her lunch Jennie was feeling quite tired but much more presentable.

In the back of her mind however she was desperately trying to think of what she could possibly say to Ellie. Part of her was longing to see her daughter but she was also terrified at what Ellie might think of her. She was left to have a doze And Albert, after pottering around went off to get something to eat.

Mary remained on duty and had brought some sandwiches with her. Jennie saw her by the door and relaxed. She was actually glad to see her there and know that she would be there when Ellie came.

It was almost two when she woke. Mary came over to her. "Did you have a nice doze? You are actually beginning to look more relaxed."

"Relaxed! My mind's been going round like nobody's business. I'm nearly shitting myself with worry about what she will think of me." Mary smiled. "She can't think any worse of you than you do yourself."

Her quiet words struck a nerve and Jennie felt a strong urge to cry. "You've got no idea, no idea at all what it's like to have been treated like shit all your life. I'm not used to people being nice to me and I'm terrified that I will hurt my little girl. I've had her picture in my purse all these years, but I never dreamed that I would ever see her again. Now I don't know what to do or say."

Mary put a hand on her arm. "She isn't a little girl anymore. She is a young feisty woman who is engaged to my brother. To find out that you are her mother is a shock to me as well but I know she can cope with it probably better than you can. It's strange how small the world can sometimes be. I can't imagine that you would have expected your daughter to marry into a family with a police officer in it?"

Jennie was quiet for a while. "You don't mind my daughter marrying your brother even now you have found out about me. I'll be your brother's mother-in-law. Bloody Hell! I could be a grannie before long!"

Mary did wince at the thought but only briefly. "I don't think they will be able to afford that for some time. Andy has only been at the bank for eighteen months and he can't get a mortgage for at least a year."

"What about your family? What will they say if they know about   me?"
"My parents are both dead and we don't have anyone else very close."

"Oh, I am sorry."

"It was a while back now. My father was killed in an accident and mother died of cancer when she was only fifty."

"How did you manage?"

"I was seventeen when my mother died so I helped out and Andy did his bit even though he was only fourteen at the time. We've been very close since then."

"Don't you mind him being with her now you know about me?"

"Don't take this wrong Jennie but Ellie is not you. She is a really nice, caring young woman. I think Andy is very lucky to have found her. Whatever else your mum did she did a good job raising Ellie."

Jennie was quiet again then she murmured. "I suppose it was me. I just wasn't any good, though me and my dad got on ever so well except that he left. My mum and dad were always fighting and I suppose he looked to me for emotional support and he offered me the love that my mother never could. I suppose we got too close and it broke my heart when he left. That was because of me."

243

"How could that be? You were only a child at the time."

"I know, but I knew we were doing wrong and I could have stopped him, but he loved me and I just wanted to love him back.. I think he was sent to prison. I know he died there. Mum told me; she said he was in hell and that was where I would find him. That's when I left. No good, I just ran away and left my baby behind. Now she has found me and I don't know how I can face her."

"Well it won't be long now. She's due in about an hour. She is really looking forward to meeting you. You are the only close family she has now. I know how important that can be."

"In an hour! Why didn't anyone tell me? Oh God I'm not ready for her. You will be here won't you? I really will need help. Is Albert around? I would like him here as well. Oh God what am I going to do?"

"Don't worry Jennie, I will stay and I expect Albert will stay. I expect he has gone off to have a nap but he will be back. He knows she is coming. You know he met Ellie last night don't you? Unfortunately it didn't go quite as well as I had hoped but in a funny way I think that will help today. Have you had any more thoughts about his offer?"

"His offer; Oh that! How could I impose myself on him? Do you know he even offered to leave his house to me! I mean to say I only talk to him and give him a bit of massage. It's not as if we've ever done it. He told me his wife wouldn't like it. Can you really see me being able to stay there? I can only just manage with my drugs and he's old enough to be my father, even my grandfather. I would be the death of him if I moved in and I don't want to be responsible for any more grief. It's just that he is so bloody-minded and very fit for man of his age but

244

he has no idea what goes on in the real world. If you try to tell him he just says 'I'm an old soldier you know. Heavens, that was over fifty years ago."

"Do you think you are living in the real world Jennie?"

"I suppose not but it is the only one I know. It's not the world I want for Ellie, or for Albert. It's a world of people like me, pimps and prostitutes, no hopers, lost souls, druggies looking for the next fix and a bit of sex without any promises. If I tried to live in your world I would feel dirty all the time."

"Surely it doesn't have to be like that?"

"Maybe I don't want to change. I fit in where I am. Nobody cares what I do or where I've been. Anyway I'll be dead soon if you don't find Karl or Johnny. You haven't found them yet, have you?"

"No not yet, but we have closed most of their escape routes and thanks to you we have the rest of the gang in custody. I shall be around as long as you are in danger and when you leave hospital we will arrange a safe place for you out of town."

"Out of town! I don't want to go out of town! I would rather stay at Albert's than go out of town. I don't even go over the river."

"Well it's up to you, but if we can't catch Karl or Johnny then your life would obviously still be in danger. Oh I've just remembered. You gave us the name of Steve O'Brian. We had a file on him so we called and found him dead behind his front door. We arrested two men who were in the flat ransacking it. We knew both of them as people involved in drugs."

"Oh no! Steve was my dealer. Where can I go now? Did they kill him?"

"No it seems he was dead before they got there. Looks as if he sampled too much of his goods and died by accident. The next door neighbour said he had a strange man staying there the night before and it sounded like Karl."

"Are you saying that Karl killed Steve?"

"No; like I said the evidence is that Steve died from an overdose washed down by too much alcohol. If Karl was there he must have known about it and moved on."

"Who was there then?"

"Two black guys. Like I said they were searching the flat when we turned up."

"They must be part of Smokey's mob. Steve did some trading for him; he must have had a package for them otherwise they wouldn't have been there."

"We only found some traces of coke but nothing else."

"That means Karl must have nicked it; he must be desperate because he will be a dead man if Smokey finds out. That would solve my problems wouldn't it?"

"We would rather catch him ourselves. There are enough dead bodies around already."

Jennie suddenly became anxious. "Here didn't you say Ellie was going to be here soon? I need to posh myself up before she gets here."

"Gracious; you are right. She should be here in less than an hour. I'll leave you to get ready."

Mary went to the nurse and asked her to help Jennie prepare then returned to her seat by the door.

Chapter thirty-three

The meeting

Fortunately a bus came along just as Ellie turned the corner. At least she would get to the hospital reasonably dry. She wondered if it was ever going to stop raining and hoped that the funeral weather might be dry. As the bus reached the hospital she could feel herself shaking inside. All the warnings she had been given began to flood back into her mind but she steeled herself and walked up the stairs to the ward where Jennie lay.

She paused for a while and then pushed the doors open. Mary was there waiting for her. "Hello Ellie. I'm glad you got here without getting too wet."

"I was lucky with the bus today."

"Good; we've managed to get Jennie ready to meet you and she is in a chair rather than still being in bed but I must warn you that she is very worried about meeting you while at the same time she is looking forward to it."

"She's worried? What do you think I am? I'm scared to death. Now it's happening I keep remembering all the terrible things people have said about her"

Mary smiled. "This is going to be some meeting. Just remember that I am here with you. Think of her as a normal human being who has done some not very normal things."

"I know that. I think that is why I am here. Better get on with it. The sooner we meet the quicker the fantasies can be sorted."

"It's just down here in the second room. Albert is there as well to give Jennie some support. He's a good man you know, whatever you might think."

Mary gently led Ellie by putting her hand on her arm. "Are you ready Ellie?"

Ellie nodded and they went in together.

Ellie stood in the doorway looking at the woman who was sitting by the bed. She seemed smaller than Ellie had imagined though the bandages that still adorned her gave little impression of the whole person. She spoke. "Hello, I'm Ellie; I think that you are my real mother."

As she spoke tears began to well up inside her and Mary put a supportive arm around her and led her to another chair close to Jennie.

Jennie had been dumbstruck at the sight of this attractive young woman but when she saw Ellie's tears she beckoned her over to the chair.

"Here, come and sit next to me dear. I can't believe what I am seeing myself. I mean to say, you are a woman. I just hadn't ever thought of you as all grown up."

She gazed at Ellie in amazement. "I can't believe it is really you. If only you knew how many times I've dreamed of this moment, but you were always a little girl with a pony tail. Here; Albert, she has my dad's eyes, soft and loving."

Albert shuffled his feet not wanting to intrude. "I don't know your dad but her eyes are kind."

Ellie stopped crying and wiped her eyes. "I did have a pony tail but I had it cut off after I left school. I've been at work now for three years, in a supermarket. I expect Mary has told you about her brother Andy. We are going to get married quite soon."

"Get married! Surely you want to enjoy yourself a bit before you get hitched."

Ellie felt a twinge of annoyance at this comment but ignored it and went on. "Well now that I am on my own it seems silly to wait. We get on so well together that I wouldn't want to wait too long."

She suddenly wondered if she should be so frank . "Oh; I am sorry, I didn't mean I was alone because I have found you now."

Jennie sat back in her chair. "You might as well be on your own dear. I can't do anything to help you and I expect they have told you about the sort of life I have led. I am everything I don't want you to be."

She paused and then continued. "I can see that my mum has done a great job in bringing you up. I thought she might do much better with you than she ever could with me. She always resented me because she had to get married to my dad and they never got on with each other. She could only be happy when we were both gone. I am glad you knew her when she was happy."

There was an awkward silence as Ellie looked down at her lap and tried not to cry again. Mary realised how she was feeling and tried to steer the conversation.

"You do know that her funeral is on Thursday, don't you Jennie?"

"Yes, you told me. Albert was trying to persuade me to go but I wouldn't want to embarrass you. After all I did to her it would be a bit of a cheek to turn up at her funeral."

Ellie pulled herself together quickly and blew her nose. "No I would like you to come. The Reverend Brian Evans is taking the service and he says it is a good time to bury the past and to think of the future. I want us to be together to say goodbye to her. You say she did a good job in bringing me up, then I think you should be there to thank her for what she did as my mum."

It was Jennie's turn to become emotional. "I don't deserve this. I've spent over twenty years being angry with her and now for the first time I see what she has done and it's too late. Anyway, how can I go? I can hardly get to the lav without help."

Mary told her of how she had arranged for an ambulance to take her and bring her back and how Albert had agreed to go and push the wheelchair she would need.

Ellie leaned forward and held Jennie's hand. "I want you to be there for me. Apart from Aunty Flo you are my only relation still alive and I don't plan on losing you now I have found you whatever you have done in the past."

Jennie looked alarmed. "Did you say Aunty Flo? She's not going to be there is she?"

"Yes; she's been trying to help me all week."

"Oh God; you poor girl! She used to terrify me when I was at home. She and mum hated each other. I got sent to Ramsgate for holidays when I was little. It was horrible especially when she tried to feed me fish paste sandwiches. I ran away when I was ten and hitched back to London. That stopped my holidays all right."

Ellie looked at the sense of horror on Jennie's face and began to laugh. "I was nine when I told mum I would rather stay in my room all week than go to Aunty Flo's for a day. And she is still making her foul fish paste sandwiches."

That started Jennie laughing as well though not for long as her ribs soon reminded her of her injuries.

Ellie controlled herself. "Perhaps we're not too different in some of our experiences then. Do you know what would really upset Flo and that is if we went to mum's funeral together."

"Is Muriel going or has she stayed behind to look after their dogs. They used to have a horrible poodle that always growled at me."

"No Muriel is here at present and I think she has Aunty Flo under control. I don't think Flo is too happy with me now because I told her off this morning. I almost felt sorry for her when I saw how put out she was."

"You told Flo off? Well I bet that is something mum never did. Looks like I had better keep on the right side of you. Coo; are you really my little girl? I certainly never had that much courage."

Ellie smiled. "Well she just got to me on a bad day."

Mary was sitting there quietly wondering at this new image of Jennie. She had spoken for over ten minutes without a single expletive. When Ellie mentioned her temper she cut in. "I had better warn Andy about that temper of yours. I am sorry to say that we can't stay too long as Jennie still needs to have a lot of rest, especially if she is going to the funeral in two day's time."

Jennie began to look worried again. "I'm still not sure if it would be a good idea for me to go. What if Karl is out there?"

"He would be a fool if he tried to come anywhere near as he would be spotted."

"But he is a fool! And if he wants to kill me it won't matter to him if he gets caught because he would just be happy that he had killed me. You don't know what a madman he is and how devious he can be."

Ellie squeezed her hand and Jennie tried not to wince at her daughter's touch. "It would really mean so much to me if you would come."

Jennie's eyes began to mist over. "I really don't want to let you down my dear but it's very frightening for me to even think of facing people like Aunty Flo apart from Karl."

Ellie looked at Albert. "If Albert came would that help?"

Albert nodded at both of them and Jennie realised that she had little option left except to hurt Ellie. Somehow she couldn't think of that. There could be a hundred Karls and Flos out there. Suddenly she felt very calm.

"If you really think it will be all right?"

"I shall be there as well and we will have other officers around the grounds as well."

Ellie hadn't thought of this as being a problem. "Police?" she queried.

"Yes," said Mary, "Jennie's fears about Karl are well founded. He has made two attempts on her life in the last few days and we still haven't caught him. We are keeping a guard on Jennie until we are satisfied she is no longer at risk. They will be very discreet and it won't stop Jennie coming to the funeral. As I said I doubt if even Karl wold be mad enough to start something there."

"I am sorry Jennie. I hadn't thought that it could be actually dangerous for you. I was just thinking of myself and how much it would matter to me."

Jennie slipped briefly. "Fuck Karl," she snapped, "my daughter wants me to be there and so I will even if I have to wheel myself."

"That is settled then." said Mary. "I will make arrangements for you to have transport there and back again. Now it really is time for you to say goodbye. We all have a lot to do before Thursday."

Ellie got up to leave then bent down and kissed Jennie lightly on the forehead. "Not goodbye Jennie but I'll be seeing you. I am so glad I have found you." Then she turned and walked swiftly out of the ward dabbing her eyes with a tissue. Mary went with her leaving Albert alone with Jennie. Jennie too was dabbing her eyes with the hem of her nightdress.

"Albert, do you really think that I could change if I take up your offer and come to stay with you?"

He looked at her. "Do you mean that? That's wonderful."

Jennie repeated her question. "Albert, do you think I can become a different person?"

Albert continued to chunter. "O you don't know how pleased I am at the very idea of you coming to stay with me. I will do all I can to help you but I like you as you are, I don't like what you have been doing with all these terrible people but you have always been kind to me."

She stopped him. "Albert, I don't think I can change now, but I do want to be different."

He grabbed her hand making he wince again. "If you are ever going to change this is the time to do it and I will be glad to do anything I can to help. Just think what a nice girl your daughter has turned out to be. It just shows what you could have done. There must be time to change."

"Thank you Albert for being such a good friend but you had better go as well. I feel very tired and I will need all my strength to get through the next two days."

"Don't you worry about that my dear, I will be with you all the time. I'll see you after lunch tomorrow. You get a good rest now. Don't you worry about your Aunty Flo, just leave her to me. I'm an old soldier you know."

"As he left Jennie whispered. "All the time, that's what I am afraid of." She gave as deep a sigh as her ribs would allow as he walked away. "You'll need to be a whole regiment for Aunty Flo."

*

Mary reported back to the police station to find everything in uproar as Timber had been arrested and two bodies had been pulled out of the Thames that afternoon. Both had been shot and the description of one sounded like Johnny. The other man had been identified as a well-known criminal from East London. He had links to the drug trade and one of the major gangs. Jane Marriner went to the morgue to see if the other body was that of Johnny Morris.

As she looked at his lifeless body she felt some frustration as she had so wanted to get him sent down. Three bullets had robbed her of the pleasure and it was definitely Johnny.

Chapter thirty-four

Reflection

Ellie's mind was humming as she made her way home. What on earth had possessed her? Jennie was like a caricature and her injuries only made the image more striking. She had wanted to know for her herself so it served her right for not listening to all her friends. Even Aunty Flo had been right. Then she thought again about the compassion she had felt beforehand. Surely that could not be wrong, and whether she liked it or not Jennie was her mother in name if not in deed. That did not mean they had to be close friends. Poor Jennie; how could she have got to the state she was in? It couldn't have all been her fault.

She was home before her mind had made any sense of it all. Muriel was in the kitchen preparing a meal.

"Hello dear. Are you all right after your visit? You were very brave and I am sure you feel quite exhausted. I took the liberty of doing some shopping this afternoon. I bought enough for Andy as well because I thought you would want him with you. Flo has gone down to the church as she discovered that the Women's Guild was meeting this afternoon. She thought it would be useful to meet them and find out what is planned. I just got some fish for this evening as I didn't think you would want anything too heavy."

Ellie stood for a while. The thought that Flo might go to the church today hadn't occurred to her. She took her coat off and hung it in the peg before replying. Muriel was right. She didn't feel like eating much at all and there was nothing she could do about Flo and Mrs Wagstaff meeting. It was probably better that they met now than later.

"Thank you Muriel. That is kind of you. Andy will be coming this evening but I must phone him first."

"I am glad. I am looking forward to meeting him after all I have heard about him. He seems to have made quite an impression on Flo. Why don't you pop up and have a relaxing bath. I bet you could do with a time of relaxation after today. I'm longing to hear how you got on today but I'll wait until the others are here so you don't have to keep repeating yourself."

Ellie wondered if Muriel could read her mind. As a hot bath and a good soak was just what she wanted. She rang Andy. He was just finishing at work.

"How did it go?"

"It was OK but not what I expected. She is probably going to come to the funeral with her friend Albert and Mary."

"I'll be finished in ten minutes and I'll come straight over."

"No Andy; don't hurry. I'm just going to have a bath and Muriel is cooking some tea for all of us, including you. She really is sweet. Come over in about an hour and I should be decent by then."

"Sure you don't want a back scrubber."

Ellie giggled. "Not today, but I'll keep it in mind. See you later."

She called through to Muriel. "That bath sounds like a good idea Muriel. Andy is coming in about an hour so you will get your chance to meet him."

As the bath filled she undressed and stood in front of the long mirror. "Goodbye little girl, you have to be a woman now."

The bath helped her relax and all the turmoil seemed less important. There was nothing she could do to change it. Que sera, sera. It would be nice when Andy was there to scrub her back. She stretched out in the warm bubbly water. Most days she just had a shower but she did enjoy a good wallow every now and then. Today it gave her mind a chance to clear and to go calmly over the events of the week. It had just been one shock after another. The surprise of discovering she now owned the house and had enough money to get married was balanced by the loss of her 'mum' had been a good surprise but the rest had been an inheritance of secrets, of a history of unhappiness and even worse.

Thank God for Andy. She smiled as she thought about making love to him for the first time but had a brief tinge of guilt as her 'mum' had always been so strict about anything to do with sex. But making love had been such a wonderful experience and it was only ever going to be Andy.

Her mind began to think of what she could do now. Even though Ellie had a GCSE in computer studies she had been refused permission to get a computer. She had enough now to get herself a little car so learning to drive was a target.

She heard the door opening downstairs and Aunty Flo's voice boomed up the stairs. It seemed clear that her meeting with Mrs Wagstaff had been fraught as the words 'that woman' echoed through the house. Ellie wondered how long she could stay in the bath but the water was already getting cool. Even the bubbles had flattened out. Ruefully she got out and dried herself and then dressed slowly.

She timed her journey downstairs to perfection as Andy rang the bell just as she reached the bottom of the staircase. She opened the door and pulled him in. Quick Andy, think of a reason why we have to go out."

"That's easy," he said as he leant forward to kiss her. "I met one of your old school chums in the bank today and it's her birthday today. I said we would be glad to go."

"Oh! I'm not sure if I should go to a party with the funeral and all that?"

"It's Helen. She was really sorry to hear about your 'mum' and it is just a few friends, not a rave up."

"Helen! I haven't seen her for at least six months. I thought she had gone to Australia with Luke."

"She did but it was a bit of a disaster. They broke up after only three weeks and then she had a rough time getting the money together to come home, so I said we would go but she does know that you may not be in party mood."

"Ellie!" Flo's voice ripped through their conversation. "Is that your young man again?"

Ellie began to giggle. "Yes, he's just taking his coat off."

They joined the two older women. Muriel step forward and grabbed his hand. "I'm so pleased to meet you Andy. You probably guess that I am Muriel, Flo's friend. I have heard so much about you. You are just in time to eat. I do hope you like fish. I got some skate wings with black butter, peas and a light garlic mash. If you would like some tomatoes as well I am just doing some for Flo."

Andy was slightly taken aback at such a different approach from Flo's. "Why yes; thank you. It's nice to meet you as well and some tomato would be good."

"Stuff and nonsense," Flo interrupted, "stop faffing around and let's have our tea. Ellie, I am afraid that Mrs Wagstaff is an ogre of a woman. She orders everyone around and expects everything to be done just as she wants. I will have to go down to the shops to get food for the funeral tea. Your ladies were hardly going to do anything so I have told them what I want, though I must say Mrs Wagstaff was quite offensive; not at all what I expect from a Christian lady."

Ellie drank her tea to hide the smile on her face. The concept of Flo and Mrs Wagstaff head to head over the sandwiches would have been a sight to behold.

"Anyway, we did agree to divide the work and she will do cakes and I will organise the sandwiches."

Ellie couldn't help herself. "Not fish paste. Mum hated fish paste and I don't blame her."

Flo stopped and peered over the rim of her glasses. "Your mum is hardly going to object and there is nothing wrong with fish paste. It is nutritious, contains good oils and fats and is cheap."

"Well I do hope you haven't upset them. It was so kind of them to offer in the first place."

"Well most of them seemed to be very glad to see me and to listen to what I was saying but Mrs Wagstaff seemed quite determined to disagree with me."

Muriel put her hand on Flo's shoulder. "Flo my dear, shall I say grace and then I am sure we all want to know how Ellie got on today."

Flo immediately stopped talking and Muriel blessed the meal.

As they ate Ellie told them about her visit to see Jenny amidst much snorting of disapproval from Flo and gentle encouragement from Muriel and Andy. Then she told them that Jenny was going to come to the funeral.

Flo gave an extra loud snort and declared "Come to Rosie's funeral indeed. How could she even think of that? I wouldn't want to be anywhere near her."

Her outburst came as a rude awakening after Ellie's story.

Ellie felt her anger rising again but Muriel quickly intervened. "Come now Flo; this has to be Ellie's decision and I wouldn't want her to have to choose between you and her mother."

"Mother! When has that woman ever been a mother. What has she ever done for you?" Ellie was by now ready for a fight. "She gave birth to me and from what I gather she was never given a chance to be a mother. I will always love my gran; I shall always think of her as being my mum, but Jenny is my flesh and blood and whatever she is, I cannot deny that. She has every right to come to the funeral. It is her only way of ever making some peace with her past and giving her the chance of a future that is different."

The tears glistened in her eyes as she tried to stop them from bursting out. Andy came over to her and held her in his arms while Muriel held her hand and reassured her while at the same time giving Flo a disapproving look.

Flo was quite nonplussed by Ellie's outburst and unusually was lost for words.

It was Muriel who found them. "We will honour whatever you want my dear and if you have managed to persuade Jenny to come to the funeral then we will treat her with the respect that you want her to have. Won't we Flo?"

Flo shuffled in her seat and looked very uncomfortable at being so directly challenged by Muriel.

"Yes" she muttered, "Oh yes, but I hope she won't want to sit next to me or talk to me."

Ellie had calmed down again after her cathartic outburst and felt sorry for being so direct. "I'm sorry but it's all been far more stressful than I can cope with. I'm not usually so rude."

Muriel smiled. "You don't need to apologise my dear. You have been through so much in the last week that I'm surprised you haven't gone to pieces altogether. I am sure that having Andy to help has given you a lot of strength. Being loved is so important, and loving is a wonderful gift, but it can also be quite distressing when someone you love is doing things that are so contrary to their own interests and your own way of life."

Ellie looked at Muriel and was surprised to see that she had tears in her eyes.

"Thank you Muriel. That is just how I feel. I cannot bear what Jenny is doing but I feel a love for her as my mother. It's like she has been a prodigal mother who was lost but now I have found her, I don't want to lose her again."

Andy was standing quietly waiting for the moment to remind Ellie that they could go out. "Are you going to be all right to go and see Helen. He turned to the others, "Helen is one of Ellie's school friends and she has been in Australia for some time. She has invited some of her friends round to her flat this evening. I said we would try to go but I don't think we will be out for long."

"Of course you must go." said Muriel. "It sounds just the thing to lift Ellie's spirits. We oldies will be fine with the television and each other. It's Holby tonight isn't it Flo?"

"If it's Tuesday then I expect so." Flo was still looking sulky but rallied as she was brought back into the conversation. "Of course you must go Ellie. You need your friends around you at a time like this." Then she turned to Muriel "I must tell you all about this terrible woman at the church."

Muriel looked as if she gave Andy a wink as if to say go while the going is good. Ellie ran upstairs to wash and put a pair of jeans on as she was still dressed for work.

The meeting with Helen was indeed just what Ellie needed and she tried hard not to think about the funeral but some of her friends there knew about her mum dying. Andy protected her from most of the questions but Ellie seemed relaxed about talking without going into the details of what had been happening.

By the time they got back home both Muriel and Flo had gone to bed. He kissed her and then walked back to his flat as he had drunk too much for driving. Ellie was glad enough just to go to bed and to let her mind idle over the events of the day.

Chapter thirty-five

No Prunes!

The sound of a tea cup on a saucer was always enough to alert Flo and she was in the kitchen before the tea was poured. She took over the tea pot.

"What are you doing Ellie? You know you don't need to go making your own meal or tea while I am here. We must look after you and make sure you don't waste away."

Like a slender shadow Muriel appeared behind her and deftly laid the table for three.

"You don't have any prunes do you dear?"

"No, mum never had prunes."

"O good, perhaps I can have some fruit instead."

"I am sorry but I hadn't realised you were coming back until yesterday and I haven't got much shopping in. I was planning to do it today."

Muriel coughed gently. "I did some shopping yesterday but I must confess that prunes were not on my list either."

Flo sniffed, a sure sign of her disapproval. "I don't know what you live on normally Ellie but when I'm in charge we always have prunes to start with followed by bacon, egg, and toast."

Muriel smiled. "I prefer grapefruit myself."

Ellie felt herself beginning to bridle at the thought that Flo was in charge of her but she knew better than to have a pointless argument especially first thing in the morning.

Flo went on. "Anyway I shall get some in for tomorrow. We will need a good breakfast to set us up for the day. By the way Ellie there is a lot of post for you from yesterday."

Ellie hadn't even thought about the post. It was just another thing that mum had always sorted out. She took her tea into the front room and looked at the post which Flo had put in a neat pile on the coffee table by the television. She began to check it. Most of it was letters of commiseration but there was also one from the bank asking mum to come and talk to one of their financial advisers. She put that to one side for after the funeral. Brian had already told her to keep all financial matters separate to let him sort out as executor. There was a scattering of adverts which she dropped on the floor for recycling and one letter from a woman who signed herself as Aunty Jean.

She took it back into the kitchen.

Flo was standing over a pan full of bacon and another with what seemed like half a dozen eggs. Muriel was sitting at the table. She looked up as Ellie returned. "Anything interesting dear?"

"Not really, except a letter from an aunty Jean. I don't remember having an aunty Jean."

Muriel turned to Flo. "Flo, wasn't there a Jean who was related to Reg?"

"Yes; she was his sister and just as bad as he was. She used to live in Watford if I remember, but Rosie never had anything to do with her or any of that family."

Ellie was surprised by the thought that she had more relatives than she knew about. "She has written me a very nice letter. Are there any more people in my family that I don't know about?"

"Not on our side. Both my parents were only children and I don't think we had any distant cousins though there was a maiden Aunt called Nelly, but she must be dead a long time ago."

"I don't even remember your parents."

"Ah!" Flo hesitated. "Well it was like I told you. They were very angry with Rosie because she had to marry Reg, so they never spoke to her again after the wedding. My father was a very religious man and he was a member of a very strict sect that shunned people who didn't do what they wanted."

"How about you?"

"Well I was older than Rosie and at work in a job he approved of. Mind you I was always arguing with him. Then I met Muriel and we became firm friends. When I wouldn't give her up I was shunned as well. You're lucky you didn't know him."

"But what about your mother?"

268

"My mother was kinder but totally dominated by my father so she always had to do what he said. Women were not allowed to have an opinion in his church. She rarely got out and he wouldn't let anyone else in except for others in that group. She died ten years ago and neither of us were allowed to go to the funeral. He blamed us for breaking her heart. Now perhaps you see why I don't like men."

"But that is so wrong. Surely it can't have been anything to do with his church?"

"Well I'm afraid there are some very strange sects with very hard rules. They think they are right and don't want to be contaminated by any other thoughts. It's pathetic really but that's men for you."

"But why did they turn against mum when she needed them most?"

"Poor Rosie didn't know what had happened. She didn't even like Reg very much but he forced himself on her once and she became pregnant. That made her a sinner so having made sure they married she was then cast out as they call it."

"Surely they can't have forced them to marry just because of the baby?"

"I suppose my father thought it was a kind act to frighten Reg into marrying Rosie but there was no way that he could then have anything to do with her or the baby. Poor Rosie ended up with a man she hardly knew and didn't like and a baby she didn't want and which she had been told was the spawn of the devil. She was very naïve then and her life had been totally dominated by her father. It might have been 1972 then but it might as well have been 1700."

269

"But what about Aunty Jean and her family?"

"I don't really know except that Reg was one of about seven children in a family that was always in trouble, and Jean was a sister who was about Rosie's age. She used to call round to see the baby sometimes but Rosie didn't like her and then she got married and moved to Watford."

"I wonder how she found out about mum?"

Muriel chipped in. "She was a very lively girl who had two children before she was married so must have seemed very alien to Rosie with her limited experience of life. I believe a lot of the family still live in the Battersea area so one of them has probably seen it in the paper."

"I wonder if any of them will turn up at the funeral?"

Flo gave one of her snorts. "It wouldn't surprise me especially if they think there will be a good tea afterwards, at least it would have been a good tea if your Mrs Wagstaff had listened to me."

"I thought you had sorted that out with her."

"I don't know how you can stand that woman Ellie, she is so rude and thinks she can just take over."

Ellie and Muriel looked at each other and tried not to laugh.

Suddenly Ellie sprang to her feet. "I must dash otherwise I will be late for work. I was so interested in what we were saying that I forgot the time.."

"Surely you don't have to go into work today?"

"Yes I do. I need to keep myself busy today so that I don't think too much about tomorrow and I'm working through to 6.30 to try and make up for some of the time I have already taken off. My boss has been so good to me but I don't want to take advantage of her so I'll see you about 7.00. Andy will be coming this evening as well so we can order a takeaway to save you having to cook."

As she was almost out of the door Flo called out. "I shall be down at the church helping to get things ready and I must do some shopping for the bread and the fillings."

Ellie turned briefly and called back, "As long as it isn't fish paste." Then she was gone before Flo could reply.

"What is wrong with Fish Paste?" Flo asked Muriel.

"I think we need to be a bit more adventurous my dear. Perhaps salmon or tuna, ham and different types of cheese. It is a funeral meal not a trip to the beach."

"Oh very well; I suppose you know about these things better than I do."

"Not everything Flo, but this is for Ellie as well as for you."

Ellie was just in time and soon became quite busy especially when she was asked to check the deliveries. In her break she sent a text to Andy as she knew he would be busy then. 'Same place, same time x LE'.

By lunchtime he had replied 'OK Luvu ND'. She smiled. Thank god for Andy.

The rest of the day went smoothly and she was able to cope with the customers who wished her well when she was back on the till. She was even surprised at herself, even a bit shocked at how quickly she was able to take mum's death so dispassionately. Still, she thought, there will be plenty of tears tomorrow.

Chapter thirty-six

Meanwhile

Following the murder of Maggie the hunt for Karl and Johnny had become London wide and the word on the street was that both the North London and the Brixton gangs were also looking for them. Now that Johnny had been found it was clear that the gangs did not want to talk. In Brixton the gang had called in a specialist marksman.

Elroy's military career had not been very long but he had served as a sniper in Iran before they had found his lack of discipline unacceptable. He found that having a career as a petty thief was good cover for the occasional contract. This one would be a pleasure as he knew and disliked Karl. Elroy already knew where Jennie was and it didn't take him long to guess that Karl knew as well. All he had to do was to follow Jennie.

*

Karl was now completely paranoid having been on the boat when Johnny was shot. They had been promised a trip to the coast and passage to Belgium but it had turned out to be a trick to get rid of them. Johnny had been shot just after the boat had left the shore. Luckily for Karl the boat had lurched as the second shot was fired at him and he had been able to fire back with the gun he had taken from Steve's flat..

In the following struggle he had managed to get hold of the gun and kill him. He dumped both bodies over the side and then tried to flood the boat and let it drift away hoping it might be sunk as he slipped over the side and swam to shore in the dark.

He knew now that he was as good as dead if the gangs got him and being in prison would just make their job easier. He had to get out of the country. Finding his passport was his priority; it might just give him a chance of escape. He had been unable to find it in the flat and Jenny couldn't have it in the hospital so he thought it must be at Albert's house. He was waiting outside and out of sight when Albert left.

The poor weather meant there were few people out so as he stood by the door he soon obtained entry without being seen. Albert might as well have left it open. Karl went upstairs to find where Jennie had been sleeping. He tipped all the drawers out stripped the bed, emptied her washing bag and generally looked everywhere but there was no sign of his passport. He went downstairs and emptied every drawer and cupboard, even Albert's bookcase was emptied and the books just thrown into a pile on the floor. Still there was nothing. He sat down and looked at the chaos he had caused.

He talked to himself swearing violently. 'The bitch must have it. It must be in the hospital after all.' Albert's diary lay on the table open at Thursday. Jennie's mother – funeral 2.30 p.m. Karl wondered why as he knew Jennie hated her mother. Surely she wasn't going to the funeral, but why else would Albert be going. It was a chance. He smiled. The idea that he could kill her in the cemetery appealed to him. He left quickly and quietly.

*

Mary had been writing up her notes from the previous two days and had just finished when Albert rang to say that his house had been burgled. She logged it in and offered to investigate herself as it was tied in with her present duties. The news of Johnny's murder had done wonders for the information given by the rest of the gang and Johnny was firmly identified as the person who had shot the croupier and Geoff Henriques and as the killer of Maggie. Karl's prints had been found all over Steve O'Brien's flat and also from the boat found at Tower Bridge. Forensic had been working overtime to identify the bullets used on the two dead me and had just confirmed that they were both killed by the same weapon. The gun had not been found and the thought that Karl may still have the gun gave even more urgency to the hunt.

*

Albert's visit to the hospital that morning had been curtailed when Jennie had to go to then X ray department and then to have a proper bath. He was glad to see that they had got her out of bed again and into the chair.

Getting home however was a shock. Karl had searched every room and turned everything out. He was still shaking when Mary came in response to his call. He had tidied a lot of it by the time she arrived but she could see what a mess Karl had left behind. She went into the kitchen and made a cup of tea for Albert with two spoons of sugar.

"Drink this Albert. It will help to calm you down. Do you know if anything is missing.

"How could they do this. Anyone who knows me knows that I aint got much money and then only on Thursdays when I get my pension."

She held his hand and repeated. "Was anything stolen that you know of."

"I don't think so but Jennie's room was wrecked and he even ripped up the clothes I gave her. They used to be Ruth's. She always liked to dress younger than she was but it looked good on her because she never put much weight on. She was only sixty seven when she died you know. Far too young. "

"She was eighteen when we got hitched. She was expecting young Albert at the time so I did the right thing but I would have done it anyway because we loved each other. She never had any more children because Albert was such a difficult birth that they had to do an operation. Still we had nearly fifty years together and she was always so kind. Young Albert getting killed like he did was terrible but we bore it together."

Mary didn't interrupt him as she could see that this was him normalising the situation but she had to redirect him. "Albert, can you tell me anything else about the break-in."

"Sorry my dear, I don't think I can. I did ask her next door but she was listening to her wireless, but she did say there was a strange young man lurking around earlier this morning, but then she thinks everyone is strange."

Mary frowned. "Do you think it might have been Karl?"

"What; do you mean Jennie's Karl; I thought you were out there looking for him. Surely he wouldn't have risked coming here."

"I think he is getting desperate. It's just as well that you weren't here as he is suspected of two shootings yesterday."

"Oh my goodness! Do you think he will be back?"

"No; by the looks of things he was looking for something and I don't think he found it.

"Do think he will go to the hospital again?"

"Not now; I think we have too much protection in place now. The main risk will be when she leaves but I am sure we will have him by then."

"What about the funeral tomorrow? Will she be safe there?"

"We will be there and it would be suicidal for him to try anything there. We would be bound to catch him. We even have a couple of armed officers in case he tries. What I will do is to get you a panic button so that if anything happens you just press it and it will go through to the police station and someone should come straight out to you. If you come with me now I can get you sorted out at the station."

"Well, I still have a lot of tidying up to do."

"That's all right Albert. You get yourself sorted out and call into the police station on your way to see Jennie this afternoon. I may not be there but the duty Officer will be expecting you. Will that be OK?"

"Yes, thank you! I won't tell Jennie yet. It might make her worry too much and I don't want to make her going to the funeral any worse. "Good thinking Albert. Now I must get back to my bookwork before I go to the hospital this afternoon. I still have to take a turn on watch and I shall be at the funeral tomorrow. I might see you later."

"Thank you Mary. It is good to know she is in such good hands. I don't know what I would do if she was harmed again." "You just take it easy Albert. I don't think Karl will be anywhere near again today."

Chapter thirty-seven

Jennie writes a letter

In spite of her complaints Jennie felt much better after having a shower. Having help to get in and out and a shower proof cover on her leg did remind her of her need for help but it was a step to normality. She was relieved to see that her bruising was fading and even better she was able to turn without too much pain. Her head still hurt but a gentle shampoo had washed out the last of the blood and refreshed her hair. She even ate her lunch without swearing and sitting on a chair by herself gave her a sense of being in control. The wheel chair to the showers had been a bit scary but what a relief it was to be able to sit on a proper toilet again.

Sister Mackay was on duty and doing her rounds and stopped by Jennie's bed.

"So you have managed to get out of bed. I must say you are looking much better sitting up and clean. It's just a shame we can't wash your mouth out. They tell me your daughter came to see you and that you are going to a funeral tomorrow. You are lucky it wasn't your own. I will be on duty again tomorrow when you go, so I will make sure that everything is on hand to get you there. In the meantime is there anything I can get you."

Jennie bit her lip and didn't reply as she was tempted to.

"Yes" she said, "I would like to write a letter but I don't have any paper or a pen."

I'm sure we can sort that out for you. I'm glad to see that someone can still write and not just send stupid messages by text or on a computer."

Jennie did not respond. This would be the first letter she had written since Wendy was in Holloway. The paper and pen duly arrived and Jennie began to write with some difficulty.

"My darling Ellie, it was such a proud moment for me seeing you here yesterday but I don't expect you will ever want to see me again after mum's funeral but I am really chuffed that you even made the effort to find me. I wouldn't have dared to look for you.

Seeing you like a proper young woman made me feel very sad and sorry that I had missed all of your growing up, but if I had been there you may not have been half as nice as you are now. Mum did a really good job in raising you. Perhaps if I had given her a chance I might have been better than I am. But I am no good and I have never been anything else. I don't blame my dad like mum did. It was just that he showed me all the love I have ever known and I loved him back the only way I knew how.

I don't know who your dad was because I was with quite a few blokes then and I didn't know I was pregnant until I was six months gone. I was in a children's home at the time and I just thought you were all the stodge that they fed us. Somebody must have hurt mum a lot for her to be so unloving to me and I never saw her the way you do. I am so glad that she was good to you. I wish it could have been different for me but it isn't and I don't think I can change much now. I need drugs to keep me happy as without them I get so depressed.

Albert is a kind man and I will go to stay with him until I am better as long as they have found Karl and locked him up, but I know that when I am better I shall be out on the streets again. It's the only life I know and I don't have any other way of making the money to buy my drugs. But I will have one thing to be glad of now I have met you, for I know now that my baby has grown up into a fine young woman even if it was done by my mum and not me. You were my baby and I can be proud of you.

You may not believe it, but you were the only person I have ever truly loved. Even when I left you it was because I loved you and knew I was no good for you. I hope you don't get this letter until I am out of here and fit again for then I shall go away so you can't find me because I don't want you wasting your time trying to help me or to find me as I would only mess up your life as well. Let me be. It is the only way I can really show my love for you.

Jennie.

Jennie looked at the letter for a long time and tears filled her eyes. She would love to know what would happen to Ellie as long as Ellie didn't know where she was. She folded the letter up and put it with the few clothes that Albert had brought in for her. She sat up just as Mary walked in.

"Where the hell have you been?"

"Nice to see you too Jennie; especially sitting up and looking much better than two days ago. I had to visit someone and we have been very busy at work thanks to you. We think we have found Johnny and Jane has gone to check it out."

"I hope they keep a tight hold on him so he doesn't get away. He would kill me too but he has more sense and looks after himself first."

"He hasn't been thinking too straight recently what with the mess up they made of the robbery and the murder of Maggie. It looks as if he did that. Still if it is him he won't be going anywhere They pulled him out of the river this morning."

"Is he dead?"

"Well the body they have found had five bullets in it."

"Oh! It was Johnny who was my boy-friend when Ellie was born. It was him that got me started in business and looked after me."

"And I guess he got you onto drugs as well."

"I suppose so but it just made what I did easier to forget."

"How did you get away from him?"

He went down for two years and I had moved when he came out so he lost interest in me and found a younger girl who could earn more."

"So you are not sorry to hear that he is dead?"

"I guess not. It's strange isn't it. I thought the sun shone out of him once, now it's as if he never existed. You get used to people dying in this game."

"Why don't you change? You have the chance to do that for the first time in your life. Not many people like you ever get that. But now you have Albert offering you a home and a caring relationship and you have Ellie willing to let you into her world."

"Don't you think that I would do it if I could? But I don't love Albert and I could only hurt him. I would only be using him and it may be silly to you but I care too much about him to do that. It just wouldn't be honest."

Mary couldn't help smiling.

"You can smile all you like, I have my limits, and one of them is not to hurt other people especially the ones I like."

"And what about Ellie?"

"I have been thinking about that a lot and I have written her a letter to say I don't want to see her again after the funeral."

"Why not?"

"Because she is the one beautiful thing in my life. She is the one person I can truly say I love and I know I would only bring more sadness and grief into her life if I stay here. I have the letter here and I would like you to look after it and give it to her when I have gone. I also want you keep in touch with me so that I know how she is getting on and so I can keep that picture in my heart that out of my shitty life something has been worth-while."

For once Mary hardly knew what to say.

Jennie leant forward as far as she could and gave her the letter. "Here it is." Then she pulled it back, "Promise me you won't give it to her until I have gone away."

"I think it is a very fine thing you are doing Jennie. I shall be glad to help and I promise to do as you ask." She took the letter and put it carefully into her uniform pocket.

Jennie looked down. "I might wait until after the wedding. I would love to be at her wedding. Just at the back. I wouldn't want to be up there like a normal mum. You will help me do that won't you Mary?"

"Of course I will Jennie." Mary was beginning to feel deeply moved by what Jennie was saying so tried to divert the subject to a less emotive topic. "Anyway Jennie, don't you go all mushy on me now. I just need to make sure you will be all right for tomorrow."

"Yes, I will be there. I had a vicar came to see me last night. Said his name was Brian and that he knew my mum and Ellie and was glad to meet me. He seemed to know all about me as well and still spoke to me. He told me it was time to bury the past and to pray for the future and, do you know he actually did pray for me right there and then. I never thought a vicar would pray for me. He said he would look out for me at the funeral and if I wanted to know anything to just wave at him and he would come and talk to me in front of everyone else."

"I know who you mean. That is the Revd. Brian Evans. Ellie and Andy met at the youth club in his church and he will be the minister who marries them as well as taking your mum's funeral service tomorrow."

"I'm glad. He seemed a really genuine man and I don't see many of them."

"Well, he is a minister."

A mischievous glint came into Jennie's eyes. "I have met vicars before you know. Wendy and me had a very discreet service at one time, but she died and I got too old for the best money. At my age you are lucky if you get twenty quid in the back of a car. I wonder if any of the young kids realise that they only get paid well while they are young."

Mary relaxed. This was more like the Jennie she knew. "I must get back to work now Jennie, but I will be there tomorrow and there will be other police as well to make sure that Karl can't get to you. After all surely he wouldn't dare do it at a funeral. Not even Karl would be that stupid". She decided not to tell her about Karl's raid on Albert's home.

"I know him Mary, and he is that stupid. He killed one man in a police station and still got away. Anyway I have a funeral to go to and then a wedding so not even Karl is going to stop me now."

"Not if we have anything to do with it he won't. You can sit with me if you like at the wedding. I don't have a mum to sit next to so you have a seat. Now I must be off. Albert will be here this evening to keep you company and I'll see you tomorrow."

"Bye Mary. Thank you. Fancy me sitting next to a copper at my daughter's wedding. All my mates will think I've been nicked."

Chapter thirty-eight

Flo in the can

Ellie's day had gone smoothly and she had a quiet lunch break with Andy as she wanted to have a quiet evening before the funeral. She still had letters to write so she had a plan for tonight; get home, have a shower and wash her hair, then a light meal and a chance to escape to her room and answer as many messages as she could. Knowing that Flo would be down at the church made her feel more relaxed as she knew that Muriel would help her and not hinder.

She was home by seven and in the shower ten minutes later while Muriel put the kettle on and prepared a meal for them. She felt nicely warm and comfortable as she dressed. Then the phone rang.

She was at the top of the stairs when Muriel got to the phone and answered it.

"Hello; yes this is Miss Moffatt speaking; did you say the police station? Goodness me! Of course, I will come at once."

As she put the phone down Ellie called down, "What's up?"

"It's Flo! She is at the police station and they want me to go and get her. They said she is there after a breach of the peace at the church. I can't understand it. She just doesn't do that sort of thing."

Ellie had a sudden vision of Flo and Mrs Wagstaff attacking each other with their wooden spatulas. "Aunty Flo?" she said, "At the police station."

"Yes! O goodness me. I'd better turn the kettle off." As she scurried into the kitchen the doorbell rang. It was Andy.

"Thank goodness you're here Andy. You are just in time to come with us to the police station. Aunty Flo has been arrested for a breach of the peace. I must put something warm on."

"I know. Mary rang me, which is why I hurried over. I have the car with me so we can get there quicker.

Andy drove them to the front of the police station and then went off to find a parking space.

Muriel went straight to the counter. "Hello; my name is Moffatt and I believe you have my friend Miss Florence Newton with you. I had a call asking me to come and collect her."

The desk officer looked up. "Right, are you sure you want her back? I must say we'll be glad to see her go. She's done nothing but argue ever since we brought her in. She only shut up when we warned her that anything she said could be used in evidence against her, but don't worry she isn't going to court." He turned slightly and called through a hatch way behind him. OK Sally, you can bring her up now."

There was a pause and then the unmistakable voice of Flo could be heard. Ellie felt a hand on her elbow. She turned to find that Brian Evans was there.

"Hello Ellie. I see you got here before me. I was just coming to try and sort out this unfortunate matter. It was really Mrs Wagstaff's own fault. She was so annoyed with your aunt that she went over to have an argument with her and then she slipped, crashed into a table and knocked her own cake onto the floor. She thought your aunt had pushed her over but we found later that she had stepped on a gherkin that had somehow fallen on the floor. It was pure accident that the coleslaw ended up on her head."

Ellie listened to him with amazement. "I think you will have to say that all over again Brian."

Just then Flo appeared through the security door. "Muriel!" she screamed and enveloped Muriel. O my dear, this is so dreadful. I feel so angry. It was all that terrible Wagstaff woman's fault but I was the one who was arrested and taken away like a common criminal. It's a disgrace. I shall write to the Chief Constable and my MP."

Then she spotted Brian. "You, you, you awful little man! How dare you come here to mock me?"

Ellie stood in front of Brian and Muriel grabbed hold of Flo, but Brain stepped out from behind them and faced Flo directly. "Of course Miss Newton I can understand your distress at this very unfortunate incident and I have come her to explain that you were not in any way directly responsible for what happened, except for having upset Mrs Wagstaff in the first place. The police were already in the hall trying to make it tidy for tomorrow. One of them is Sergeant Wagstaff, Mrs

Wagstaff's son. She was blaming you for what happened and so he brought you here to avoid further disturbance and to give us all a chance to find out what had happened."

Flo was only half listening and still sobbing. "How could you let them bring me here among all these common criminals."

"I think Sereant Wagstaff was afraid that you might cause some damage as you were flailing your arms around and getting very agitated. In fact I think you did hit him when he tried to calm you down."

"As I was just telling Ellie, Mrs Wagstaff wrongly thought that you had pushed her over but you didn't. She had trodden on a gherkin and slipped. Everything else sprang from that and her mistaken thought that you had assaulted her. She is very embarrassed by it all and we are all very sorry that it got out of hand."

"Do you mean I am exonerated? Free of all blame?"

"Apart from telling Mrs Wagstaff that she was a stupid woman."

Muriel looked at Flo. "Florence, you really ought not to have said that. I think you owe her an apology. After all, if you hadn't insulted her, the rest might not have happened."

Flo hung her head. Muriel's reprimand was far more effective than any police action.

Ellie asked "Do you need some help to get things sorted out at church."

"No, it is all in hand again and Sergeant Wagstaff is staying on to make sure all the work is done. He said it was the least he could do to apologise. Mrs Wagstaff has gone home but the rest of the ladies have worked hard to sort things out and even saved Mrs Wagstaff's cake. Fortunately her icing is quite firm. Last year we had to cut the cake out of it and break the icing up with a hammer for the sweet counter. As you know it is very hard to tell Mrs Wagstaff that she has got anything wrong."

Ellie smiled at the thought. "I know somebody else like that!"

By now Andy was back with the car so they drove home. Andy left them at the house. Muriel went back to the kitchen to finish preparing their meal while Ellie sat with Flo watching the television. Flo was very quiet all evening and Ellie was eventually able to get a lot of her letters done.

She went downstairs for a drink as Flo and Muriel were retiring. As they were going up the stairs Ellie thought she heard Flo say, "I wondered where that gherkin had gone."

Chapter thirty-nine

Preparations

Karl had slept badly. Now he sat on the edge of his bed checking what he still had. There was five hundred pounds in his wallet. He also had the gun but there were only four bullets left. There was no room for him to miss. He would have to get as close to Jennie as possible.

"Jennie, Jennie, Jennie" Her name kept ringing through his head. It was all her fault. He knew he was as good as finished. The episode on the boat when he and Johnny thought they were being taken to safety showed him that there were no friends anymore. If he hadn't taken Steve's gun from the flat he too would be dead by now but Johnny had been shot first and he had time to shoot. Albert's flat had produced nothing except the satisfaction of wrecking it but the passport he so desperately needed was gone. It was all Jennie's fault. Shooting was too good for her. He fantasised having his hands around her throat and watching her slowly choke, or better still being able to carve her up bit by bit and hearing every scream. But it had to be the gun if he was going to get away.

The more he thought the more manic he became. It didn't matter if he got caught any more as long as he had the satisfaction of killing her first. Now he knew where she was going to be and when he could prepare his trap. Let them all go into the chapel and wait as Jennie came out. She would have to come out first because she was family and everyone else would be stuck in the crematorium. He counted the bullets again and kissed each of them as he loaded the gun.

*

At the hospital Jennie had also been restless and twisting in her sleep had made her back and leg ache. She woke with a strange sense of unreality. Had she dreamed about Ellie? She was brought back to the present as the nurse came to change her bandages and to get her out of bed. It was more painful than yesterday and it was just as well that she was in a private ward because she did not cope with pain quietly. Soon she was in a chair and began to feel more comfortable. The sister came to see how she was. Jenny told her.

"Really Miss Burns, you are one of the most foul-mouthed women I have ever met, but I'm afraid it doesn't impress me one little bit. I just need to be sure that you will be fit for the funeral this afternoon."

Jennie's mind focussed. "Shit! It's my mother's funeral today. Did I say I would go? Why, why did I say that? It was the shock of seeing Ellie, but I can't go out as I haven't any clothes to wear for a funeral. The stuff I came in with is all torn and messed up."

"Don't you worry about that! Mr Smith is bringing fresh clothing for you to wear. We have a car ordered for one thirty which should get you to the crematorium in good time. You will have a wheel chair to get you around and we will give you an injection before you go to mask the pain. I think that will cover everything."

Before Jennie could think of what to say she swept out of the room greeting the police officer who was on duty as she did so. It was obvious to Jennie that she was completely trapped. She couldn't even stand for long never mind running away. She just managed to get her bag and take out the cherished photograph of Ellie as a baby. Then she slipped it back into the bag and relaxed into the chair. Soon she was asleep again. She was still asleep when Mary came to relieve the duty officer and to help with the escort in the afternoon. Mary checked with the sister that Jennie was fit enough for the journey and then made herself comfortable for the morning vigil.

*

Ellie slept until the ringing of the telephone downstairs disturbed her. She woke up and was amazed to see that it was nearly nine o'clock. She heard Muriel answering the call then as she was not called she washed and dressed. When she went down Flo and Muriel were in the kitchen with a tin of red salmon and a bowl of sliced cucumber.

Muriel poked her head round the corner. "Good morning my dear! We let you sleep in as you will have such a trying day today. You will need all your energy. That was Mrs Wagstaff on the telephone to apologise for not being there today as she has a bad headache. I doubt if it's in her head but I am sure it is tender."

The humour in what she said was so unexpected that Ellie didn't respond for a while, then she nearly choked herself. "Muriel !" she gasped, "that's not very kind."

"It's as kind as I feel towards this lady. Fancy getting poor Flo taken to the police station when she had only slipped. That was unkind. Now do you want toast or full English? Flo is making a sponge cake and we are busy doing salmon and cucumber sandwiches."

"Thank you Muriel I will just have toast today but I can do that for myself."

"No dear, you sit down and sort the post out. There is quite a bit today."

Ellie looked at the pile of letters and quickly sorted out the adverts for recycling. She opened the others with mum's paper knife. Sure enough there were two bills and three letters from old friends who could not come.

The last two had a legal look to them and one of them was from mum's solicitor giving her condolences and asking her to make an early appointment.

Flo suddenly appeared and placed a plate of bacon eggs, beans and the toast in front of her. "Only toast, what nonsense. You need to be well fed today my girl. There you are, and I don't want to see any of it again. Ellie sighed, thought for a moment and then capitulated. Eating the breakfast was less exhausting than arguing with Flo. Still a little dig at her might make her feel better."

"You know that big policeman, the one with the handlebar moustache fancied you Flo. He kept asking about you, didn't he Muriel."

Flo rose to the bait. "I've never heard anything so ridiculous, how dare he have such thoughts about me. What did he say? I have a good mind to report him to his superiors. The insolence of it! Men! They only ever have one thing on their mind."

"He was only admiring you."

"I have better things to do in my life than to worry what a stupid man thinks of me. What did he say?"

"He said that in twenty years of being a policeman he had never seen anyone like you."

"Really! Why, maybe there are some perceptive men after all. Muriel, did you hear that?"

But Muriel was in the kitchen with a tea towel in her mouth trying not to laugh out loud. Ellie saw her and that set her off as well. Poor Flo stood in the middle wondering what on earth she could have said that was so funny. "Well, I don't think it's funny for a man to appreciate me."

They were brought back to reality by the door bell ringing. It was Andy, looking very smart in his best suit. "Sorry I'm so early. I just couldn't sleep last night with worrying about Ellie being all right for today especially with her mother being there as well."

Oh Andy; it's so good to see you." Ellie flung her arms around him and kissed him. "We've just been teasing Aunty Flo about the policeman saying he'd never met anyone like her."

"Oh yes; I remember him saying that. I thought it was funny at the time."

Flo stared at him. "Funny! What is funny about being appreciated?"

Fortunately his mobile rang and saved them from hysterics. It was Mary.

"Hi Andy; can you do me a favour because I'm on duty at the hospital and can't leave Jennie. It's Albert. Someone broke into his house yesterday and searched it, especially Jennie's room. All her clothing was in a pile on the floor, the bed turned over and so on. He is in a bit of a state because he thinks it might have been Karl looking for Jennie. He has just brought some new clothes in for Jennie but he is obviously shaken by what happened. He's gone back home now but I have told him you will pick him up and take him to the crem. Are you all right with that? I don't want to have to have him held up by having to wait in for one of my colleagues at this stage."

"Sure, I'm OK with that. The car will be a six seater so there is plenty of room for him. It's collecting us at ten past one so we will pick him up on the way. Ellie is fine so we will see you at the Chapel."

He explained what had been said to Ellie.

"Oh that poor man; And I was so rude to him the other evening."

"What man is that?" asked Flo.

"His name is Albert and he is a good friend of Jennie's, and I mean a good friend, not one of the nasty people she has been around with. He is an old soldier and used to be a magician."

Flo looked worried. "He's not going to sit next to me. I don't trust men who do tricky things."

Ellie smiled at the idea of Albert and Flo doing tricks together, but the look on Flo's face made her curtail her imagination.

After the breakfast things had been cleared and the house tidied to Flo's satisfaction, just in case anyone came back later, Andy ran Flo and Muriel down to the church with the sandwiches and sponge cake.

Molly Evans was there and she had a brief word with Muriel just to be sure that Flo and Ellie were all right. She had come down that morning to make sure everything was ready having heard that Mrs Wagstaff was indisposed. They were all home in good time for any last minute preparations. As the time came closer to go so Ellie lost all her humour and started to feel quite tearful at the thought of what was happening.

*

Karl checked his gun again then slid it into the pocket of his raincoat. He caught a train to Clapham North and then walked to the Windmill. He felt safe as he had never been there before and the normal clientele were unlikely to recognise him. He bought a steak and kidney pie and washed it down with a pint of beer. By one the pub was quite full so he slipped out to the car park. It didn't take him long to steal a car and drive to Roehampton and to park it among the cars already there for another funeral. He made sure he knew the time and where they would be coming out of the chapel, then he returned to the car and waited.

*

Albert spent a lot of the morning clearing up after Karl's visit. He was unable to see if anything had been taken. He had been told by Mary not to let Jennie know what had happened and that worried him. That, the thought of going to a funeral and the raid all played havoc with his bladder all morning. The trip to the hospital with the clean clothes was about all he could

297

cope with. Jenny was still asleep when he arrived so Mary took the clothing from him and suggested he go home and relax before the car came for him that afternoon. He was relieved to do so as he would have found it very hard not to tell Jennie about the raid on his house. He continued to tidy up but was finished by midday and then got out his best suit, then sat in it for an hour before the car came.

Chapter forty

Death in waiting

Albert had nodded off and woke with a start when the door-bell rang. Still in half a daze he got into the car. Ellie and Andy he recognised but there were two older women there as well, one of whom scowled at him. Even so he tried to be polite.

"Good afternoon ladies and Andy. Thank you for calling to pick me up. I've been all over the place today and Mary has had to go with Jenny in the ambulance car."

To his relief Ellie smiled at him. "Hello Albert. This is my auntie Flo and her friend Muriel. "

Flo interrupted, "Miss Newton and Miss Moffatt."

Ellie smiled and then continued. "and this is Albert Smith, one of Jennie's friends. He's been very kind to her recently."

Flo gave one of her disapproving snorts. "He's old enough to be her father."

Albert gave a little bow. "Possibly even her grandfather. I am so sorry about your sister. It is your sister that was Jennie's mother?"

Before Flo could make some unsuitable retort Muriel leaned forward and shook Albert's hand. "It is nice to meet somebody who knows Jennie. It's been such a long time since we saw her or even heard about her."

Albert smiled at her and Flo turned round and scowled at Muriel. "Muriel! Don't encourage the man." Muriel sat back in the seat and smiled at Albert.

After that nobody seemed inclined to speak until they reached the hospital. They were slightly late and Jennie and Mary were already in the hospital car with a wheel chair in the back. The two vehicles then headed towards the crematorium. Ellie was by now quite emotional and Andy kept a protective arm round her. The silence was only broken when Muriel offered everyone a mint. Only Albert accepted with a smile,

The cars drew up in front of the chapel. Brian Evans was already there as were a number of mum's friends. The ambulance drew up round the corner where there was a slope for the wheel chair. Fortunately it was far enough away for Jennie's comments to be unheard except for those trying to help her out of the car. Always polite, Albert excused himself to the ladies and went to help. The ambulance driver was looking a bit shocked.

"Blimey!" he said, "You have a right one there. I thought I'd heard it all before but she's a new education that one. She ought to have an X certificate label stuck to her."

Jennie calmed down when she saw Albert. "Take me back Albert. I've changed my mind. I can't do this. Mum will turn in her grave if I turn up and she'll probably haunt me for the rest of my life."

Mary was also looking a bit nonplussed and the police escort was a few yards back trying not to laugh. Albert bent over the wheel chair and gave Jennie a kiss.

"Gerroff. I want to go back to the hospital."

Albert looked at her intently. "There is no going back now Jennie. You can't run away any more. Now I am going to wheel you into the chapel and you will be like the proverbial church mouse. Not a single squeak." Jennie was so surprised at this streak of assertiveness that she sat back in the chair.

"You heard me Jennie. We ain't going to let your little girl down now are we? She is in there with her eyes full of tears and she is expecting her mother to be there as well. We'll sit at the back of the chapel so people won't be looking at you."

Jennie looked at Albert as if she was going to cry as well. "All right Albert. Don't shout at me. I don't like it when you get angry."

Mary looked at Albert with a new sense of admiration. She put her hand on Jennie's shoulder. "Here we go then, head up, mouth shut."

The chapel service wasn't very long as they were going to have a service of thanksgiving at the church later. Even Jennie had to borrow Albert's handkerchief as Brian spoke movingly of the selfless sacrifice that mum had made in raising Ellie and at the same time alluded to her great sorrows in the past.

At the end of the service Jennie hung back with Mary and Albert to let all mum's friends out. Ellie with Flo and Muriel led the party out. As Jennie left Mary walked ahead and Albert pushed the chair.

Outside, Karl's expectation that Jennie would come out first was spoiled and he had to stand with the crowd waiting for the next funeral. The gun in his hand was ready to fire.

It seemed to be ages but at last the wheel chair appeared. He recognised Albert and there was his target. He moved quietly behind them and then moved to the side so he could get a clear shot.

Albert heard a noise behind him and turned to see what it was. He saw the gun rising and immediately stepped in between Jennie and Karl. The first bullet struck him in the shoulder and sent him tumbling into the wheel chair knocking it over. Jennie fell out and Karl moved out to make certain he would get her this time. In the corner of his eye he could see the police officer racing towards him. He fired just before Mary hit him with a tackle that took them both to the ground. His second shot clattered over the chapel roof.

Mary grabbed his arms and twisted them round to his back. The gun fell to the ground. The other police officers came running over to support her and the funeral party were all standing around wondering what had happened.

Karl lay there without struggling, except for a twitching of his left leg. Mary thought he must have hit his head and been knocked out. The blood around his head seemed too much and as she looked more closely she realised that Karl was dead. Jennie was yelling with the pain of falling and Albert was slowly sitting up clutching his shoulder.

By the time they had called for ambulance and police support Elroy was on his way home by bus with his gun nestled among the clubs in a golf bag with a yellow club cover hiding the top.

The ambulance man and Mary got Jennie to her feet and back into the chair. She was still yelling with her pain when she saw Albert bleeding badly. Muriel was with him as was a member of the congregation who was a nurse. Brian and Molly Evans went round making sure everybody was all right. Ellie was huddled in Andy's arms shocked by what she had just seen.

Jennie and Albert were taken in the ambulance car with the nurse stemming the blood flow. Jennie by now was more concerned about Albert than her own pain. She kept saying to the nurse "He saved me, he stopped Karl from killing me, you can't let him die, please don't let him die, not for me, he can't die because of me."

Even when the nurse assured her that it was just a flesh wound and she had that under control, Jennie was almost hysterical and when they got to the hospital she had to be given a sedative both for the pain she was in and to calm her down.

There was a wide space around Karl's lifeless body. The bullet wound in his head now more obvious. Elroy never missed his target. The police escort searched the grounds for him but there was no sign he had ever been there.

Flo was looking very dazed as she had fainted when the shooting began and had been left on the ground by Muriel when she had realised that Albert had been shot, but she was now being comforted by Muriel. Brian suggested that the service of thanksgiving should be held later in the month as the events of the day would be too confusing for anyone to concentrate. The tea however had been made and at gave the rest of them a chance to talk about what had happened. It also provided a place for the police to interview everyone about what they had seen. Flo was still so shocked that the only thing she ate was a piece of Mrs Wagstaff's rescued cake.

Jennie had also burst some stitches when she landed and had to put up with the hospital for longer than she wanted. The memory of Albert taking the bullet meant for her was something she would never forget, even if he had dumped her out of the wheel chair. Somehow she couldn't even see her beloved father doing that for her.

Her mind was as serious as it had ever been. The shock suddenly hit her and she wept profusely even though it hurt. At the back of her mind the realisation that Karl was now dead as well as Johnny gave her the first sense of peace that she had known for a long time.

Albert's injury was rapidly treated as only cleaning, stitching and bandaging were necessary apart from a tetanus injection. They offered to keep him in overnight but he chose to leave and go to the church to let everyone know that he was all right. Mary went with him having reassured herself that Jennie was safe.

He was applauded when he arrived and was soon surrounded by ladies offering him tea, sympathy and cake. Ellie and Andy were there and very relieved to know he and Jennie were safe. Nobody knew how Karl had died until Mary told them some of the details. Many of them still saw it as a miracle. Mary took Albert home and made sure he was going to be all right. The next day he was at the hospital to reassure Jennie that he was OK and to see how she was.

Ellie and Andy went home with Flo and Muriel. The house seemed very quiet and peaceful. Next day Flo and Muriel returned home to Ramsgate and Andy and Ellie returned to work before going in to see Jennie that evening. Life began to return to normal and the events of that week retired into the past.

Chapter forty-one

Epilogue

Like many stories this tale has been based on fact, but fact is often much stranger than fiction, so a lot of fiction has been added to make it more realistic.

The future, which is also now the past had mixed fortunes for the main characters. Ellie and Andy married six months later and Jennie did go to the wedding and sit at the back of the church with Mary having stayed with Albert since coming out of the hospital.

Her evidence to the police enabled several crimes to be cleared up and to close a vicious ring of drug and vice merchants. Timber wasn't the only officer to take an early retirement but few of them were charged as the corruption had spread widely and even now much of it is undiscovered.

Andy was offered a posting to a branch of the Bank in Northampton so they moved there and were able to buy their own home. Their daughter, Jennifer Hope was born recently.

It would have been nice to think that Jennie would have a happy ending as well. She did stay with Albert until after the wedding but then she moved away as she had planned.

It was Mary who told them that Jennie had died. She had kept in touch as promised and her address was the only one they found on Jennie's body. One overdose too many killed her. Her room had many pictures of Ellie, Andy and the baby so maybe she died happy in the knowledge that the inheritance of the past was well gone and the secrets were out in the open and could not hurt anyone any more.

There were four people at her funeral apart from Brian Evans who took the funeral, Ellie, Andy and Mary and the ever faithful Albert. Mary gave Ellie Jennie's letter as she had promised.

Albert was never alone after Jennie had gone as he began to attend the church and recently he married one of the members, a widow who was ten years his junior. He was awarded the humane society medal and a Police award for bravery for his action at the funeral and he treasures them to this day. Mary became a sergeant in the CID and has recently become engaged to a local vicar and Flo and Muriel are still Flo and Muriel.

34929909R00174

Made in the USA
Charleston, SC
23 October 2014